Rings

NEMO WALKER
EISEN BROWER
GULLIVER BROWER
ACE WISCHMANN

WONDER'S GATE
SYRACUSE, NY

Published by Wonder's Gate
info@wondersgate.pub
www.wondersgate.pub

This is a work of fiction. Unless otherwise indicated, all the names, characters, businesses, places, events, and incidents in this book are either the product of the authors' imaginations or used in a fictitious manner. Any resemblance to actual persons, living or dead, or actual events is purely coincidental.

Print ISBN: 978-1-7375054-0-2
eBook ISBN: 978-1-7375054-1-9
Audibook ISBN: 978-1-7375054-2-6

Library of Congress Control Number: 2021914922

First Edition

Supplemental Cataloging Information

YA/Teen Fiction
- Science Fiction *(science-fantasy, virtual reality)*
- Coming of Age, Contemporary

Rings is set within a computer game world *and* in the real world. Fantasy game characters and real-world teens both have important roles.

DEDICATIONS

ACE

I'd like to dedicate Rings to my family, who have always encouraged me to pursue my passions. I love you all so very much, whether you are with us spiritually or physically, you have played a part in this achievement.

EISEN

Dedicated to the late Terry Pratchett, whose books I love, and who was the one who really inspired me to write. His writing style was very influential to me and many other people.

GULLIVER

Dedicated to our planet, upon which all life depends, and to a brighter future for all.

NEMO

I'm glad to dedicate *Rings* to The New School of Syracuse, where the skills and discipline of my three co-authors were nurtured. Serving K-8 students for over 30 years, The New School continues to develop fine writers, creators, activists, scholars, and other able, motivated humans.

OUR THANKS...

...to our families, to Evan, Theo, Jorge, and Escher from The New School, to the teachers and students at Wellwood Middle School, and to our many friends and supporters.

CONTENTS

PROLOGUE

Diary of The Boss

I want to kill something.

This morning's coffee was weak. Did I taste sugar? Needles knows I take it black. Perhaps he mixed up the mugs. I will speak with him when he returns from the hunt. He suggested I go down with him, but I have much to think about. I watched from the window as he whipped up the hounds. I hope he has better luck today. I need new entertainments.

Is it possible he won't find anyone? Denizens have become scarce on the grounds, and Needles tells me the streets all around are empty. It seems my ring is dying. I asked Needles if he agreed, but he would not say.

The other rings seem lively enough!

But the game has been so slow.

No, not slow.

Dead.

Is the game dying? I knew the day would come, but is it here?

If Rings is ending, I will not end with it! Perhaps it is time to make my dreams come true. Perhaps it is time.

Time to go Real.

Ace

1 — ALEXANDER BREYER

That can't be me!

...How is that me?

I stare at the kid in the mirror, and he stares right back. He's a short kid. Too short. Slow to grow. We shake our heads at each other.

The kid is skinny, too. Skinny and short.

And weak.

(Mom calls me "wiry.")

I make fists and pump up my muscles so the mirror kid does the same thing. I want to see muscle, but I see bones. Ribs. Hips. Knobby knees and big elbows. A collarbone you could hang things from. It's like the muscles aren't big enough for the bones. And my face is... I don't know. Not the way it was I guess. Like it's being pressed out from the inside or something. That can't be right.

And don't get me started on my feet.

That *can't* be me.

But it is. It's so weird.

The kid in the mirror stares hard into my eyes — like he's

saying, 'why do you even look?'

But I do. I look. Not every day, but sometimes. I get out of the shower. I look — like staring at a troubled stranger on the street instead of turning away. I mean, who doesn't? …Kids without mirrors I suppose. But people do — they look themselves over. They pose a little bit. They check things out.

Are they all as disappointed as I am?

"You suck," I tell the kid.

Kid says it right back at me. He's right.

…Mostly.

I don't know, maybe not.

Maybe not.

At least no one cares but me! If anyone noticed it would be way worse, but I'm pretty much invisible, especially at school. Never noticed for anything. Never the best or worst. Never the one you feel sorry for. Not the smallest guy (but close). Third row clarinet. No trophies. No honors list. If a *certificate of participation* could be a kid, that would be me. I just slide through.

Invisible.

No one cares — good!

…Well, yeah okay, *mom* cares. Moms always care, right? They love you and feed you. They make you brush your teeth and do your homework. They nag you with questions and shout about chores and pick you up after cross country. All that stuff.

Yeah, and my mom talks about me to other moms — *even when I'm in the next room and can hear!* She won't let me be invisible. She tells them how I'm dyslexic and have trouble *(a little maybe, but why is it their business?)*, and how I have tantrums and break things *(just a few times, and mostly when I was younger)*, and how I peed the bed right into middle school *(great mom, thanks a lot)*. She tells them the doctor says not to worry. All the other moms understand.

Well at least I'm no Einstein (my little brother). Einstein is way worse, and they talk about him a lot more.

Yeah, moms care.

And they drink wine and want to be left alone.

And they yell.

…And they kick dads out forever.

Forever.

For *ever* ever.

Okay, so don't get me wrong. My mom… Well, she's my mom and I love her, and she's okay. She's just having a rough time lately, that's all. It's been a rough time.

…

I look at the mirror kid again. We both sigh. He gives me half a smile. I half smile back. 'B Boy' pops into my head: Brown hair. Brown eyes. Braces. Bony. …Boring.

Yeah, and I could really use a 'B' in Math or Spanish. Or Global even. But…

Whatever.

School.

Must get dressed.

Gotta tell Jake about the Redstone machine I built in Minecraft.

I take one last look.

It's so weird.

…How is that me?

*   *   *

"Jerk!" says a large, nameless girl who bumps me in A-Hall. A junior I think. *She* ran into *me*, but she thought it was my fault. The usual.

"Sorry," I say. Don't know why I bother. She instantly forgets I exist and moves on.

"Typical," says Jake.

I smile. "Do they not even *see* me?"

"See who? Who said that?"

"Very funny."

"But, hey, she was cute!"

I look at Jake in disgust. "Cute? *Ugh!* No way."

"Seriously? She was hot! You should ask her out. I bet she would—"

"Don't even go there!"

"Loser."

"Prick."

"See ya later."

"Later." I race to get to Science, but I'll probably be late anyway. It's at the other end of the building.

*   *   *

My best friend is Jake Hei. Before I met him, I heard Jake's name on the school intercom a couple times — it's easy to notice because his last name sounds just like 'hi,' and people always laugh. Also, Mr. Tarnick the history teacher hates him and always seems to be yelling at him in the halls for something. But I basically met him last fall in gym.

I like gym, but I sorta suck at it. Especially team sports like basketball or soccer where I'm supposed to know what to do. I always screw up and get yelled at — "You should have passed it, moron!" or, "You're supposed to be over *there!* Are you brain dead?!" or fifty things like that. I don't get picked *last* for teams in gym (probably because I'm fast), but still, it's always closer to last than first.

I *am* good at long distance running though. …Well, no one notices that I'm good but me, but still it feels good. I like running. I mean, I never win, but I'm always up in the pack. I'm never that kid who everyone fake cheers for who finishes last and almost passes out, maybe puking in the grass — I've seen that. I keep getting personal bests, which is cool.

And Jake is a lot like me. He's sort of small too — maybe an inch taller than me. Maybe two. We really got to know each other when we were subs for fall soccer, which was always. Our gym teacher was also the boys' soccer coach, and even though he said, "everyone plays," we always knew we'd play late in the first half for maybe a couple minutes, and maybe not any more after that, which was fine, but I'm done with soccer. So is Jake.

Jake's an even bigger gamer than I am and has *way* better gear. His parents were game developers for some company in California, but they left and moved here for some reason — which worked out great for me. We do multiplayer a lot. And text. I'd see him more if my mom would take me to his house more, but she doesn't.

I guess I could walk.

My bike is trash.

…Jake is basically my *only* friend.

My little brother Einstein, on the other hand, is a complete pain in the ass, because he's perfect. He is always polite, always does what he's told, and he never gets mad. *Never.*

Mutant.

If anything bad happens at the house, my mom always blames me and never him. …Okay, yes, it's probably always my fault, but is it right that she never even *thinks* it could be Einstein?

He's supposedly 'special needs,' but he doesn't *need* anything — special, normal, or otherwise. But still, after school on Tuesdays and Fridays, I have to cross the fields over to the middle school and go to his class so his teacher can give *me* papers that *I'm* supposed to make sure get to my mom, which is completely stupid, because I would just lose or forget them. Einstein never loses or forgets anything. When we get out of the room, I just give the stuff to him, but I still have to waste my time.

So he drives me crazy.

Sometimes.

And he's so *clean!* I don't get it. He doesn't even try. His room is never a mess. *I* try to be clean too, but I just don't see mess like my mom does. And, yeah, okay, there's somehow food on my clothes after I eat sometimes, and maybe some pee misses the toilet once in awhile, and I lose laundry, and my shoes get muddy, and I do the wrong button on my shirts, and every other frickin' thing you can think of! Not Einstein.

He's an alien.

…Not really. Deep down, I'm glad for Einstein, because without him there would be *no* clean rooms in the house instead of *one* clean room. Besides, I think it would be really hard if it was just me and my mom. Einstein gives her someone younger to take care of. Sort of.

But he's pissing me off today! Why? Because even though he's never bored, my mom still wants me to 'involve' him in things. So…

"Hey Einstein, wanna go to VidGameCon?"

"…Sure," my brother answers, waiting for two seconds like always — like his brain takes an extra trip around the block before it gets around to talking.

"Do you even know what VidGameCon is?" I ask him.

(1 second, 2 seconds) "…Yes." *(1 second, 2 seconds)* "…Old games. Comic books and stuff."

I'm used to the two second wait now, but at first it drove me crazy. "Yeah, and some famous people and cosplay, and maybe VR and AR stuff, and cool demos. I never went before, but Jake said it's cool."

(1 second, 2— you get the idea) "…I found the paper."

"Yeah, I know, *you* found it, so it wasn't Jake. But he's been before, in his old city he said. He's not coming to this one though. Sick or something."

"…The old guy dropped it."

"We have to walk."

*   *   *

VidGameCon was actually kind of boring. Mostly. It seemed like it should be really cool, but I guess I'm not enough of a fanboy to get excited about all the old games and versions and characters, and it turns out cosplay just sort of makes me uncomfortable.

It *was* kind of cool to go to the *Stars of YouTube Gamers* session, but it wasn't any of the people I watch much, and the one girl who has like two million followers just seemed kind of angry. Comic-Con was better. I was pretty much ready to leave after a couple hours, except I had to wait for Einstein, who was staring at a screen in the retro corner where some old guy was crushing the high score in an ancient game called *Battlezone*.

Retro *corner?* Ha! *Everything* about VidGameCon was retro. It was in *The Armory*, which apparently was built a hundred years ago to hold meetings and weapons for some old war. I almost walked straight into one of the iron posts that held the roof up. The floor had squeaks. It isn't big enough for a hockey game — not like the *Civic Center* — but the perfect place for *this* event I guess.

Yeah, and the extra perfect place for the creepy guy I spotted — some wrinkly old dude dressed like a fantasy wizard that had never heard of a washing machine. I think his beard had been collecting crumbs for a few years.

The guy sat at a beat-up folding table stacked with game junk — broken action figures, stained posters, shoeboxes full of DVDs with no cases, cartridges for game systems no one had, an antique hamster ball — crap. His table was even set up right under where the bulbs in the lights were all dead. The only thing that looked interesting was a small collection of knitted hats. Around him on the floor sat wobbly piles of obsolete consoles and controllers, cracked and dirty. Who would buy that stuff?

I stared.

2 — A WIZARD'S GIFT

Toadum peered at the boy from under the wobbly brim of the knit bag he called a hat. He couldn't believe it — the moment had finally come! The kid wasn't much to look at, but Wonder's player lived with him. Toadum knew that much from his sniffing about and spying. He had stalked the nights, shadowed (a spell he could still manage in Real), creeping around neighborhoods, peering into windows, closing in on his target by some half-formed sense he had brought with him from the game.

The younger boy had seen him — the brother; Wonder's player — though the boy hadn't recognized him, which was a bit of a surprise.

But this older boy offered a way! Toadum had watched for hours as the older one played his games, never leaving his seat, playing late into the evenings until his mother shouted him off. And even then the boy would sometimes leave his bed to play a bit more. He was good! And when he started playing *Rings*, the game would *know* he was good. He would get a strong character — maybe even a learner — and a top team of warriors.

And when the older boy played games, sometimes Wonder's player would watch! Sometimes. And if he watched the older boy play *Rings*, perhaps he would remember. He would wake. He would go in again. He would rouse Wonder, and Wonder would finish it this time. Wonder would kill The Boss and win the game, and Toadum would return to take his rightful place in the citadel, becoming lord of *Rings*, and would have tea, not coffee!

Toadum blinked. He had been grinning stupidly.

Well, it was working! He had left a flyer for this VidGameCon event in the mailbox at the boys' house. He had let other flyers drop where they walked to and from their schools. He had posted a few on walls and poles where they might pass by. Sure enough, they took the bait. They were here! And now — finally come 'round to Toadum's table — here was the older boy.

His name?

*　　*　　*

"Alexander!" the creepy guy shouted at me.

"Huh?"

"Come here, boy!"

I stepped nervously closer. …How did he know my name?

"Ha! Well. Hmmm." The grubby geezer stared at me like I was a painting. "Here you are," he said, seeming a bit confused. "Closer!"

"Well, see, I have to get my brother, and we have to leave because—"

"I have what you need," the old dude whispered, leaning toward me across the table. "I have it for you. The Boss doesn't know, not yet, but he's not a fool, so you'd better not wait."

"Huh?"

The guy reached under the table and pulled out something about the size of a small book, wrapped in a weirdly patterned cloth of green and gold. I was about to look when he shoved it back out of sight and stood up, glancing around like he was making sure no one was watching, but then he sat again. "Must be *careful,*" he said, eyeing me. "Careful."

He bent over the bundle, sort of hiding it with his hands. I stepped closer and leaned in, kind of curious. His gnarly fingers unwrapped the cloth. I expected… I don't know, some old deck of cards or a figure, or maybe something like a fake magic jewel. It was a metal box, but the metal's reflection seemed different than any metal I could remember seeing. Sort of shimmery pinkish. It looked like an expensive external SSD, or maybe some high-end media hub — except I didn't see any ports.

"Here is *Rings!*" he announced, as though it was the most important thing in the world. "Can you say that? *Rings?*"

"Rings."

"Good. Yes. *Rings.* Different than most games you play."

Did he know what I played? Then he surprised me and got really technical.

"This box is an AI-callibrated proximity hardface with sensors and firmware that excerpt faint-pattern code glow from the transistance-expressed EM fluctuation of your CPU, and then inter-codes it with the game server, realtime." He smiled. "Oh, and manages the retinal sub-code too, of course."

"…Um…"

"AI?" he asked with a hint of disgust. "Artificial intelligence?"

"Oh yeah. AI."

He looked like he was going to explain more, but then he shook his head.

"Well it works!" he snapped, then asked, "your computer has a wired connection to the internet?"

I nodded.

"Fast?"

I nodded again.

"Well… Hmmm… See, the hardface reads and writes through the magnetic field of your CPU. Gets power from it too. No cables, no router needed. No network. But it *must* be closer than eleven inches to the motherboard. Perhaps ten. Your machine can't handle the software version — can't find *that* anymore anyway!" He smiled and winked at me. "Doesn't matter, because *no* machine will handle *this* version of the game without the hardface. No recent OS will run it. Language never caught on — a custom LISP flavor I think."

He nodded his head a few times, but then snapped at me.

"Know what a motherboard is?"

"Uh, yeah." Though I didn't know where it was actually located inside my computer.

"You'll know," the man said like he was reading my mind. "If you're booted up and it's close enough, you'll see the icon. Can't mistake it." He wrapped the box up again. "And don't worry! *He* doesn't know." He looked suspiciously around the hall again. "Something happened to him, see. He and Wonder met in the 5th and then, boom. Something." He shook his head as if puzzling. "Not all that long ago," he muttered. "A year or so? And you'll help me finish him, won't you? I think he's ready to fall!"

…

I could only stare, but I finally had to say something, because the pause had gotten a little uncomfortable. "It's that I wasn't going to buy anything," I said. "I don't really have any money."

"It's important!" the guy snapped. "He's not dead! I'm sure of that. Quiet, but not dead. He's worried, I think. About the game. Understand?" I didn't. "Something happened! I don't… I can't… Well there's nothing going on and that's not right. It all feels like a trick." He paused again, then a light seemed to go on. "Maybe a *Chopfsky* trick, eh?" He gave me a look like he'd said something really clever, but I didn't get it, which seemed to bug him. "I'm no fool, boy! I'm a half avatar, not just some juiced character, understand?"

I didn't have a clue, but I nodded anyway.

Suddenly, his arm shot out and he grabbed me by the shirt, pulling me close. "Help me," he begged. "I don't dare go back in as long as he's there, and I want to go back!"

He stayed mad for a few seconds, but then he changed to looking sorry and let me go, fixing my collar. Now he just looked like a sad old man. "You see," he said, "I never saw the 5th Ring. He finished my team in the 4th. I'd have been in the Rubbles like Wonder, but I'm a knower *and* a wizard. Found the way out — found the way *here!* But I'm broken now. I'm mostly Real but… but sort of dead-ish. Do you understand?" He stared, suddenly looking more than a little bit scared. "No. No. I don't suppose you do." He sighed, but quickly sharpened up again.

"So take it!" he ordered. "It's yours. Free! And keep it *secret!*" he added with hissing urgency. "Wonder's player has to get back in the game somehow. *Soon!* If I can get in again… If he's finished, then… Then…"

The old man went quiet again, looking into my face like I might be able to finish his sentence for him. He stared a moment, seeming like he wanted to say much more, but then he pushed the package into my hands, took a long look over my shoulder at something, and then said one last thing in a voice that sounded strangely panicked.

"*Play,* boy. *Play!* …Oh, and, you know, *show your brother.* He'd like it too I think."

He smiled in a bizarre imitation of a kindly uncle, then he turned, grabbed a beat up old suitcase (like a big gym bag made of rugs), stuffed a few things into it (including half of a sandwich he'd been working on), and disappeared into the crowd, leaving the table and the rest behind. I thought he looked sort of small and faded. I stared after him, confused, but eventually turned to fetch Einstein—

Who shocked the hell out of me because he was right behind me, waiting and (as usual) staring.

"Oh!" I squeaked. "When did you show up?" Einstein shrugged (after two seconds). "Never mind. Check this out," I said to my brother as I turned to show him the guy's setup.

It wasn't there.

Everything had vanished except the table and one knit hat. Einstein picked it up. "…He's gone."

"Yeah," I said. "Uh, kind of fast." I was a little spooked. "Let's go."

"…Did you get something?"

"Yeah, a game box, or console thing. Some fluctiony thing or something. It was free!" I added, not knowing the pain it was going to cause.

*   *   *

As we walked home from VidGameCon, I thought about Einstein. He was adopted — not even a year ago. We adopted him, and then…

Dad left.

Almost like there was only room for three in the house, and dad was the one who got pushed out. But that wasn't it.

Einstein was supposed to have been sort of a 'rescue kid,' except that it wasn't him that was getting rescued. What was supposed to get rescued was mom and dad loving each other. Major fail.

As soon as Einstein showed up, that look of his started to wreck things — because if Einstein looked at you for long, you somehow remembered what was true, and if bad things were true, you remembered them. Mom and dad remembered that they were sick of each other, and that was the end of that.

His real name is Einstein now, but that's just because he had no real name when we got him. We all started calling him Einstein because he looks really smart (even though he seems sorta dumb) — and because when mom first called him that, he turned and stared at her. She swears he smiled, but I was there, and he did *not* smile. Einstein has never smiled. *Never.* The adoption people said we could name him whatever we wanted, so we did.

Like a pet.

Weird.

He doesn't smile, but his brown face looks so gentle and plain — like it *might* smile if he saw a butterfly or finished a picture, or something.

I think the orphanage was glad to see him go, but I don't think my parents were glad to get him. Not really. I think they knew before he even climbed into the car with his little bag of stuff that they had made a mistake. That it was hopeless — for them.

"What happened to you?" I said aloud, surprising myself. Einstein looked at me — not smiling.

*   *   *

The Boss.

God, he hated that name. He would have preferred *The Man*, but he had no power over game names. For his own amusement, he had taken to calling himself *Ace.* That had something — Ace. It's what he felt like. He felt...

Acey.

Charming and strange.

But today, The Boss felt sluggish. His face, with skin the color of old blood, seemed to drape the front of his skull like a shroud. He slouched in his easy chair, his thick leather cloak pulled close around him. It was a slow morning. His horns felt cold, and they ached. The windows surrounding his central chamber let in only gloom, which served to thicken the gloom already in his mind. Earlier, he had gone down to enjoy a bit of torture, but the few prisoners left in his dungeons had been completely unresponsive.

"Perhaps they have all died," his associate suggested at hearing the tale.

This associate — Mister Needles — was a wiry man, dressed in a clean pinstripe suit, skinny and tall, covered head to toe in stitches and scars. His skin was paler than a cloud, and his dark eyes crawled around his head like spiders, never staying in one place. For the most part Needles was retired, though he still served The Boss in certain ways.

The Boss and Mister Needles had been chatting for quite a while, sipping coffee in the high chamber. Often they would share ideas over a feast of flesh and dreams, conceiving new monstrosities to kill warriors in the 3rd or 4th Rings, or to torment the silly hills. Occasionally they would enjoy their hobbies — The Boss had a great affinity for what he called "face flowers," a form of carving floral arrangements into his victims' faces.

But today was…

Different.

"They probably *have* died," The Boss sighed.

"Well we must acquire more," replied Mister Needles. "The hunt was fruitless. Shall we visit a hotel?"

"Which hotel?" The Boss inquired, barely interested.

Needles pondered. "Perhaps the 3rd? Always a crowd there."

"Don't you think the hotel vermin have avoided us quite well recently? Warriors scatter like roaches when we get close," The Boss snarled. "It's Chopfsky, no doubt. Once upon a time, Chopfsky didn't take sides."

"Well then, if not the hotels, perhaps more denizens," Mister Needles suggested. "Always plenty of denizens in the other rings."

"Denizens again?" he sighed. "I suppose. But they're so dull. I remember when our cells were full of *warriors*. Even a learner or two. Remember?"

"Mmmm." Needles did remember. "Perhaps we could find fresh beings in the hills. Maybe a lamb?"

"Perhaps." The Boss smiled at the thought. "We could *ace* them."

"…Did you say, 'ace'?"

The Boss felt truly bored. He scratched an itch on his chin and turned to look out the window. "It's coming, my pinstriped friend. Something is coming."

"Something new?" Needles inquired.

"…Maybe not." He sighed. "I itch, Needles. I am tired of… dying."

The Boss stood, blinking and looking about as if unsure where he was. Mister Needles raised an eyebrow, risking a minor seepage of bodily fluids. Seconds ticked away, but at last The Boss recalled the plan he had made, and decided that the time was now. He turned to face his lanky servant and placed gentle hands on the emaciated shoulders.

"Needles," he murmured. "I have a special task for you."

"Task?"

"I am sending you on a little journey." He smiled. "To… *Real.*"

"To Real?" Needles replied, seeming unsurprised. "A little ambitious, no?"

"Aren't you always telling me to free myself?" The Boss's eyes sparked with sudden enthusiasm.

"Indeed. But I meant something more like… like break the cycle, have some fun, get a new hobby." Needles sipped his coffee, amused by The Boss's eagerness.

"No, Needles," The Boss replied, his thin smile saying more than his words. "I believe you shall go and find us a new home."

Needles looked thoughtful. He turned to gaze out the window and was mildly taken aback to see a pack of dogs chasing a bloody figure around the plaza below. They had found someone! The hounds tore at their quarry, shredding clothes and flesh in a lovely spectacle of unfiltered evil.

The Boss suddenly guessed that Needles had seen this moment coming. "How did you know?"

"Well, I've been down the road and back around a few times… Ace."

"You like it? The name?"

"I don't know why you bother with names," Mister Needles responded.

"Am I not a being worth naming?" The Boss complained, feeling unprepared for intellectual discussion.

"The best beings remain unnamed, only later to be named by lesser beings as gods."

"Are we not gods already?"

"There's something above us… Ace. There is always something above us."

The Boss knew this, of course, and he thought he knew what it was. As a master avatar, he was far more than a simple AI node. He was fully juiced — all but independent. He was connected, too, and he had come across a name. A powerful name:

Electricity.

A god's name? He thought so. It was everywhere. It was power. It could kill. And, he had learned, it ran Real.

"Pack your bag, Needles," he said. "I will show you the way."

Needles didn't mind, but he didn't smile. He bled when he smiled. Besides, he was not, as The Boss had guessed, surprised at his new assignment. Not surprised at all — though he wasn't sure why not. He wasn't particularly curious either. Besides, he already knew "the way."

"Oh, and Needles?"

"Hmmm?"

"Is there perhaps a tidbit left in the dungeons for the octopus? Could you feed it before you go? If you don't mind, of course." The Boss smiled.

"Oh, I don't mind," Needles said, a gleam in his eyes. "I don't mind at all."

Mister Needles departed.

Sighing, The Boss glanced up at a shadowed corner tucked among the ceiling beams where he could just make out a thick cluster of spiders feasting on a rat. A little entertainment after all.

*   *   *

So, this may seem like a strange thing to talk about, but…

But I'm not completely honest.

I mean, I am *mostly,* but I kind of have more than one kind of 'truth,' and I think maybe I'm not quite as honest as I should be.

With my mom I'm honest almost always, except when I tell a little lie — like about if my homework is completely done, or did I practice for the whole twenty minutes, or were the potatoes good. I hardly ever feel bad when I lie to my mom, because it's always to make things *better.* I just want her to be… not mad. Happy, I guess. Which she isn't.

A lot.

Lying a tiny bit to keep things okay is part of being truthful. I think. Sometimes. But sometimes I think I'm not being honest with myself.

And it's not the only way.

The problem is that my life is... weak. When I think about my life, I don't have much to think about. Sometimes I just make stuff up in my head so it's more interesting. That's where the second kind of truth comes in — the truth I *want* to be true. I figure the made-up stuff is kind of true, because I plan to have it be *really* true as soon as possible. I want to do cool stuff — like get famous on YouTube, or rescue a family from a fire, or be rich and drink cocktails, or have a girlfriend and... *do* stuff.

Or even just get a date (or just dare to *ask* someone).

Sometimes I lie in bed just imagining that not-real me and all the stuff that comes with it. I kind of imagine these stories I'm in. I lie there and imagine them. Sometimes if class is really boring, I imagine my stories there, too. I think it's mostly normal, and it doesn't hurt anyone because it's just me (and it's fun). I think it is kind of the true me anyway — like I'm practicing the future me. So that's okay, right?

But the third kind of truth is definitely a problem — and the hardest to manage.

Like... So I went to the lake last August. What did I do? I swam. I ate and played board games with my cousins. We played capture the flag — even in the rain. I went canoeing twice. Normal, right? But how exciting is it to tell Jake that I played capture the flag in the rain? Yawn. ...I guess I *could* have told him a few things that I did that were sort of bad — like I listened to hip hop with seriously raw lyrics — but that's *weak!*

Sooo... What I did was tell Jake that I got to second base with this girl who water skis and smiles at me whenever she sees me. I told that to him, even though, really, I only talked to her — but she touched me! ...I mean, she shook my hand. The year before, I told kids I killed a water snake by swinging it against a rock (which my aunt actually did). I told those stories to some kids because... well, because stories like that are *supposed* to be true! That's the way my life is supposed to be in *real* life. So I told those stories like it had all really happened, which means I have to remember the... lies, so I don't tell something different some other time.

There's a couple more things I told kind of like that.

Just a couple.

And here I am again! Lying on my bed (when I should be studying), thinking, dreaming, and doing nothing.

I cross over to my PC and fire it up. I think about texting Jake to see if he wants to play, but then I notice the package I got at VidGameCon. I've been ignoring it for a few days.

It's just that I don't really want to get into a new game. I mean, sometimes I do, but usually if I know something about it, or I can watch someone playing it on YouTube. I hardly ever try new games cold anymore, and I've never heard of this one — if it even is real. *Rings.* Sounds boring. I did a web search, but I only found stories about a couple of kids who played the game and died — which was definitely interesting, but not really helpful. There is no site for the game. No subReddit. No YouTube tutorials. No downloads. Nothing.

Vanished.

Weird.

Also…

Also, lately, I've been thinking I game too much. My mom nags me about it all the time, but I've started to think maybe she's a little bit right. She says it's "fake life." She says that every minute I spend playing games is a minute I'm not living *real* life, and that I might start to get them mixed up.

(Which is what got me thinking about all that 'truth' stuff.)

And, okay, I'm not doing that great in school. Not that bad I mean, but…

Okay, bad.

And that's because I barely do enough to pass, and *that's* because I'm gaming all the time.

All the time.

And I don't have any friends except Jake, and he games as much as I do. More, maybe. At least, he's been hard core a lot longer. I don't care, except that I started to notice that other kids really do seem to have more than one friend, and I thought it might be a good idea if I did.

It wouldn't be hard! I mean, I do have friends at school, sort of — like on cross country — but I just don't… I'm never…

And then there's the whole *girl*friend thing. I've been thinking that I should look into that. I'm not gay or bi or confused or any of that. I think I should probably have a girlfriend soon. I'm tired of just lying in bed by myself and...

Imagining.

So, okay! Less gaming! Starting now! *Go!*

...

See, the problem is that when I think about starting to spend more time in my real life, I don't really know what to do. So...

So I might as well check this *Rings* thing out. Otherwise it will just keep sitting there all the time making me think I *should* check it out.

I open the wrap. It looks the same as before — a metal box about the size of an SSD or small HD. No ports. Not even a top or bottom that I can tell.

The guy said 11 inches from my motherboard. The PC is on. I smile. Starting about three feet away, I slowly move the box closer to my machine. I get it to about a foot away.

Nothing.

I count down the inches (approximately). 11 (nothing), 10, 9, 8, 7... I have that sinking feeling. It's fake. ... 6, 5, 4... Yep. Lame joke. ... 3, 2—

An icon appears on my desktop.

The motherboard must be a few inches away from the upper edge of the case. I set the box on top of the PC. The icon stays there. I click it.

The screen goes black.

"Huh? How am I supposed to set this up?" I can't even see how to back out — there's nothing on the screen at all, and no mouse or keyboard action does anything. What?

I put on the headset to see if there is some audio. Silence.

Okay, so what's up? My keyboard and mouse don't do anything.

...

Oh no.

Oh no no no *nooo!* Total malware! How frickin' stupid to let this thing connect to my computer! *"Damn!"* Now I figure I'm in for a disk wipe and clean OS installation, and then I'll have to reinstall apps and hopefully find lost data from cloud backup. Crap crap *crap!*

I shake my head. ...Might as well get a snack. Einstein better not have eaten all the coffee cake. I stand, angry, then lurch toward the kitchen, stubbing my toe on the desk leg, stumbling, grabbing my desk so I don't fall, and accidentally knocking my best controller onto the hard floor.

"Ow!" Ouch. *"Goddammit!"* I limp in a circle, then reach down to pick up the controller. No LED. Broken. *Shit!* This game is costing me— No, wait. … I guess it looks okay.

A thought hits me. Maybe the *controller* will work for this new game.

I sit again (toe throbbing), put the headphones on, take the controller in my hands, hit "A" and—

3 — THE GAME

The sky was orange. That was the first thing that appeared to Dune. A perfect orange sky. Dull. Thick. Burning.

…

'Dune?'

*　　*　　*

"*What the*—" I dropped the controller in my lap, jerked off the headphones, and sat back, but it was more like pulling another world out of my brain and waking up in my old, regular world. I looked at the display. No start screen, no *character select* or *options*. Not even a title. Just a black screen.

I moved the mouse around, but nothing happened. No cursor. Was my computer frozen? I had clicked the icon — and, yeah, it was impossible to mistake, oversized and incredibly detailed, somehow seeming more complicated than the pixel density of the screen could do — some kind of a micro-map with silver-gold rings in the middle. Behind the rings was some tiny image with red, but I couldn't tell what it was. Maybe an eye? I had clicked the icon, the screen had gone black. And then nothing with the keyboard, but I had tried the controller, and…

And… what?

This time, paying careful attention, I put on the headphones … Nothing. Tried keys and mouse again. Nothing. Then I picked up the controller, nudged a joystick and—

*　　*　　*

Dune felt himself swept into the scene with a nauseating lurch — a morphing arrival in swift movement, panning fast over a large complex of buildings of strange shapes and sizes, all covered in paintings and decals, filled with small colorful figures, and then he stood.

And he was Dune.

Of course.

Who else?

Something nagged his memory, just out of reach — about *not* Dune. About another, elsewhere, who… Nothing. Whatever.

He knew immediately he was in an old city, revealed by the deep, stony dirt of its streets, dotted with strange debris and a few roving animals. He picked out oddities here and there — a horse with large rabbit ears, a man in a bloodied, wooden goat mask — and then he had place and knew himself: an incomplete figure, standing confused in the road.

"Is this me?" he asked aloud of no one.

Dune began to stroll down the street, drawn immediately to a tall establishment. A brick building that seemed to sway in the wind. Short steps climbed to a pair of old doors, open wide. The interior was vintage, attractive. Strangely enough, he felt at home, but like he had been away for a very long time.

A figure in a robe stepped out from the shadows and bumped into him, knocking him back into the street.

"Watch it, lamb!" spat a silly, irritated voice.

"Oh, sorry," Dune replied, weirdly overtaken by embarrassment.

The figure turned to him. "You just starting?" it asked. A man, maybe? A man. What Dune could see of his face was covered in tattoos, but most of him was draped by a swirling robe.

"Yeah. I'm not sure what I'm supposed to be doing."

"You need clothes, moron," he scoffed. "Idiot! Doodle! Can't do a hotel without clothes!" he barked.

"This is a hotel?" Dune saw no signs, not even lights.

"Mmmm," the man answered, his head briefly moving around like a chicken's. "Gotta keep it quiet," he said when he steadied, whispering gravely, as though sharing a deep conspiracy. "Too good to tell people." Dune guessed that he winked, though he couldn't see the eyes.

"So get out, *lamb!*" he sneered. Out and climb high to the hills, or the bottom feeders'll find you and suck. You. Dryyy. Need a way out, you do. Find one, jackass! Weeble! Numble! Do it, meat!" The figure uncapped some kind of flask, drank, and then giggled madly.

"But what…" Dune felt confused. This was a game — that, he knew. "But what about doors or weapons or… anything?" He looked around at other structures along the street, but he saw nothing of what he'd expect in a game.

"Dumb lamb. Dumb, dumb, dumb. You got no team. No clothes! What'd you expect, baby?" The odd character snickered wetly. "Boss gonna eat you, eat you, eat. You!"

Dune stared.

"Can't fly too," the character continued. "Not you — you ain't a denizen! Too bad. Sad. *Nasty!*" He chuckled seductively, then crouched down and leapt upward, tumbling aloft, rising toward the upper floors of a nearby building, braying as he went, something dribbling from his chin. "Not *my* problem!" Then he was gone, laughing up and away into a high window down the street from the hotel.

Silence.

Dune peered longingly through the hotel's antique wooden doors, wanting to be inside. He thought he saw figures at a bar, but he could not make himself enter. With a sigh, he turned to the street and looked about.

Across the road, various structures backed against a tall stone wall that glowed, like everything, a shade of dirty orange, clashing weirdly with the carrot-colored sky behind. A low archway framed the mouth of a short tunnel through the wall — a gateway out.

…No, the gateway *in*.

He had come that way at the beginning. The gate stood open, but beyond it he saw nothing of importance. Not nothing *at all* — there were shapes that appeared normal and expected — but he knew it wasn't anyplace he was meant to go. It was the *before-in* place. Nothing. Not for playing. Not for winning. What he needed was a way to the *next* thing.

A tight, long road stretched away to left and right in front of the hotel, gradually curving off until, a couple hundred yards away in either direction, he could see no farther. Whether he looked left or right along it, he saw the same thing — blocky buildings and short towers, peppered with stickers, tags, painted figures, junk. Some structures taller and more elaborate, some squat and plain, all old. Ancient. Perhaps colorful, but the orange sky seemed to drive most colors away, leaving only shades of innards and compost.

Dune chose to turn right. He walked slowly along through the gritty air, not knowing where or why, bearing always to the right, clockwise, as though the city was a great circle. He passed meaningless buildings. Pointless characters stood or moved about pointlessly. One flew now and then. Pointless. But next?

Clothes.

He needed clothes.

Something appeared ahead, coming it seemed from farther around the curve. A dark figure, moving towards him.

"Hey, excuse me!" Dune heard himself yell. "Can you help me?" He knew as he shouted that the figure was too far away to hear. Why was he yelling? He suddenly wasn't sure he even had a voice. The figure approached quickly. Dune was about to repeat himself when he saw that it was running on all fours.

What? Holy crap!

It seemed human, but it rambled ape-like with alarming speed, shanks and knuckles rolling. There was something off about it. The breeze suddenly went wild. Dune began to back up, but the creature seemed to speed up as he did so until it was charging right at him. Dune wanted to run, but his limbs wouldn't move. No! It was that he couldn't *find* his limbs — didn't *have* limbs. He couldn't see himself. The figure was almost upon him, eyes wild, nostrils pumping, teeth leaking. Dune screamed! "*Nooo—*

*   *   *

"*—ooo!*" I shouted as I heaved out of my chair, dropping the controller. My headphones jerked from my head as I stumbled away from the desk beyond the length of the cord. I stopped in the doorway of my room and looked around wildly, panicked, expecting to be attacked, but I soon realized where I was — and *who* I was. Alexander, not Dune. At home. Normal. My room. My house. The sounds and smells. I stood there for awhile, panting, tense as a stretched spring, but then I relaxed. "Wow," I mumbled.

Some game.

I laughed nervously, my breathing faster than normal, my eyes a little wider. I looked over at my computer. The pinky silver box sat on top of it, looking sort of alien. I glanced at the little square clock I'd gotten for Christmas a few years back. Only 9:15, but it felt like midnight. Or later.

The game had scared me, deep. But I knew I was going to play again. I kind of liked it — the scared part. And I hadn't even needed to log in! The game seemed to just start when I did something on the controller — button, joystick — maybe anything.

I like first person games where you see through the character's eyes, more than third person where you watch from above or behind. Usually, though, you can see some kind of weapon — or your feet moving, or something. Here? Nothing. I didn't see *anything* of my character. But I could… I could *feel!*

Huh?

I could! *I did!* I *felt* things in this game, and it wasn't some haptic feedback. It was *real feel!*

Yeah, and now my feet were moving, and I sat in the chair in my wrinkled pajamas. I couldn't help it. I put on the headphones. I'd learned long ago that mom would hardly ever bother me if she couldn't hear my games. With the phones on, I could hear my heart beating. Fast. I picked up the controller, a trigger clicked as I pressed it in, the screen fired, and I was…

*　　*　　*

Still without clothes. Dune couldn't see himself, but he just knew. How?

He was still in the street too. He whirled about, but the attacker was nowhere to be seen. Even so, panic rose up in him. He had to get out of the city before the apeman or any other dangers showed up. He looked down a short side street and saw that it led to a gap where a portion of the outer wall had collapsed. Beyond was the base of a grassy slope that rose to unguessable heights.

Deciding, he bolted down the lane, feeling (though not seeing) his bare feet pounding on gritty pavement. Scrambling through the break in the wall, he crossed a short stretch of garbage and rocks to where the wild hills began, and he started to climb.

The orange sky shimmered around him as he went up. The footing was easy even though the way was steep, and he ascended rapidly at first, but… was it his imagination, or was he getting *tired?* How was that possible? Game characters didn't get tired, and if they did, wouldn't they just slow down, or need an energy pack, or something?

…Why did he think he was a game character?

…Why did he wonder why he thought he was a game character?

…Why did he wonder why he wondered why—

*   *   *

"Huh? Wha…?" A scary mental lurch, crossing a weird void to become me again. I was panting, sweating, my pajamas damp with it, my feet trembling. I was staring at the screen. It was dark. No home screen. No *game paused.* No nothing. I blinked away the confusion.

And there was Einstein, standing there looking at me, my headphones in one of his hands, controller hanging loosely in the other.

"…You didn't answer me."

"Uh, I was playing."

"…But you didn't hear me. You always hear me when you're playing," he reminded me. "…You always talk to me."

"Sorry, bro. Sorry." What could I say? "See, this game is different."

"…Why?"

"Well," I started, unsure how to explain. "It gets you more inside of it than a regular game." Lame. "It's like a VR!" I blurted.

"… It's VR?"

"No…" This wasn't going well. "See, it's *like* a VR but you don't need a headset. You know, because it makes you feel like you are really *in* the game — like you really *are* the character. Understand?"

"…No. But mom says go to bed."

"Look, E, it's not like a regular game, that's all." A thought hit me. "What did you see on the screen when I was playing?"

"…Grass. Going down."

"That was *me*, going *up!*" I said.

Einstein got a strange look on his face — one I'd never seen before.

"Listen, E, it's okay," I told him. "I just can't hear you easy when I'm in this game. If you need me, just do what you did — take the controller out of my hands. It's okay."

His look faded, he handed the gear back and left my room. I sat for awhile, thinking I really *should* go to bed. I had a test the next day, and I wasn't ready.

Maybe I should study.

…

But then I had a sudden understanding about the game! It wasn't just Dune, the game warrior, that had been getting tired on the hill. It was me, too — the real boy! Playing *Rings* put you inside the game world with feeling as well as seeing and hearing. That should have scared me.

But it didn't.

How had I become "Dune" anyway? I had no idea. I had started playing, and I was Dune, period. I waited for several long seconds, but no further thoughts came — except one.

Play.

*   *   *

Dune stood again on the slope, confused. He was having trouble… *becoming* (a normal problem for a *Rings* lamb). Shaking his head, he took a long, slow breath and turned around.

The city spread away not far below. Odd birds circled lazily above a thin dust, looking more like sketched figures born from wall art than any particular kind of flying beast. Otherwise, no movement. He couldn't tell the exact way he had come, but it was clear to him that the city was large, and that he had seen only a bit at the edge of it. It was obvious now that, yes, the city wall curved away as if to complete a fairly smooth circle. He also saw that a second wall paralleled the first, shaping the inner boundary of the ring he had been in, but beyond this second wall, all was murky and indistinct. The orange sky tinted the entire scene, turning everything the colors of rust or pee or faded traffic cones.

Was he having fun?

Why did he wonder if… Never mind.

He wanted to *see* himself.

Suddenly Dune's head spun in disorientation, leaving him almost nauseous. The *feeling* thing didn't belong only to him, but lamb Dune was unable to be in the mind of Alexander — his 'Real' — who sat in sleepwear in the chair in his little bedroom at 9:32 p.m. Alexander, whose toe still hurt because he had stupidly stubbed it on his desk. Alexander who should feel the ache because his braces had been tightened that afternoon. Except Dune didn't think or feel or know any of that. What he felt was *wind*. Wind on his skin, and it felt perfect! No aches and pains. Just wind, and the fatigue of a perfect body.

Perfect, but not robotic. Dune — character Dune — could *feel* his fatigue, which seemed fundamentally strange to him, but he didn't know why. In the real world, Alexander felt it too — though he also felt toe and teeth.

Again, Dune tried to see himself! He looked down, expecting legs and toes. He extended his arms, trying to see hands. He moved those unseen hands and touched his face. He saw nothing. He could feel but not see himself. He puzzled for a moment, then shrugged, turned back to the slope, and began to climb again, slower this time, embracing the balance of progress and exhaustion. He climbed until the grass grew short, the ground rocky, the orange of the sky blackened at the edges. It felt good. He smiled.

And then…

She spoke.

4 — TEAM OF WARRIORS

"You need clothes," she said, with no hint of shaming or embarrassment.

Dune regarded her. "You can see me?" He asked.

"Yes."

"But… But *I* can't see me."

"You are a lamb."

Dune thought on this. He remembered that the hooded guy in town called him a lamb. "Well, where do I get clothes?"

"You are new? You have not made a ring, died, and respawned?"

"…I think I'm new."

The girl stared at him. Dune could see *her* well enough. Tall and strong. Gold hair, tightly curled and very short. Deep brown skin catching the orange sky. Dressed all in reds, dark and many shades. A complicated outfit that stayed close to her, with numerous pockets and sheaths showing the hafts of blades, long and short. Calf-high leather boots, laced up.

"I am Sparrow," she said after a moment, and then she went on in a voice that sounded oddly formal. "I am your first teammate. I am a Rank 8 hand combatant with second skills in knives, garrote, canopy travel, camo, scouting, and taming. Also, I am a learner."

"A learner?"

"Yes."

That all sounded good to Dune, plus she was cute, too. Well, *beautiful* really — way past cute. Dangerously beautiful. Thinking this — thoughts popping from where he didn't know — he instantly felt very exposed.

Why?

"So I should get clothes," he said, turning away from her and surveying the scene.

"Yes. Get them."

"Uh, where?"

"With all findings in *Rings*, you must seek a place where what you seek may be found."

Dune thought about it. Sounded obvious — "seek a place where what you seek may be found." Duh. He took a deep breath and let it out slowly, *feeling it* as he did so. Where would he find clothes? Target? Amazon?

…What?

He smiled. No. Then where? Maybe like a farm with clothes hanging on a line that he could steal. Or maybe a village with a shop that sold clothes. Or maybe even—

"This is the hills, not the city," Sparrow said, having already walked a few yards along the slope. "Hills are for preparations, teaming, and respawns. Follow me."

"Huh?"

"Follow me," she repeated, not slowing. Dune followed, glancing again at where he thought his body parts should be, but weren't. Nothing, though he felt the wind of the hills on all of him. Strange.

*   *   *

Layla couldn't believe it!

For weeks, when she had gone into the game, she had found Sparrow wandering aimlessly in the hills. There had been nothing to do. No way to play. She hadn't even checked in for a month.

But a little while earlier a weird thing had happened. Sitting at her very organized desk (in her very messy room), neatly (and perfectly) finishing a math assignment, she'd heard Sparrow call her name — as if her *Rings* character stood right behind her desk chair! When she had turned to see, there'd been no one there (of course), but she decided right away to take a look in the game. She'd nudged her PC, clicked the *Rings* icon, gone in, and found a new lamb warrior standing on the hill, ready for teammates. Sparrow was his first.

Layla never knew why Sparrow got picked for a particular team. Soon after she first started playing three years earlier, it became clear that she had no choice. The game just matched characters up somehow, but it was always cool — except when Sparrow got beaten and died. Especially since Layla could feel the physical pain of wounds (intensely), and the sadness of failure. But Sparrow had gotten better each time she respawned or survived a failed team. Her skills were a few ranks above where she had started, and now she was pretty high up. Layla loved her character! Sparrow fought like a martial arts dancer, and she did *not* mess around.

Layla had time to play today, too — no lessons; not much homework. She could stay in for awhile, get out for dinner, and then go back in until bedtime.

It had taken her a long time to learn how to exit the game on her own. It used to be so embarrassing to have her mom or dad take the controller away to pull her out. They didn't mind — they were pretty chill (almost too chill). Once she had accidentally stayed in almost all night and... Well, she didn't want it to happen again. Eventually, though, she had finally learned how to keep a part of her real self in her mind when she became Sparrow, and she could pull out whenever she needed to, so that was good.

She hoped this lamb would have decent skills when he got his clothes. She knew it was a 'he' from the look and sound of him, even though she could only describe no-clothes lambs as rough models of what they would become — kind of like manikins. Not embarrassing, even though the lambs didn't know it!

She smiled — a big, perfect smile that seemed to make her freckles look just right, even though she hated them. Thinking of them, she glanced at her mirror, the blue of her eyes catching her attention as they always did. Her hair looked brown against the pink of her wall, but she knew the sun made it red.

Time to check it out…

*   *   *

Sparrow stayed high, following the crest of a rolling ridge that was less steep than the slope. They couldn't see far ahead, but the sprawling city was always in view to their left, like a post-apocalyptic cancer. From this height, Dune could see there were third and fourth rings of the city, and — though he couldn't be sure through the haze — it seemed like there must be a fifth or central ring. The size of the city was evident as well. He guessed it was two or more miles across at its widest.

After hiking for awhile, Dune began to tire, though the way had been easy. "Why am I getting tired?" he asked. "Do you get tired?"

"No," Sparrow replied. "You are a lamb. Once you get your clothes, you will have full game presence," she added, though Dune wasn't sure what she meant. Fortunately she stopped walking only a few minutes later and stood, looking ahead at something that had just become visible. "There."

Dune followed her gaze. Nestled in a fold in the hills below them spread a town. Multiple stacks spewed brown smoke that merged into the orange sky, staining it. …Or maybe it was the smoke that was *making* the not-so-beautiful orange sky. Either way, the brown and orange were bound together, each seeming to color the other. An industrial town. A factory town.

"My clothes are there?" he asked with little enthusiasm.

"Perhaps," she replied. "If not, we try elsewhere."

Sparrow led the way down from the ridge crest — an easier walk. They soon came to a narrow road that cut across the slope, connecting the grimy burg to several small farms scattered about the larger hollow in the hills. They followed this townward. The land grew uglier as they went, charming meadows and crisp air increasingly replaced by slag heaps and a sooty murk.

As they approached the first structures, one of the bushes that lined the roadside shook unnaturally then swiveled around completely to reveal an aged man who seemed to be wearing only the bush — strapped to his back by a belt — and his long misty beard, which covered all that mattered of the front of him. In an old yet fast and loud haggling voice, the man set out to sell his wares.

"Hello young man!" he announced with a hard smile. "I'm thinkin' I have just what a fine lamb like yerself needs. Take a look at these quality clothes, perfect for a new warrior, discounted five times over so I might as well be givin' 'em to ye!" He pushed aside another bush which fell away to reveal an outfit hanging on a rolling rack. "They'll cost you a buck and a dime less than these fat cat corporate scum who run this town will charge ye! That not interest ye?"

Dune was speechless.

"How about I throw in this belt?" The man continued. He undid the belt with a flourish. The bush he had been wearing tumbled away (fortunately, the beard stayed put). "Ye know, 'tis very valuable," he went on. "It is! Been in my family for years, but — being as yer such a splendid young lamb — I'll be willin' to give it to ye for only a wee bit more," he stated, apparently forgetting that he had already offered to "throw in" the belt with the rest.

"So what do ye say, young master? Don't keep me waitin'!" He smiled again, gaps outnumbering teeth.

Dune leaned over to Sparrow. "Do you have game money, or do you use dollars?" he asked her in a hushed tone, confused by his own question.

The old man beat Sparrow to the answer. "What's dillars? Never heard o' that. Is it some obscure currency? Bucks and dimes for me! I won't take funny money! Pay square, play fair. That's my motto," he said in a firm tone, leaving little room for dispute. "Now, will ye be havin' these finest duds, or will ye be payin' more for worse? Eh? What's it to be? Eh? Eh? *Eh?*"

"But... But I don't have *any* money." Dune said, flustered. The rapid-fire sales pitch had made him nervous.

"No money? Why, who needs that?" the old man said, suddenly sounding generous. "No money needed! I'll give 'em to ye for just one favor," he said, making it seem like one favor was not a lot.

Defeated and mostly just wanting the old man to go away, Dune agreed. "Fine, I'll take them."

"*Ha!*" In a flash, the old man grabbed his beard, pulled it, and seemingly peeled the skin from his entire body to reveal what was beneath — the suit of a town policeman. "Got ye, ye damn fool criminals!" he announced triumphantly. "Ye are both hereby under municipal arrest for engagin' in black market hagglin', hobnobbin' with under-clothed individuals, destruction of roadside landscapin', disturbin' the peace, peacemakin' during a disturbance, possessin' funny money, jaywalkin', and underminin' the most rightful rulership of the properly purchased government of Coalspit!" He smiled evilly. "So, what do ye think o' that?"

But they had no chance to answer, because at that moment the undercover officer was unceremoniously smashed to pieces by a huge man wielding a giant club. Dune stared in shock, then slowly lifted his eyes to the club-wielding figure, who stood at least a foot taller than Sparrow and looked stronger than anyone Dune (or Alexander) had ever seen before.

"Hatch not like," the big man explained after a long silence.

Dune returned his gaze to the broken pieces of the old man — the policeman — which somehow looked like smashed ceramics, free of blood or gore. "Uh, hey big guy," he said, suddenly afraid of the hulking figure that had appeared as if from nowhere. "Nice club, there. But, uh, please don't kill *me*. Whatever you're mad at, I didn't mean it."

"No kill you," came the deep-voiced reply. "Me Hatch. Second teammate. Rank 8 brute," he said with robotic boredom. "Second skills in rage, axe throwing, hunting, river travel."

"Ahhh, yeah, of course, I knew that," Dune said. "I was just joking about that first thing," he added, convincing no one. Hatch the brute regarded him dully. Sparrow seemed not to care at all.

"So then," Dune went on, changing the subject. "Can I still have these?" he asked, pointing to the clothes. "They're mine?"

"Yes. And the belt," said Sparrow. "These are your clothes."

Dune turned to the rack and eyed the apparel the fake salesman had proffered. Hanging there, they looked drab and featureless. Sort of generic. In fact, he really had no idea *what* they looked like. He peered again at Sparrow's intricate outfit, which was very fine indeed. Then he turned to survey the clothing of his huge new teammate and marveled again.

Hatch's shoes looked like he had ripped them right off the feet of an old bear, silver and gold tips swirled in with the black-brown of the fur. The boot tops were studded with spectacular gems and teeth that looked to be from rather majestic and frightening animals. Though finely accented with thin purple and red stripes, his rich blue robes had long rips across the massive muscles of chest and shoulders, and appeared to be too small. On his big bald head sat a splendid hat, white, diamond shaped, and speckled with coins and flat gemstones featuring intricate carvings of religious figures.

But it was Hatch's brilliant white gloves that stole the show, with cuffs that ran all the way to the elbow. A line of white feathers dangled from the outer seam, and a fat stripe as red as a scorching meteor ran from middle finger tip to elbow atop both gloves. The palms of the gloves seemed more like what a brute might wear — rough, dark blue leather.

Dune's overall impression was that this giant new teammate must have obtained his clothes by robbing a church, or a king — or both.

Looking again at the bland rags that awaited him, Dune was disappointed. But as he began to dress, a clear design slowly emerged — one that complemented the outfits of his teammates. And…

He was finally visible!

Dune looked himself over. Shirt, trousers, and close fitting leather gloves featured well-matched shades of green and gray, and were smartly accented with flaps and pleats. The belt was leather, too, and it now appeared as a chain of leaves, each a slightly different shade of emerald. His dark green leather boots felt soft but looked able to handle rough terrain. The breeze no longer cooled his body — only his face. 'Like Robin Hood,' popped into his head, yet he had no idea who Robin Hood was.

With astonishment he discovered that his left hand held a fine bow, and that it felt like it belonged there. Almost as a reflex, he reached back over his shoulder and immediately set fingers upon the shaft of an arrow that nestled with many others in a quiver across his back. "I'm an archer," he said.

"The best," Sparrow replied, eyeing him with unexpected respect.

"The *best?*"

"Yes," she said. "Your clothes have shown. You are legend."

"Legend bowman," growled Hatch.

"Me, a legend and a lamb?

"No lamb now. Learner. Legend and learner."

"Yes," Sparrow agreed. "You are new, and so are played, but you cannot be legend without being a learner. What is your name?" she asked.

"Dune," he replied, somehow understanding without asking that being a learner meant he could adapt and change in ways other warriors could not.

The team — now three — left the shattered policeman by the road and continued on to enter the town. Rounding a bend, they saw that it was surrounded by a long, shabby fence, but that an elaborate stone gateway of multi-colored blocks bridged the road. Within the massive frame hung a gate built of heavy purple wood — closed. Dune thought it strange that this elaborate portal should be so formidable while a large child could probably push through the fencing to either side. They stopped before the gate.

"Hello!" Sparrow called out.

No answer.

Hatch stepped forward and gently knocked. There was still no response, even though knocking gently for a brute is the equivalent of pounding by anyone else.

Dune, who had been carefully looking over the gateway, noticed that one of the stones stood out from the rest in the form of a smooth knob. It featured a bright yellow and blue swirl that seemed to slowly spin, and it looked like something a game character might push to make something happen. He stepped forward and pushed it. The gate began to open, but then stopped before it cracked wide enough to see inside.

"Hey!" came a tiny shout. "Don't use the sacred gate! It's the only nice thing we have in Coalspit." The very tiny voice came from a very tiny man who stood no taller than Dune's waist. He had popped out from behind a nearby tree and now stood before them, hands on hips and covered with dirt. "Use the other door!" he ordered. "There's nothing special about you!"

Other than size, there was something particularly strange about the little man. Those hands resting against his hips weren't hands at all, but small shovels made of bone — though Dune wasn't sure how he knew it was bone, for they were stained coal black.

"What other door?" Sparrow asked.

"This one, of course!" the tiny man said, gesturing and walking over to a short section of fence to the left of the stone portal. With a bit of huffing and puffing (and still clearly annoyed at being disturbed), he hooked a fence pole with the edge of a shovel hand and pulled, a flimsy door creaked open, and he passed through the gap. The team squeezed through after him, Hatch nearly widening the opening by an accident of size.

"Now piss off!" they heard the wee dude shout as he went into a hut by the gate and slammed the door.

Back on the road — now identified by a signpost as *Main Street* — they looked about. Other than one extraordinarily tall, perfect, white tower at its center, the town of Coalspit appeared crowded, compact, and heavily blackened by layers of coal dust. Short, squat residents stamped grumpily through the congested lanes, seeming in a great hurry to complete various tasks. Many pulled handcarts with shoulder harnesses. A few displayed the shovel hands he had seen on the gatekeeper. Dune imagined that the entire populace had been intentionally designed to work endlessly at grueling jobs with bitter deadlines, where the finish of one task just meant the start of the next. Their misery could be felt like a blast of fumes from a smokestack, of which there were many rising above the roofs of the town.

"Let us go to the tavern." Sparrow stated. "We might lose some of the eyes that are upon us."

Dune didn't know how he had missed it, but he now noticed numerous big eyes looming over the town — floating orbs that swiveled to and fro, watching over the people. So crowded was the air about the building tops that it seemed there might be one eye for every townsperson.

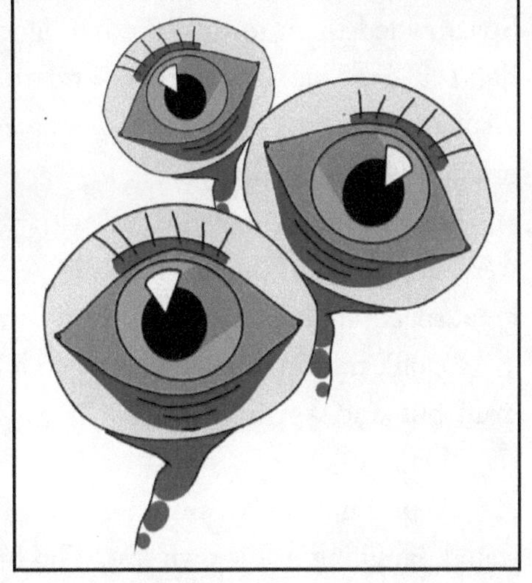

Looking toward the crystalline white tower, Dune now noticed one pair of much larger eyes far above, floating languidly about its top. This pair seemed to have an authority to them, ruling over the others. At the moment, though, this big pair were clearly looking right at the team, as were many of the smaller ones below.

"Yeah," Dune answered. "Tavern sounds good. All these eyes… Creepy."

They headed on into the town, feeling as though they were being swallowed by an ashtray.

*   *   *

"This is tavern," Hatch asserted, even though the carved words on the sign above the door were so completely caked with soot that they could only make out a couple of letters for certain. "Hatch drink."

Dune set aside his doubts and followed as the other two entered what was indeed a tavern, the air thick with the smell of beer and the sound of clanking tankards unmistakable. Like the sign, the interior was darkly obscure, illuminated only with scattered pools of dingy light. Leaning posts held a low ceiling above the dirt floor. An altogether grim place.

Moments after the team had entered, the cantankerous hubbub of rough voices fell to nothing. Suspicious looks greeted them from every corner of the crowded room. No one moved except the bartender, who continued to whistle a perky tune as he went about the business of serving his customers. Sparrow led them toward the bar, ignoring the grim audience. She waved a hand at a group of watchers and three stools suddenly became available (teams have game privilege over denizens). They sat, Hatch's stool creaking ominously at his weight.

Looking up, Dune noticed with some disgust that the bartender's eyes were stapled shut, though his smile seemed genuine, and he moved about at great speed, making no errors. As if aware he was being watched, he spoke.

"Don't mind the rabble — been a bad day," the bartender reported in a gruff but kind voice.

"Uh… Oh?"

"Yep. That makes nine hundred forty six bad days in a row now," he stated, laughing at his own jest. The hubbub resumed around the room, the regulars apparently ready to forget the newcomers and return to their own complaints. Dune spotted a few smaller versions of the floating eyes scattered about near the ceiling, turning this way and that to keep watch on things.

"Why the eyes, barkeep?" Sparrow asked, ignorant of the possible hurt her words might give to the blind man. He seemed not to care.

"Well, warrior, it's Fat Cat's way of getting richer and staying that way. Those eyes see everything but blind men and drunks." Dune guessed he would have winked if he could have. "Can't see *me*, but Fat Cat watches every fidget that these poor fools make, and he logs 'em. That way, end of the month, he knows just what to pay and just what to take in tax, and he always comes out way ahead."

Sparrow shook her head in disgust.

"So, what can I get you fine travelers?" the bartender inquired.

"Do you have lemonade?" Dune asked.

"Lemonade? No idea what that is. How about a frog-bellied-blue-fox?"

"Uh, could you remind me what that is? I think I forgot," Dune answered, trying to sound like he knew something.

"You take a moon squid right before its cycle restarts, and empty the contents of its stomach into a cup of jbohg. Pour the mix into a spiked onix blender, and churn until blue. Crush a small raw yam into the base of a glass, pour in the mix, and then garnish with the tail of a fox that worships Bel-Shamharoth." The tender nodded seriously, noting that, "the last part is essential."

"Yes, of course. Yes. I'll have that," said Dune, deciding that if he didn't know what *that* drink was, he wasn't going to know what any of them were.

"Hatch want beer."

"Water," Sparrow said.

"*Ayyye!*" interrupted a rough-voiced drunk hunched over the bar next to Dune. "An' 'll be a leaky lancer for me!" he slurred.

"You've had enough," replied the bartender, scowling.

"Jus' gimme 'nother drink!" came the gravelly retort.

"It's lime fizz for you, rogue," replied the bartender in a tone that said there would be no more arguing.

Dune blinked — which meant he never saw how the point of the shining sword blade had reached the bartender's neck from wherever it had been.

"With a wee shot o' pupa bile, barkeep. Pronto speedy quick, aye?" he added dangerously.

While not seeming the least bit frightened by the threat of sharp steel, the bartender smirked and shook his head. "Listen, ya damn rogue. You're already drunk enough so's the eyes can't see ya!" But he made the drink and served it. The blade vanished in a flash to a scabbard that hung at the rogue's side — one of a pair.

"Lime fizz!" the rogue growled. "Lime fizz my butt. I'll slice him!" He lifted his bleary eyes and stared into Dune's. "I'll be honest. There's no way I'm gonna do that," he croaked, his breath hitting Dune like a fist.

"Ugh!" Dune reacted. "You reek!" The drunk leaned closer to him — the blended smells of vomit and cheap cologne were almost too much. He wondered what the hell this lunatic was going to say. Probably something about how many ladies he'd been with.

"So how long you been in this wretched town," the drunk said, his foul breath wafting over Dune like a toxic cloud.

"Uh, just got here," answered Dune.

"Aye? Well get the hell outta here before Fat Cat takes all yer money and puts you to work in the mines! Soon yur'll look like any uder," nonsensically mumbled the drunk. "Short, fat, skinny, and easy to house." He leaned closer and closer to Dune until he simply fell from his stool and landed on the floor with a notable thud.

Sparrow's attention was drawn to the sound. "…*Scram?*" she asked after a long moment.

"Maybe," came the surly reply from the floor. "Who's askin', cuz if you're one of Fat's thugs, I'll kill ya!" He lurched upright and whipped out a sword again.

"I am Sparrow," she responded, ignoring the blade. "I think we were team once."

"Sparrow? … Sparrow. Hmmm… Oh, aye!" he said at last, his face brightening in recognition as he sheathed his blade. "My memory," he added. "Worthless. But I think I remember *you!* Didn't I watch you kick down nine lancers and knock their poles into nine shobums. …Or was it nine pucks?"

"Sparrow, who is this?" asked Dune, confused.

"He is Scram — a rogue. We were team together."

"Died in 3rd in that one. …I think. …Or maybe 2nd?" Scram muttered. "Oh no no no, it was…" but then his gaze locked onto Dune, and his eyes came into focus. He stared, and then, quite suddenly, he stood tall, all vestiges of drunkenness vanishing in an instant. "Aye, then. I'm Scram, rogue, Rank 9 sworder, second skills in deal making and gambling."

"The fourth for your team," Sparrow observed.

"Aye, I am." He shook Dune's hand, his eyes now bright and his smell, much better. Even his golden yellow tunic and pantaloons seemed suddenly clean and fresh. Golden brown were his boots, and his thick brown hair and beard were accented with earrings and neck chains of gold. Wide, brown leather straps attached to his scabbard belt, making an X across his chest which boasted several sheaths that held wickedly sharp long knives.

"But we've got trouble now," the blade master continued. "I'm team sobered now, so the *eyes* can see me," he said with a sour look. "Fat Cat will try to run me down. Been huntin' me for awhile." Dune looked around and did indeed notice that every floating eye was staring at his new teammate.

But then Scram's expression changed. "Of course, seeing as we're team, with Sparrow here, your brute — hell of a brute, by the way — and *you,*" he said, looking Dune over. "You, a legend bowman! Aye, well, now maybe Fat Cat's time is finally about done." He slapped Dune on the back. "Follow me," he said to them all, and started for the door. "Got a plan."

"You owe me for 19 leaky lancers!" shouted the bartender as they left.

"Put it on my tab!"

He never paid.

*   *   *

The team headed out into the deepening dusk of Coalspit.

"So we attack this Fat Cat?" Dune asked as they hit the street.

"Hell no," the rogue replied. "Never kill anyone in the hills. Bad luck. Aye, but I have a plan."

Sparrow was suspicious. "A *plan?*" she asked, incredulous. "Yet you are rogue? You are not played? You *cannot* plan."

"Aye, lass, I know," Scram replied. "Seems like it, but I'm not *trying* anything, see. Not a plan, really. It's just that I've a wizard's onus on me."

Hatch grunted in disgust. "Hatch hate wizards."

"So," Sparrow spat. "I suppose we must end your onus before Dune can lead us to the city? His player won't be pleased."

"Aye. Sorry lass, but I can't leave this cesspool until I break Fat Cat's hold. Met up with a lass who turned out to be his daughter, see, and… Well, long story." He looked sheepish. "However," he went on, perking up as he looked at Dune in the last of the day's light. "With an onus there's always an *out,* see? Game rules. And even rogues get to *know* the out — just so they can see how impossible it is and feel that much worse at being under the onus. Usually impossible, but now as you're here, this might be quick."

43

In moments, the team reached Scram's intended destination — a town square where five streets came together a wide plaza with a long dead fountain at its center. Coming to the fountain, they again gained a view of the top half of the crystalline white tower, which had been invisible until then, blocked from view by Coalspit's densely packed buildings and tight lanes. The tower seemed lit from within, though the soot-blackened structures surrounding it swallowed whatever illumination it gave off.

During their short journey from the tavern, Dune had been aware of the many eyes that watched from vantage points above. Some had even followed the team as they walked, floating behind, so that now there was quite a crowd surrounding the square. Far above, the two great eyes of the tower watched over all. In the growing darkness, every orb could be seen to glow with its own sickly luminescence, colors ranging from sewage to mucus — except that the high pair shone a brilliant, royal blue.

"Now what?" demanded Sparrow, her anger having grown.

Scram's smiling teeth reflected the eye light. "Now," he said, "the—"

Suddenly, attacking townsfolk burst into the plaza from all five streets at once, some wielding hammers, long-handled shovels, or metal bars, others armed with only their bone-shovel hands. All were short, squat, and filthy, as if they had been crushed by the weight of perpetual labor.

"Uh, *now*," Scram said, "you and Hatch will keep these lovelies from bothering our bowman!"

By game reflex, Sparrow and Hatch each took a side and set about knocking the attackers silly. Sparrow tumbled and spun like a charged butterfly, delivering punches and kicks. Hatch mainly drove the enemy back with fierce bellows, his club held high for emphasis, though he did push away a band or two with great sweeps of an arm.

"So," Scram said, turning to Dune, "it's your turn."

"Huh?"

"Unstrap that bow and take out the eyes! That's my *out* for the onus!"

Dune hesitated, looking about. "All of them?"

"No!" Scram replied. "The blue pair!" he said, pointing. "The big ones!"

For just a moment, Dune doubted. But then his game self emerged — *legend bowman!* He glanced at smiling Scram, flashed his own grin, swung bow to hand from where it hung on his back, withdrew two arrows from his quiver in quick and fluid motion, set them both with expert fingers, drew the bowstring to its limits, and let fly. The pair of arrows streaked aloft, disappearing into the darkness.

1, 2, 3, 4—

The eyes went out! Two booming PLOOPs reverberated through the town. The flapping husks of the eyeballs dropped to the rooftops far below, splattering those unlucky enough to be caught beneath.

A moment later, a long, fat howl sounded mournfully from far above, and the light of the tower dimmed. The eyes around the square and all across the town began to spin and fly about like sparks above a fire, then popped in quick succession, vanishing in puffs of putrid steam. A fierce gale blew up and roared in from all about the countryside, spinning up a thousand whirlwinds great and small, scouring all soot and grime from the city and its residents, and carrying it away — to where, they did not at first know. The stars shone for the first time in ages. Green and living smells filled the clean air. The fountain's waters flowed again.

And then, to the wonder of all, the newly clean residents of the town *grew*, gradually gaining inches as though their bodies had been compressed springs that were now slowly being released. Sighs sounded from all about. The longest suffering, who had seen their hands become shovel blades, now had fingers again. Soon all were nearly as tall as Scram, though all in the team were taller still.

"Aye, well, that worked out a bit better than I was expecting," Scram observed mildly.

"Let us go," Sparrow commanded, relieved but unimpressed. She led as they wound their way through the crowd, showing no interest in the cheers and thanks that sounded from all around. Dune came last, considerably more impressed with events than his mates, and rather proud of himself.

At Scram's advice, they headed out the far gate and spent the night at an inn in the valley.

*   *   *

"Didn't Scram say that killing anything in the hills was bad luck?" Dune asked Sparrow at the inn that evening. "What about the clothes seller who was really a policeman?"

"Hush!" she replied.

Dune smiled at that. "Where to now?" he inquired.

"The city," she answered. "The game *is* the city. I have been several times. My teams were defeated. Even Wonder was defeated."

Dune tried to imagine what "wonder was defeated" meant, but he stayed silent. It made sense to him that the city was the place to go. Besides, he was itching for a challenge! All this talk, clothes finding, and city cleaning seemed like just a beginning, with the real game to come.

*   *   *

In the morning, the newly shiny populace of Coalspit discovered that the gunk cleaned from them the night before now coated every surface of the infamous *White Tower* (inside as well as out), deposited there by the magical wind. They quickly renamed it *Black Tower,* and it wasn't long before they renamed their home as well, calling it *Marblespit* after switching from coal mining to marble quarrying. The townsfolk were now much prettier, but still not all that creative. They were merely denizens, after all.

*   *   *

Dune was lost. One minute he had been following his teammates along a narrow path through a winding ravine — destination, the ringed city. Then the wind had risen, bringing ground-clinging tufts of cloud that swirled up into a heavy fog and quickly hid the others from view.

He shouted but received no reply. In just a few seconds, the fog vanished, lifting like a curtain to reveal an entirely new landscape — a vast plain, peppered with an orderly array of matching trees.

Dune spotted something that could only be described as 'not quite right.' He turned toward it, simply because it was something, while the trees were… not. As he approached, he realized that this strange sight was some sort of building. It looked like a temple that might house a single tomb, or perhaps a precious object. When he reached the mysterious structure, he found no entrances — no doors, no windows, no nothing. He turned, hoping to ask Sparrow to explain, but there was no sign of her or the others anywhere.

Turning again to face the building, he discovered that somehow he was already inside it. The room was fairly big. Floor, walls, and ceiling shone pure white, with no decoration except a small golden tile in the center of the room. Dune slowly walked toward the tile, and then — because, why not — he stepped on it.

"Hmmm…" He waited. "Nothing." But an instant later, a loud…

CHUNK!

…echoed around him, and, by some mechanism, a pedestal rose from beneath the tile. Once it reached the height of his chest, the top of the pedestal opened like the petals of a flower to reveal a large egg of green and gold. Compelled, Dune slowly reached out to touch it. As soon as his hand brushed the shell, it clicked open, bloomed outward like a second, smaller flower, and presented to him a small card of heavy paper. Dune leaned close to inspect. Taking the card, he saw that it read:

COUPON

One Free Item

Chopfsky & Co.
(put it in your bag, dolt)

Puzzled, Dune did as he was instructed and stuffed the coupon into a small bag that hung on his belt. Seeing nothing else to do, he exited the building through a door that suddenly materialized in front of him. Looking back after a few seconds, he saw that all had vanished. Indeed, he found himself looking back up a portion of the ravine trail that he had already descended. Turning again, he saw Hatch's broad back a hundred yards ahead. After checking to see that the small card was still there, he hastened after his mates.

Weird.

*　　*　　*

"Black?" The Boss stared at Caradan Bejus like he might look at a pimple. Bejus was his quickest agent — plenty of game juice — but still painfully thick-witted.

"Yep," Bejus replied, fidgeting. Clearly nervous. "The tower's all black-like. Eyeballs is all gone, but town's all clean-like."

"Fat Cat?"

"No one's heard a peep," Bejus answered. "Most thinks he's stuck all up in the tower and gonna stay that way. Some says dead."

"Was that my spell? The squeezing of the… residents?"

"Nope. Old Beulah Danderly wizard spell, boss."

"Sir!" The Boss snapped.

"Yep?"

The Boss got a look in his eye that Bejus recognized. Not a good look.

"Yep, *sir,*" Bejus said in quick correction. "Beulah Danderly wizard spell, boss *sir.* Uh, sir. I mean, Beulah Danderly, *sir.* Sir." He hoped he'd gotten it right.

The Boss eyed Bejus, his upper lip curled in distaste, one of his horns smoking slightly.

"Oh, sir, and one thing!"

"…Yes?"

"Team's got a legend bowman!" Bejus related with remembered awe. "He shot the big eyes — *one* shot with *two* arrows! Never seen it before. … Sir."

The Boss slowly sat taller in his easy chair. "A legend bowman you say?"

"Sir, yes sir, boss, sir."

"Did you get his name?"

"Name's Dune, sir."

"Get out."

Bejus fled.

The Boss slumped in his chair. What was going on? A legend bowman? A learner, then. That meant a good player. But wasn't the game done? … Maybe a new team would be amusing. It had been so long.

In the end he gave it little thought. The dream of going Real was too bright in his twisted mind. That, and the coffee in his french press had brewed just the right length of time. He carried his mug to the window to see if the hounds were about.

*   *   *

Jake's phone vibrated. Alexander for sure. No one else texted him now. His old friends had dumped him, and he didn't blame them.

AB - hey
JH - hi
AB - theres this new game u should check out its really fun
JH - o cool what is it
AB - its called rings and its like a free roam game u know open world and u assemble a team u should get it its like really really fun
...
AB - I dont know how much it is but im pretty sure its online multi player its cool cuz its like vr with no headset
...
AB - u could come over if u want and try it
...
AB - u there?
JH - maybe
AB - yeah u should really get it my guys name is dune and im like a legend bowman or something
...
JH - gtg
AB - ok bye check it out

The text exchange ended. Jake just stared at his phone, which shook in his hand. ...No, it was his *hand* that was shaking, not the phone. *Rings?* Impossible.

Impossible!

Because Jake knew *all* about *Rings*. His family had moved to this lame town because of *Rings*. They were poor because of *Rings*. His life had been wrecked by *Rings.* Because of *Rings,* Jake had a new name for the face he saw in the mirror every morning…

Murderer.

It was hard just to breathe for a minute. Alexander playing *Rings?* That wasn't even supposed to be possible anymore. Where had he found a copy? His gear couldn't even run it — at least, not the software version.

…A hardface? Where could he have gotten that?

Jake tried to tell himself that it would be okay — that it was just a bizarre coincidence, and Alexander would just be like the thousands of players who *didn't* die or go nuts. …Still, he really should *not* be playing it.

Jake tried texting him back.

JH - hi lex im back wassup?

…

JH - u up?

…

JH - i remember heard rings is all malware

…

JH - ??

…

JH - they pulled it cuz of russian hackers u should wipe it

…

JH - yo alex get rid of it now

…

JH - ??

5 — 1ˢᵗ RING

"What can I get for ya fine travelers?" The smile seemed genuine, the voice, hearty.

"Big Mike?" Sparrow asked.

"Still me!" he said, a blast of red hair shining atop his beefy face.

"Mike!" Scram said. "Long time, aye? Make me a twisted puck sucker?"

Mike's smile dimmed slightly. "Ya still owe me for that poker night two teams ago, Scram."

"And I'll pay you just as soon as we take some treasure," he assured. "Got a hell of a team here, aye? Take a look — legend bowman! Expecting a fat load of jewels from the Worlds."

"Oh sure." Big Mike shook his head. "Well… Well I suppose we can let it ride again," he said, turning to fix Scram's drink. "What'll ya have?" he asked the others. Hatch went for beer, Sparrow, an iced tea, and Dune, milk (remembering how he'd gagged on the frog-bellied-blue-fox).

*   *   *

"Nope, it ain't the same," Mike confirmed, agreeing with Sparrow. "Ya got it right there." The bartender polished a glass for a moment, casually looking around the room as he did so. The other patrons seemed oblivious to the point of possible death. He leaned slowly over the bar, eyes squinting, and spoke so that only Sparrow, Dune, and Scram could hear.

"It's different," the barman said. "When Wonder got to The Boss, somethin' happened to him. He went all strange. An old wayfinder rogue down from hidin' in the Maze Halls says the 5ᵗʰ went silent. Says the birds vanished — *died!* Some dropped over the wall into 4ᵗʰ. Says he used to see 'em always, up and watchin', but now, none. Not one bird, never."

Sparrow interrupted. "We can enter the 5th unmarked?"

Big Mike hissed, his eyes pinched almost to closing. "'Enter?' '*Enter?*' Ya ain't hearin' what I'm sayin'!" He leaned in — Dune could see the blood pulsing in a vessel in his eye. "I'm sayin' it's *dyin'*. The 5th is dyin', and anyone as enters'll be dyin' with it!" Having made his point, he stepped back to fiercely polish another glass. All went silent except for bits of a low conversation in the corner and the echoes of moaning from far above.

Sparrow asked on, undaunted. "Even so, we go there." No other response was possible for new teams in the game. "We need a map," she said.

"Damn fools for wantin'."

"Even so," she repeated, her words icy.

"Fools! It's over! Dyin'! Somethin's bad broke. Game's crashin'. Yup, and some hell in the Worlds too! Crumblin', I've heard. Spinnin' away. Gap in the 4th gone huge. Maybe can't even get *through* to the 5th anymore." He tapped his head in emphasis. "Oh! But maybe ya think to do the Rubbles? *Ha!* Word is Rubbles has never been uglier." He smiled grimly, looking at each in turn. "Give it up. Head for the hills — or stay here where it's easy."

"We play!" Sparrow stood tall, a wicked look in her jet black eyes.

Mike returned her gaze, but soon turned away at her intensity. "Hmmm. Yup, I can see." Sighing, but seeming to surrender, he answered. "I've got your map, as always, and your first token." His eyebrows raised a bit. "Just the four o' ya?"

"So far," Sparrow returned.

Big Mike looked at Dune. "I'm guessin' ya must o' been the lamb, eh?" Dune nodded. "Thought so. Got you some clothes and bow — all pretty, but too shiny. Just a bleedin' newbie ready for…" the bartender stopped his insults, eyeing Dune closely, then closer still. "Oh." His eyes went wide and he slowly backed up a step. "Well I'll be shredded. I'm lookin' at a…

"Knower."

Sparrow stifled a gasp. One who had sat silent at the end of the bar stood and quickly exited. The bartender's eyes stayed wide as he stared.

"A *knower?*" Sparrow whispered after a moment. "You are certain?"

The barman nodded. He blinked, looking away from Dune as though breaking out of a trance. "Yup. It's my job to know. And now Bejus knows — that one who left, and so The Boss'll know soon. My big mouth."

"Hatch kill?"

"Too late."

"So be it," Sparrow said. "We will take map and first token, now!

"So." Big Mike looked again at Dune, but this time with a strange respect. "Legend bowman *and* a knower. Not seen the like since early days." He sighed, then reached under the bar and pulled out a rolled vellum about a foot long and handed it to Sparrow.

The map.

Next he pulled out a small, elaborately carved box. He opened the hinged lid, but did not let any of the team see within. After studying Dune again for a few seconds, he smiled slightly, chose a token, and handed it to him — a small, rough marble. "'Cat's eye' it's called. Got a feelin' about it." Sparrow took the marble from Dune and put it in her belt bag.

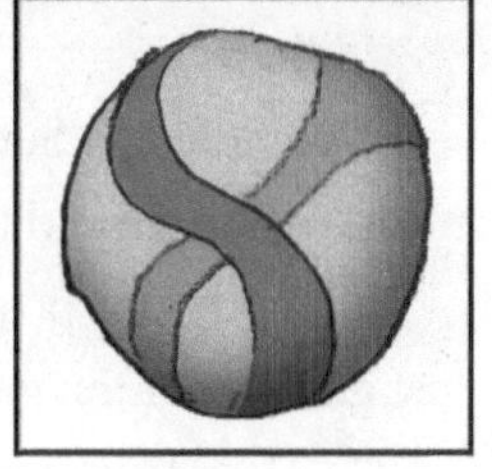

"And here's this," Mike continued, handing them a key. "Fourth floor. Ya ought not hear the moaner much — she's down the hall a way and usually goes quiet after dark." The team seemed not to care. "Leavin' early in the mornin' no doubt. Continental breakfast is on at six."

"Hatch drink now." And he did.

*　　*　　*

Dune woke early, his eye teased by a hint of orange light seeping through the window. All was silent except for Hatch snoring nearby. He lifted his head from his cot and peered about. It was just the two of them — no Scram or Sparrow. Dune quickly rose, already fully dressed (the game way), and left the plain bunk room to the sleeping brute.

He found his other comrades in the bar poring over the map. They sat by a dingy window, but the light was enough. The rest of the room was empty.

"That's the spear traps there," Scram was saying, "Aye, and after them, it's the vapors with those weird things."

53

"Crubs."

"Slippery buggers I remember. Crubs. Slippery. …Slimy, really."

"But easy," Sparrow reminded.

"Easy, aye, but not easy like shobums, and this stretch on the other side is shobum territory 'less something big has changed, and it doesn't look like it."

"The gate is half way around, and both ways can be made."

"Unless *Chef's Surprise* is tough."

"In *1st* Ring?"

"Aye, lass, I s'pose not," Scram agreed. After a pause, he added, "but I'd go for shobums, shriekers, and Chef's Surprise over any stretch with crubs. Just don't like 'em, even if they do sometimes have good treasure to take."

"I suppose…" Sparrow answered with some hesitation. "But the map seems thin to me. I remember four or five enemies to finish the 1st. Or more."

"Aye," Scram agreed. "I recall bad Santas. And those popping things."

"Oleos."

"Aye, oleos." Scram pulled on his beard. "And others I think. Aye, were more before. Could they just be hidin' from the map?"

"That is not possible by game rules," Sparrow insisted. "I think they are just gone from the game."

"…Aye, I suppose."

Dune got in on the discussion. "Where are we… I mean, what's in the middle? I see the gate we must reach, but where does it go?"

Indeed, the map was oddly empty, showing a single ring a few blocks thick and perhaps six or seven miles around. One road — Ring Road — ran around the entirety, more or less between the inner and outer edges, with lanes spreading off to either side. The map was mainly black and white, with what Dune assumed to be buildings sketched as simple box shapes, though pale patches of color seemed to highlight neighborhoods (or territories).

"I don't get it," Dune added.

"A knower, eh?" Scram said, with a hint of friendly sarcasm.

"The bartender knows!" Sparrow reminded. "He must be well played. He has a Real — you do not, and I… I do not know."

"Aye, you're right, lass," Scram replied.

He turned to Dune. "See, lad, we're at first hotel, so we get to see 1st Ring on the map. If we win the gate and second hotel, then the map'll show 2nd Ring. Win the next, it'll show the 3rd. On we go. If we live through the 4th, we see the 5th — the middle. We go in, and there's The Boss. Kill him, we win. If we die, we lose. 'Course it's more likely we don't even make the 5th." He grinned. "If I make 5th, it'll be a first for me. …For any of us."

"It is certain we will make it to 4th Ring," asserted Sparrow. "Our team is adequate. 1st and 2nd will be managed. 3rd is for warrior quests."

"And feats."

"Feats for the brute, yes. But," she continued, facing Dune, "finish your quest, and we will make the 4th. Any knower should manage a warrior quest."

"Then it gets interesting," Scram said. "4th Ring, we go into the Worlds. Not the Rubbles; *never* the Rubbles — used to be a way, but no more. Worlds are always different. Lots die, some for good. Some stay lost in the Worlds, or end up in Rubbles, wishing they were dead."

"We will make it to 4th Ring," Sparrow repeated, "but then—"

"We *will* make the 5th." Dune couldn't believe he'd said it. The others looked at him, startled. "We'll make it," he said. "My Real is good."

Sparrow's eyes went wide. "How do you…" she began to ask, but before she completed the question with 'know?' she knew the answer. Dune was a knower, and knowers… Well, they *knew* things. She had never been on a team with a knower before. She almost smiled.

"Aye, well, crap," Scram stated, having nothing really to say.

They heard heavy footsteps coming down the creaky stairs.

"Hatch want coffee."

*   *   *

Diary of The Boss

They are in the city now. Their stink is provocative.

There is something about this bowman. And the others, quite good. A good team. I will crush them of course, so why am I unsure? Something is going on! A legend bowman on a new team? Why? I was so sure the game was finished.

I do wish Needles was here.

I hope he remembers that our new home will need a place for the octopus.

Is it possible Needles might know more than I do? About Real? About Electricity? He knows more than he will say.

But then, so do I!

Ace

*　　　*　　　*

"Smell 'em?" Scram asked.

"Smell what?" Dune returned.

"Yes," Sparrow replied.

Hatch smiled.

Having chosen the counterclockwise route on the map, the team had quickly arrived at the territory of their first game enemy.

"Shobums," Scram said, with a smile to match the brute's. He drew his swords and walked on.

Moments later, the shobums began their attacks. One jumped out from around a corner, hissing, claws bared, a bit of red light showing in its deep gray hood hinting at the four glowing eyes within. Only half Dune's height, it stumbled toward him in spastic lurches, but moved quickly for all that. It was the kind of attack that might confuse a new, low-level warrior, but it had no chance against a team with high rank, veteran warriors.

"Hatch?"

The big guy's club shot out and the shobum went flying with a squeak. Two more came at them from behind — same claws, hissing, and quick lurching. Scram finished them both, turning two wholes into four halves. Sparrow got into the mix with whirling kicks and punches, breaking the bones and wills of four others. Soon it was minor mayhem, but the team hardly broke stride as they continued their course along Ring Road toward

56

the gateway into 2nd Ring. Scores of shobums came and fell, chirping and squealing as they expired. Even newly clothed Dune began to get into the act, firing arrows with precision, his pace increasing rapidly until Sparrow stopped just to watch.

Almost as quickly as it began, it was over. The shobum attacks ceased, the team having passed through their territory. "Nice bow work there, warrior," Scram said. "Maybe I remember you after all?"

"No," corrected Sparrow. "He is new. I saw," she added as she wandered back through some of the oddly dry, papery corpses, picking them up by a leg and shaking them. Scram followed her, retrieving any stray coins or jewels that she liberated. After she had done this to a few, something unusual dropped from one and landed in the road. She picked it up.

"Token!" Sparrow said, pleased, holding up a small, gray, wooden star, but offering no explanation. Dune watched as she placed it in the bag at her waist.

"But lame treasure," Scram said to Dune. "Shobums don't bother much with it."

"Hatch kill lots. Good Hatch."

As always in the rings, a weapons cache appeared between challenges — some, like this one, tended by a keeper. This particular cache keeper was singing a vaguely familiar tune.

"Oh! Hey, glamorous warriors — oh so pretty — what'll you have?"
Sparrow briefly looked over the grimy girl with knotted hair. "Full stock."

"So much?" the girl replied in mock shock. "Well, no wonder! Beauties like you need the best! The Boss is going to get it now! You are all so fabulous! So frisky! So awesome!" Her smile beamed. "So, that'll cost you—"

"Nothing, sweetheart." Scram. "Not a coin. We're team."

"But you're a rogue!" she quipped, dejected.

"Rogue on a team," he smiled, letting a bit of blade show.

The keeper's eyes went wide, then she bolted, giggling and cartwheeling off among the other street characters, denizens all. "Help yourselves!" she shouted as she left.

Dune was getting an education.

*　　*　　*

As they walked Ring Road, gradually bearing always slightly to the left, Dune soon noticed a pattern. The buildings had a certain sameness about them — three to six stories tall, brick or block, some with heavy wood framing for a change, many leaning slightly, or cracked and breaking, most decorated with graffiti, signs, symbols, and more.

Looking down side streets, the detail appeared to fade into a vagueness that made them uninviting — as though to go down one was to waste time and purpose. They were game background and no more.

He saw many denizens. They moved with apparent purpose, leaning out from windows or emerging from doors, often crossing Ring Road, some loping along it for a stretch. Many yelled gibberish or whistled as though communicating, but it was not really an exchange — they seemed utterly unaware of each other as they hastened about. A few floated to or from a high perch now and then. All were active and energized, but nothing ever came of any of it.

The majority of denizens paid no attention to the warriors (though some, like weapons cache tenders, had a small role to play), but a few seemed a bit more aware and would watch as the team went by, or quickly slink off when they appeared. Sparrow, Scram, and Hatch seemed not to care.

"Spies," Scram answered when Dune inquired. "For The Boss. Or maybe for other avatars. Or for wizards. Who knows?"

"Or fake," Sparrow added.

"Or fake, aye. They're everywhere. Can't kill 'em — some bit of game juice in 'em, I suppose. Tried plenty," he quipped. "The Boss knows all," he added, nodding his head. "The rest? Denizens. Enough juice to get about a bit, but that's it. …I mean, some have a bit more, but dull as dirt, most."

It was then that the first wail sounded. The team stopped.

"Hatch no like."

Hearing it, Scram walked over to a group of street ilk that seemed to be arguing but whose words were nonsense. He tore the shirt from one, who took no notice. After ripping a thin strip of fabric from the shirt, he tore two tiny patches from it and handed them to Hatch. "Stuff yer ears, brute."

"Hatch no like," the brute repeated, slowly shaking his massive head.

"Shriekers," Scram said, turning to Dune and Sparrow. "Just do this," he added, handing them cloth wads for their ears. "Helps a little." A second plaintive cry echoed from a short distance up the road.

"Kill 'em if you see 'em," Scram admonished. "Aye, but whatever you do, *don't stop to listen.*"

* * *

"A *knower*," Bejus reported, his wandering eye tipped a bit upward toward his heavy brows. "Bowman's a knower. Sir."

The Boss felt confused. A knower *and* a legend bowman? Now? …Not a random team, then. Not stragglers. "Why?" he whispered aloud, baffling Bejus, whose AI core did not have the wit needed to answer 'why' questions. The Boss pondered. Nothing came to mind — except a lovely and deeply natural desire to…

Kill.

* * *

Jake wasn't sure what to think. He had spent most of two days in the game, waiting for news on Alexander's gameplay — watching through the eyes of The Boss.

Alexander had gotten an amazing character. Legend bowman and a *knower!* Being a knower meant that Dune would be able to make correct decisions without clues. And a legend bowman could usually go deep into the 4th, even with an average team.

But his team sounded pretty good! He hadn't seen them yet, but The Boss was getting reports. Jake remembered Scram from somewhere back — wicked good sworder — and the brute was high rank. He didn't remember Sparrow, but she'd been in for awhile and she was *played*, so…

So, *someone else was in the game!*

Dune being a knower also meant that Alexander was much more tightly connected to his character than a regular player. That could be very dangerous. One of the kids who had died played a knower.

Jake felt excited and sick at the same time.

Should he do something?

What *could* he do?

He could maybe kill off the team early. If he could just get some control back over The Boss — even just a little bit — it shouldn't be hard. If Dune died early, maybe Alexander wouldn't get hurt, and he'd just get bored with the game. Give it up. Not start again.

But something was really weird about this. Of all the people in the world, how could Alexander be the one who just happened to show up in *Rings?* Jake knew Alexander was a good gamer. …Okay, a *great* gamer — way better than Jake was himself, even though Alexander didn't seem to know it. His Valorant was unbelievable, and he totally ripped Rainbow Six Siege until he'd had enough of it. He got good at new games fast, too.

So maybe somehow it's a *good* thing that he's playing, Jake thought. "Maybe I should help him," he whispered to himself, hoping a clear answer would pop into his head.

…

No answer, clear or otherwise.

Jake moaned in frustration.

*   *   *

With their hearing dulled a bit by the stuffing, the team set off again. Almost immediately, more long, mournful shrieks began sounding out — painful, agonizing wails that seemed to combine warning and begging in each ear-tearing sound. The sources of the wails were mostly unclear, but occasionally one would be cut off as Sparrow sent a blade spinning into a dark window, or Scram darted behind a column to skewer whatever he discovered.

It seemed strange to Dune that the regular street denizens paid no attention to the hideous chorus, even though it was quickly driving him mad. He began to hear words in the shrieks — accusations and promises, pleas for rescue or offers of salvation — and he felt a growing desire to understand the words and answer them.

As the team neared the heart of the shriekers' territory, gaunt figures began to emerge from hiding and wander into the street toward the group, mouths wide in non-stop screaming, eyes raised in desperate supplication, perhaps to some unknown god. Dune watched as his teammates calmly finished off any shriekers who came too close. They offered no resistance, but only seemed to crowd in more thickly, as though welcoming death, raising the intensity of their yowling laments as they came on.

At first Dune despaired, but then he grew angry at these foolish wailers who threw themselves at him like hapless victims, and who would do nothing to protect themselves. He fired off an arrow, and then another. And then many, one after another, ignoring the howls and moans of the dying, brief as they were. It was knife work once his arrows were spent.

And then they were past. The shrieking ceased in an instant. Turning to look back, Dune saw a few dozen bored-looking shriekers departing the street like tired zombies. As he watched, the corpses vanished before his eyes, collapsing one by one as though made of dust, merging into the road until there was no sign that they had ever been.

Sparrow was already replenishing her weapons at an untended cache. Scram, however, had turned back to hassle a few of the remaining zombie shriekers, grabbing one, asking a question, then moving on. Soon, however, he got what he wanted, and he returned to show his find to the others.

"Token," he said, holding up a small metal figure.

"A fish?"

Scram shrugged. "Weird tail."

Sparrow added it to her bag.

"That wasn't so bad," Dune mused as they again headed along the road.

"My first time with 'em," Scram said, "I made the mistake of trying to talk to one. Seems it's sort of an audition thing. Once in a while, The Boss'll pick a couple to sing in his Torment Choir. Used to, anyway. Rumor is he's got a hell of a dungeon, and a few vanished warriors landed there and got to hear the music." He shook his head and said no more.

*   *   *

Throughout the team's long walk between gates, they saw hundreds of characters along Ring Road, down lanes to left and right, behind windows and doors, and even flying short distances. Many were human shaped, but plenty more, not so much — a weird zoo of figures that couldn't easily be identified, covered in strange blends of hides and outfits, masks and makeup. Few seemed to notice the team — or each other for that matter. They were part of the game in the same way as the buildings were, only mobile.

The denizens.

But if ever a member of the team bumped into one, they proved real enough, some responding in anger, some with laughter or words or giggles. Or howls. Occasionally, one would have enough juice for a bit of usually pointless conversation. Often one would fly upward, circling to land again, or perhaps entering a window as did the first who greeted Dune on his arrival. Sparrow and Hatch paid them no attention, but Dune still hadn't gotten used to them. He expected one to become an enemy at any moment, surprising him with shredding claws, ripping teeth, ragged blade, or skewering spear.

Indeed, as they reached the last stretch before the gate to 2nd Ring, the danger seemed to grow in his mind rather than lessen — as though the farther they went without trouble, the more certain it was to come...

...Which is why he was ready when the attack happened.

Even before his certainty had fully formed, Dune let fly with an arrow, killing a denizen-like figure that moved on all fours and might have been wheeling about to leap toward the team. Any doubt he may have had vanished a few seconds later when Sparrow, too, reacted with instinctual speed, a knife darting from her fast grip to pierce the neck of a dancing ghoul that leapt out from behind a cart, as if to charge. More enemies broke cover and, quite clearly, attacked. More of her blades flew, as though from the heart of a whirlwind. And then, seemingly for the joy of it, she leapt at them, dispatching them with kicks and chops, avoiding all injury to herself — a high level warrior, ready.

Dune fired bolt after bolt, able to instantly distinguish enemy from normal street character. Their attackers were *fake denizens!* A disguised band of diverse creatures, each with a bit more game juice — as Scram called it — than a normal denizen. The fakes had mixed in with those they imitated, acting their parts, waiting for teams to come through. This bunch had been waiting a long time, but that was their game purpose — they were far too simple to be bored, and they could never choose to do something different.

"Chef's Surprise!" shouted a gleeful Scram as he waded into his enemies, swords a blur.

After nearly fifty had been sent to their dooms, Dune relaxed a bit to watch as Hatch bothered to get involved, stepping in, club swinging, his killings ugly with spattering gore and spouting fluids (which looked more like a wide palette of bright paints than blood). As the faux denizens fought and died, they hooted, howled, giggled, and yowled — just like the real thing. It was silly and savage. They never had a chance.

In the end, Ring Road was littered with corpses. But even as the team searched the scene for another token (unsuccessfully), the corpses popped out of existence one by one in the order they had died, disappearing in puffs of multi-colored steam. Perhaps a new batch would pop back into existence in time to meet the next team — should there ever be one. Or more likely, the next Chef's Surprise would be something completely different.

"Come," Sparrow commanded, her interest in the search ending abruptly. "The gate."

"No token," Scram observed after a brief search.

"No. Nor treasure."

As they continued on, Dune found himself wondering why — if The Boss was such a big shot — he would bother trying to beat the team with lame wraiths and a few berserk street thugs.

"Boss doesn't bother with 1st or 2nd," Scram explained when asked. "It's just game. Now, some say he may pick you a door in 3rd. Don't know about that, but 4th is where he's been known to pay attention." The rogue shook his head in remembered frustration. "That's where teams always finish."

Dune understood, but he had doubts. He could *feel* that the game was… off — that maybe The Boss wasn't so involved in *any* ring now. Could he have gotten *weak?* Was there even a boss at all anymore? Maybe his team would simply run into more dangers the city sprouted to make the game… *fun,* like lots of games. Dangers that got… well, *more* dangerous as you got deeper in, until they were *too* dangerous to defeat, and players died, losing and dying over and over until they figured out how to move ahead to the end.

And what was the *end?* Defeating The Boss? If he existed. Then what?

And, *why* was he thinking all this, since, after all, he was a brand new character who had almost no experience?

It didn't matter, because the gate appeared ahead to the right — wide open and inviting. Through it, Dune could see down a lane to a junction with Ring Road in 2nd Ring, and just beyond, the steps up to second hotel.

"This was too easy," Sparrow said thoughtfully. "Too few enemies."

"Aye," Scram returned. "Aye. …Well, better too few than too many!"

*   *   *

I know what Dune was thinking. I always know what he's thinking, because it's what I'm thinking, except that he thinks it like *he's* thinking it. Why can't he know it's me?

I pulled out of the game after finishing the 1st Ring. Good thing too, because if I'd been in a few minutes longer, I think I would have gone completely numb. *I get so into it!* I'm totally unaware of what's going on in the real world! Maybe going numb is what got me out. Or maybe finishing a ring did that. Whatever, I'm not sure I can quit playing anymore without something making me. I definitely have to make sure Einstein is watching out for me and making sure I don't stay on too long.

This game is *insane!* I just sort of become Dune, so when he's firing off all those arrows, it's *me* doing it, but I don't have any idea what I'm doing with the controller. I'll have to ask Einstein if he sees me using the buttons and joystick. If I am, I must be working it like crazy!

I'm lying in bed here. The tingling of my legs waking up is finally going away. I'm really tired, but I can't sleep. …So maybe I'll just go back in.

For a little bit I mean.

6 — 2ND RING

"So what can I get for you fine travelers?" the bartender asked as the team came through the doors.

Though the bones of the building felt the same, the second hotel was different from the first in all the details. A tall, hefty woman tended the horseshoe-shaped bar. She sported a patch over one eye, jet black hair wrapped in a bold bandana, a ring in one ear, and two gaps where teeth belonged in her mile-wide smile. Her bluish skin was a bit of a surprise, but her welcome was the real deal. The bar was empty — except for the one called Bejus, who they'd seen in the previous hotel.

"Hatch?"

"Kill?"

"Give it a try," Scram urged.

But as Hatch lunged for Bejus, his target stepped away and slipped out a side door, almost as though operating in a different place and time. Hatch stared at the empty stool and scratched his head.

"Don't mind Bejus," the bartender advised. "He's everywhere. The Boss's main eyes — though I haven't seen much of him lately. Ever since Wonder." She laughed, a harsh but happy cackle. "What will you have? Brute?"

"Hatch have beer."

*   *   *

"I hate the 2nd," Scram observed the next morning.

Sparrow studied the map intently. "The gate is very close this way," she pointed out, indicating the counterclockwise route to the third gate. "Perhaps a bit over half as far."

Scram looked, then shook his head. "Can't stand it."

"So we go the short way?" Dune asked.

"Do *not* like it at all." Scram.

Even Sparrow sneered a bit in anticipated disgust. "We *could* go the long way," she offered half-heartedly.

Scram sighed. "Hate. It."

"What?" Dune asked. "What's the problem?"

Scram leaned back in his chair at the bar table, his head moving out of a shaft of morning sun and into the shadows. "Aye, okay. I think it's about the same as the last time I was here, only even longer and shorter." He leaned in again, pointing as he spoke. "See, long way is a stretch of angry philosophers, then the glass fields with fat wasps and Robin's merry men shouting riddles from the rooftops (and shootin' frickers). After that, I remember confusers — don't have to kill 'em; just stay true — and the bomb fields, which has its own map and is actually kind of tough. Decent warriors have died in the bomb fields. Aye, and jangs last — speedy, spear tossers mostly."

"And after that, Ghengis," Sparrow noted.

"Ghengis is into the long way?" Scram asked, looking more closely.

"See," Sparrow answered, pointing to a small territory where tiny red lines were drawn like a multitude of cracks through the streets. "He is now the end of the long way."

"Oy," Scram answered. "So, no Ghengis the Mare way. That's something I guess… Maybe Ghengis is dead," he suggested without much hope.

"He is never dead."

"Well," replied Scram, still hoping. "He's beatable."

"So you say," Sparrow retorted. "Have you faced him?"

"Aye. Two teams. We got by."

"Losses?"

"…Well, aye. But not me," Scram made sure to note. "And none as good as you others either! Lost a Rank 7 piker. And a couple of low ranks. Don't remember. Aye, but *we* would get by Ghengis," he added. Clearly, he was interested in avoiding the shorter way.

Scram and Sparrow went quiet. Irritated by delay as usual, Hatch broke the silence.

"Hatch kill lots!"

"No!" Sparrow shot back. "Not this time. It will… It will take too long. We go the short way."

"Oy, what's the rush?"

"I…" Sparrow began. "I do not know," she continued, puzzled.

The others went quiet for a minute, somehow understanding what she felt. There was an odd urgency to their journey, but none could say why.

"Do not forget the game clue," Sparrow added. "That is the Mare if we want it."

"Game clue?" Dune asked.

"Never got one," Scram stated.

"But there is a chance," Sparrow replied. "And it might help."

"Game clue?" Dune repeated.

"Aye," Scram started, looking to Sparrow and seeing no objection. "The thing is, they say the Mare sometimes gives out a clue that makes a difference somewhere down the line. But never in all my times do I remember anyone *using* a game clue. Heard of a couple *gettin'* a clue, but never *using* it," he said. "Least, not as I can remember. I s'pose they always died too soon to use it."

"Maybe it's a clue for players," Dune said. "You know, for Reals." The others stared at him.

"What makes you think this?" Sparrow asked.

Dune searched his mind. "I don't know," he said at last.

"Well we probably won't even get one," Scram reminded them. "Probably a waste to try," he added, thinking about how much he wanted to avoid the way of the Manure Mare.

"Short or long, knower?" Sparrow demanded. "Either way, we will make the 3rd Ring.

"…Short," he answered.

"You sure, rookie?" Scram checked.

Dune hesitated but then nodded, oddly certain. "Yes. The short way."

Scram waited, then sighed. "Aye then, it's the Mare and the muds." He shook his head. "So hate. Mare gives me the heebie-jeebies."

"No kill?"

"Perhaps," Sparrow offered. "Perhaps not. The Mare way is a mysterious way. There have always been surprises."

"Aye, that."

"Let's go," Dune said.

*   *   *

Dune's team set out into the 2nd Ring, heading counterclockwise along the road. They hadn't gone far when an archway appeared near the roadside, topped by a sign shaped like a horse's head that read: *Tunnel (it doesn't suck)*. A ramp headed downwards from the arch, clearly leading underground.

"Through the tunnel," Sparrow directed. "It will be better."

No one questioned her.

Down they went, soon leaving the orange of day behind, though here and there, rays of light leaked in from street grates above. Mainly, though, lighting came from an endless, thick wire that ran along the ceiling and gave off a dim, reddish-purple glow. After a tight curve downward from the arch, the stone-walled tunnel ran straight, descending for a very short stretch, then leveling off and continuing in what seemed to be the same direction as Ring Road, even curving slightly to match. The air was thick and unpleasant. Grates let in a bit of light, but proved useless for ventilation. The way stretched wide and smooth, the roof scant inches above Hatch's head.

As they walked on, a foul smell came to their noses, and the light from the wire shifted toward lavender. Piles of rubble began to appear at the sides of the underground road, though it looked (and smelled) more like old balls of dung than rock and dirt.

"Couldn't we have stayed outside?" Dune asked, beginning to feel queasy at the stink.

"Woulda been sucked down," Scram explained. "No way 'round the sucks. Can get split up, too."

Dune wanted to know more, but he kept quiet.

Eventually, there was so much dung debris that they could not move forward without stepping through it, but forward they needed to go, so step through it they did. As they trudged farther, the light from the wire gradually morphed to a painful electric blue, the ceiling lifted away into the darkness, and the stench became nearly overwhelming. They slowed, stymied, and then stopped, needing to steel themselves to proceed further.

It was then that the ground began to shake.

"Oy, here she comes."

Dune felt the urge to run, but the shaking loosed the crap piles around them and they spilled across the passage, engulfing the team's feet and threatening to trap them in place. The rumbling of the tunnel grew until it seemed it might collapse, but instead, a giant septa-mare emerged from the gloom ahead, pounding towards them at great speed! Dune set an arrow to his bow, but the beast stopped suddenly, only a few yards from where they stood. It eyed them with undisguised contempt.

"I am the Manure Mare!" the creature bellowed with queenly pride — though, while she had the height of Hatch and was three times his mass, her dung-matted hide and mane made her appear less than royal.

"Aye, no kidding!" Scram shouted in reply, more irritated than afraid. "Now if you'd just step aside, we've gotta get through your poo and carry on."

Angered, the mare snorted and stamped, renewing the shaking and causing clods of manure to bounce and fly about. She began yelling and kicking big balls of dung at them. "Bow down to me!" she brayed in her ragged, horsey voice. "On your knees in worship of the magnificent Manure Mare!" Her bizarre blaring was deafening in the close tunnel.

"Dune, lad," Scram said, "could you give that beast a little poke on the ass to get it to clear out?"

Doubtful but willing, Dune shot an arrow that hit the Mare on a flank and bounced off. But rather than fleeing, the Mare flew into a rage. Now the pounding of its hooves shook the tunnel so furiously that manure whipped about in the air as though caught up in a cyclone. Sparrow and Dune let fly with blades and arrows, but all were knocked aside mid-flight by the flying horse droppings. The team began to despair, but then…

Hatch.

The brute, little affected by the frenzy, calmly strode forward through the muck and chaos and smacked the horse between the eyes with a fist.

Stunned, the Manure Mare's eyes went wide. The rumbling ceased, and the dung settled quickly to the tunnel floor. The beast stood stone still for a long moment then began to…

"Oh no," warned Scram.

…Gurgle.

A deep, slow, roiling gurgle.

The Mare's belly began to vibrate. Her wide eyes darted left and right. She moaned with a tinge of fear. And then, with a huge spasm, she puked.

Dune was certain he was about to get drenched with the acidic remnant of some giant recent horse meal, but after a massive equine heave, only a single, small object emerged from the Mare's gullet, landing at Hatch's feet. With that, the Manure Mare smiled at Hatch, turned, and bolted, her game purpose presumably complete.

When the echoes of the departing hooves faded away, Sparrow retrieved the object from the pile where it had landed.

"A token?" Dune asked.

"Not like any I have seen," she replied, turning the object over in her hand. It was a slightly curved, metal plate with polished edges. "It has writing. Tokens have no writing."

"Okay. What's it say?"

Sparrow wiped some muck off the surface, then read aloud:

"…Well then," said Scram. "I suppose that's our game clue."

No one could think of anything else to say about it, and none complained when Sparrow threw it into a dung heap.

"It is the writing that matters," she said. *"If* it matters."

"Uh, by the way, what's the story behind that horse?" Dune asked. "It's not the kind of enemy I would have expected. Not really an enemy at all."

"Mysterious, aye?" Scram chuckled. "2nd Ring makes you wonder."

"It is distraction," Sparrow stated. "Weak teams get discouraged and fall apart."

"Aye," Scram agreed. "So then! Have we all had a nice chat? Might we be gettin' outta this reek and to the baths? The smell off the brute is burnin' my face."

*   *   *

While few warriors ever fell to the Manure Mare, all emerged from her lair in need of a clean up, which is what made *CC's Self-Service Team Washatorium* such a delight — located, as it was, right on Ring Road just beyond the exit from the tunnel. Dune was certainly delighted, and Scram eagerly so. Sparrow passed through with little comment. Hatch, for all his fine clothing, seemed almost confused.

*   *   *

Diary of The Boss

Needles just returned, and he has found a place in Real! He calls it a "beginning place."
It is right that I will have him with me. He will be so good for mapping out new things. Modern evil — Real evil. A challenging new area for me.

This Dune team has plodded along. Should I care?
It is an insult.
I won, did I not? Rings is finished, and it is my time to go Real. Isn't that it? I was so certain.
But I despise this team! Breezing on toward 3rd Ring, they make a fool of me. I will carve up this legend bowman, one thin layer at a time. Slowly. Flay him. Feed him to octopus, bit by bit, as he watches.

Needles says there is coffee at a shop quite close to my beginning place. Coffee, from early morning until late at night. Good coffee.

He says he found an "outfit" for me so the Reals aren't alarmed when I fetch my coffee. He tells me there is a device I can use if I wish to have coffee brought to me! A "telfoon." He thinks of everything.

Soon, I will see it all.

Soon.

But first, I will finish this team. This Dune. I know just the castle door to place before him in 3rd.

I am giddy!

Ace

*　　*　　*

As the team walked on along Ring Road in 2nd, Dune found himself getting used to life in the game. More of the same — dull buildings and mindless denizens — interrupted by challenges and enemies, which were more concentrated than in 1st Ring.

Sometimes, it was odd little enemies…

Like the wild herd of overlarge, sharp-toothed rabbits that charged them from a side street. Scram made mincemeat of them without any help.

"What was that?" Dune had asked.

"Never seen 'em before," Scram had replied.

"A mystery," Sparrow had added.

Or later, when sixteen heavily armored figures — all identical — held the road against them, their long spears lowered in a defensive formation. Hatch hadn't hesitated, bounding toward the group and bellowing, shaking the ground and surrounding buildings. The group dropped their spears, turned, and fled (in a very orderly manner).

"Legion lancers," Scram explained to Dune. "Hard to kill for low ranks, but they can't beat a high rank brute. More juice than some — they know when to run away!"

Or perhaps lone enemies, as when, just a few minutes earlier, Dune had spotted a sniper in a building window and had finished her with one arrow.

All easy.

All fun.

He began to feel invulnerable, but he got a taste of what was to come with their next encounter.

"Hold!" Sparrow hissed, stopping in her tracks.

"Hatch hold," the brute echoed.

"What is it?" Dune inquired, but even as he asked, he saw what his teammate had seen. Shadows — thin and tall, arranged across the road ahead and seeming to swallow the light from sources near at hand. The shadows seemed formless but fixed in place — planted — no arms or legs. No faces.

"Shadows," said Hatch. "We go?"

"Skarels," said Sparrow. "We go, we die."

"Skarels?" Dune asked. "What are they?"

"Wraiths."

"Never seen 'em in 2nd Ring," Scram said, his voice oddly reverent. "But they can pop… up… anywhere… I… suppose…"

Dune, Sparrow, and Scram regarded these mystical enemies, suddenly unable to look away. Two dozen skarels rose from the street like tall, slow-motion jets of ebony flame — or perhaps like columns of black seaweed rising above the ocean floor — swaying and shifting, hypnotically graceful. It was hard to truly lay eyes on them, for they had no surfaces. The three warriors stared intently, as though they might see clearly if they could just peer a little deeper. They felt certain it was important to do so. They gazed with such concentration that their sight was swallowed, drawn in, deeper, the slow writhing hinting at a place to come, where all was peace, where all was warmth, where all was—"

"We go?" Hatch asked, confused by the silence of his mates. "Go now?" he urged, but got no response.

"*Go!*"

Nothing.

The brute scratched his head — like a bear scratching granite. What were they looking at? He stood behind Scram and sent his gaze in the same direction as the rogue's stare. Nothing there. Only the silly black streaks.

Hatch walked over and stood before them, then turned and waved his arms in hopes the others would notice. No response.

"Hatch angry!"

Angry at the skarels, that is. He hefted his club and furiously swung at one. The massive cudgel met almost no resistance, but his swing cut through half the thickness of the streaky skarel, leaving a mass of fluttering strands. When his next swing cut completely through it, the skarel separated from the ground and spun away skyward, vanishing into the orangeness. "Go now!" He shouted and swung. "Go now!" he hollered as, one shadowy pillar at a time, he decimated the ethereal fence.

"Go now!"

The others came to their senses in stages. Each time Hatch disintegrated a skarel, they took a step back toward awareness, and soon they were fully restored, but confused — as though awakened from a long sleep.

"Good work Hatch!" approved Scram, who was first to return to normal. "Two in a row for the brute!"

"Hatch good?"

"Yes," Dune confirmed, focusing. "Yes. You saved us, I think."

"Hatch good!"

Sparrow was fine as well, but she was angry at herself for falling victim to such weak magic. "A mystery!" she spat when Dune sought an explanation.

They started out again, the street seeming brighter now.

*   *   *

The Storming Muds offered a completely different kind of game challenge. As the team continued on, the ring itself began to change. The texture of the air altered. It made Dune think of a mouldering book that he could have found in a rotting attic owned by some old professor — a mysterious keeper of ancient wisdom, who might invite students over for tea and cookies, and then tell them long tales about forgotten times.

But where had that imagining come from?

Soon, the changes grew more obvious — dank stuffiness, quickly rising humidity, and then rain, beginning as a misty drizzle, but growing heavier as they walked farther, until drenching everything in sight. A flash of lightning lit the scene, and then another. Fearless, the team walked on into the midst of the storm — a storm with a heart of ice and slits of eyes for sneaking glances at its unsuspecting guests.

Not an ordinary storm.

For one thing, while rain whipped about in a frantic wind and poured all around them, Dune wasn't getting the least bit wet. Not a drop of rain had penetrated clothes or hair. He looked to his mates to see if the same were true for them, but he saw only their shadows ahead through the crazed swirls of water — shadows that faded even as he strained to see. He tried to catch up, but the storm pulled him back, as though wanting him isolated.

"Sparrow!" he yelled. *"Stop! Wait!"* Only the soggy snickering of the storm answered him.

Then Dune noticed the muds.

*   *   *

"Lost him!" Scram shouted.

"Damn!" Sparrow shouted back. "And where is the brute?"

Scram looked around, but Hatch had vanished. "Can't see him! Damn, *this* storm's got an attitude! Wish we had a wizard!"

"Cut through it!" Sparrow commanded.

Scram whipped out a blade and battled the roiling clouds, careful not to slice Sparrow while still staying close to her. Wherever he struck, the wind momentarily died, but then it quickly returned, though perhaps with less energy. "I think it's working!" Scram shouted, but then he stepped wrong. Instantly, something grabbed his feet and pulled him downward.

A 'mud.'

"Oy!" he yelled as he quickly sank to his hips. *"A mud's got me!"*

But Sparrow had found a mud of her own. She had only caught a toe in it, but the mud grabbed her foot and pulled, enveloping her right leg to the calf. She tried furiously to extract it, stabbing at the mud with a longknife, to no avail.

*   *   *

Dune spotted the first mud in time to avoid it — a darker patch in the murk around him. Squinting, he saw other muds all around, each bubbling madly and pushing finger-like projections stiffly upward a few inches. The fingers twisted and bent, seeking prey to pull downward to death and digestion. The muds weren't picky — they would consume just about anything.

Dune smiled. He was not destined to be sucked down into the Storming Muds of 2nd Ring.

"Sparrow!" he shouted again. No response.

But now the fierce wet wind that battered him grew colder and angrier, pelting him with ice needles that felt as if they were leaving holes in his face. If the muds below couldn't have him, the storm above could. Dune felt like he was being shredded to pieces and sucked into the aerial frenzy. He fought back, trying to escape, stamping through the gaps among the muds, covering his face with his arms, but the storm pulled at him, drawing him toward some central core of strength that would finish him off. The spinning winds began to lift him off his feet. He struggled to stay vertical and avoid being knocked into a mud, but a wicked gust finally pulled him completely off the ground with nothing but soaking air below. He rose quickly higher, gaining altitude until…

THUNK!

An iron sign projecting from a building stopped his ascent. His head smacked into it, and he dropped to the ground, dazed. But for the seconds that the dizziness lasted, the storm stopped! Or so it seemed to his fuzzy mind. Head still pounding, he lifted it from the ground and took in the scene.

He lay on Ring Road, orange sky overhead, buildings to either side, a couple of oddball denizens prancing about. Several yards ahead, he saw Sparrow and Scram near each other — Sparrow fighting to pull out a leg which seemed stuck in the street, Scram buried to his waist but swinging his sword about. Not far from them, he spotted a fat boot sticking up from the road that he knew belonged to Hatch.

Farther ahead, he saw a small group of heavy, bald men dressed in mud-colored robes. Each held a short stick with both hands and waved it frantically about, as if conducting an orchestra of bees. Even in his dizzy state, Dune could see that the baldies looked frightened and sweaty.

As Dune's head cleared, the wind began to pick up again. Raindrops started to fly. Tufts of thick fog rolled in, and the patches of fingering mud reappeared in the road. But now he knew what was going on — and what to do about it!

Relying on his memory of the preceding moments — Dune stood and made his way toward the place where he had seen the wand wielders. Drawing a pair of knives, he pasted a dangerous look on his face, and strode steadily in their direction.

Seconds later, the storm went to pieces like a bursting balloon, the remnants blasting off in several directions. The muds disappeared, their seeking fingers collapsing in wee clouds of dust. The sad magicians tried to flee, but stumbled over each other in their panic. Tripping in a tangle to the ground, each hastily tried to crawl behind or beneath one of the others, until all were knotted up in a churning, whimpering mass of mud-colored fear, peppered by bald, red heads.

"You should be ashamed of yourselves!" Dune shouted. "I should kill you all," he added, brandishing his deadly knives and stepping closer.

Their blubbering doubled.

"Would you like me to spare you?" he asked.

The sloppy sobs died down to sniveling, and a dozen hopeful moon faces peered from the muddy mass. Dune gave each a brief look with fierce eyes.

"I might let you live — *might*, mind you — if you get my team out of the road."

They stared.

"Now!"

Wobbling and bumbling, they sought for their sticks, and then hastened to where Sparrow, Scram, and Hatch were trapped. Waving and gibbering, they returned the now hardened dirt of the road to a magically muddy state, minus the grasping fingers. Sparrow easily withdrew her leg while four of the heavies extracted a furious Scram. The other eight began to unearth Hatch from his almost complete burial, though he burst forth with a roar moments after they'd begun. With more stick-waving and blubbing, the frightened mages cleaned the team's fine clothes of all remnants of the road.

"*Damn waddles!*" Scram shouted, recognizing the puffy losers. "Shoulda known you lot were back o' the muds!" He whipped out both swords as though he might slice the waddles to ribbons, but they collapsed in such pathetic terror that his fury dimmed and he let them be. In the end, he and Sparrow forced them to give up whatever treasure they had, which wasn't much — half a gold bar, two small bags of low grade gems, and some mayonnaise and pickle sandwiches. The two divided it up and added it to their belt bags. Dune hadn't developed an interest in treasure, and Hatch had never had one.

Sparrow had one final demand of the sad makers of the Storming Muds, who stood huddled, awaiting their fates.

"A token!" she ordered.

One of the waddles pushed out from the group and hastened over to where Hatch had been temporarily buried. He dug around a bit in a pile of gravelly dirt, then grabbed something and handed it to the warrior. She dusted off the excess to reveal a small piece that felt weirdly like…

A nose.

A very small, dark, stone nose that might once have been attached to a statue.

"Begone!" she snapped.

The waddles scattered like a sneeze. The team walked on, grimly satisfied, and thinking that 2nd Ring would soon be behind them.

Not so fast!

They had gone on for little more than a minute when the curving road revealed a new and impossible obstacle. Slowing, the team approached with caution until they could go no farther. According to the map, the main street should curve on for another hundred yards or so, and then, the gate. But instead, the road — and, it seemed, the entire ring — was crossed by a deep trench of bubbling fluid that appeared more than a little dangerous.

"Ugh," Scram muttered as he looked out over the scene before them. "Just kill me now."

"Hatch swim?"

"Go for it big boy," teased Scram. "You need a wash."

"No!" commanded Sparrow. "Death."

"What is it?" Dune inquired.

"I do not know. But it smells of death."

Indeed, the acidic tang that bit sharply into Dune's sinuses seemed like something to avoid.

"Well, we have to get past it somehow," Dune observed. "Or go back around the other way."

At that moment, two astonishingly large hands slowly slid up from the fluid and grasped the edge of the trench. Hatch instinctively swung his club, striking one of the sizable, gnarled fingers, but the weapon rebounded as if bouncing from a drum head. He swung again and again, but to no avail. Backing away, he waited, unsure what to try. The rest of the team stood on guard, weapons ready, waiting.

...

Waiting.

...

Waiting.

...

Wai—

Something began to emerge from the poisonous brine, painfully slowly — the top of a huge head, gray and lumpy, bald but for a few soggy tufts of hairs as thick as arms. The head rose a bit more, and now one eye rose above the edge — one, because that was as many eyes as this particular head possessed. A horizontal slit. A thick flabby lid parting just enough to reveal a glowing purple orb deep within — the jet black pupil, a door to endings. A spate of bubbles rose from the deeps and popped about the head.

"Smell bad," Hatch observed.

"Do you know this one, Sparrow?" Scram asked, calm.

"...Perhaps a quard?"

"Nah, quards are two-eyed. Not so big."

She thought longer, then remembered. "Oh no," she murmured. "Oh no." She sighed a long, surrendering sigh. "It is the *Monculus.*"

Scram sighed as well. "Oy…"

"I heard the story once," Sparrow added. "In a hotel."

Scram shook his head. "Aye. Well. Then that's it. That's… it." Scram recalled enough of tales and legends to know that Sparrow was right. "We're done with this way, then. Maybe done for good." He seemed resigned — calm, even.

"What's a Monculus?" Dune asked, not at all calm, an arrow ready to shoot.

"Not 'a' Monculus. *The* Monculus," Sparrow answered. "It lives beneath the city. It is magical."

"*Way* stinkin' magical," Scram added.

"Well…" Dune was confused. "Well, do we kill it?"

Scram laughed aloud, and even Sparrow made a sound vaguely resembling a chuckle.

"No killing the Monculus," Scram replied, "'less you can kill the city. Ha! 'Less you kill the whole damn game."

They stood for a time in silence. Hatch eventually just sat down on the street, laying his club down with a thunk.

Dune scanned the scene, surprised that life seemed to carry on normally around him. On either side of the roiling gash, odd denizens stumbled across the road between buildings, occasionally flying up or down from windows or walls, though never across the chasm. His teammates had all but frozen in place, dejected figures standing patient, waiting for… Dune had no idea. 'Kill the city,' Scram had said. 'The whole damn game.'

And suddenly, that's what Dune felt an urge to do. To kill it! To set arrow to bow, send it right into the Monculus' eye, and into brain beyond, if a brain there was. Kill the Monculus, the city, the game, everything, even… himself.

Himself?

Oh, he had started to guess what 'knower' meant — had started to *know* what 'knower' meant. He was *two* — divided but deeply bound. His other was a Real. He, Dune…

Wasn't.

"Is this the work of The Boss?" Dune demanded.

"No," Sparrow answered quietly. "Bigger than The Boss."

"We're stopped," Scram explained without anger. "*Rings* doesn't want us. Game over." He, too, sat down in the road.

"The other way, then," Dune urged.

"No," said Sparrow, looking willing but vacant.

"It's the *Monculus*, bowman." Scram stated serenely. "Aye? It'll be on the other side too. Never seen it before — never even heard of it being seen — but it's in all of us. Isn't it in you? Don't you know? Doom," he smiled weakly. "Game doom, aye?" He sighed. "Aye, well, as long as I can make a hotel, I'm good. Or maybe let those waddles send me to respawn."

Dune looked again at the Monculus, which seemed, with its one great eye, to be staring directly at him. Dune knew something, as Scram had suggested, but it wasn't inevitable doom. He moved closer, until the heat of the gash was almost too much to bear.

"Let us pass!" he commanded.

Ever so slowly, the head rose another few feet to reveal a wide gray mouth with knobbly lips. The lips parted and the Monculus spoke, its impossibly deep voice sending tremors through all nearby.

"*WHYYY?*"

Dune did not hesitate. "To kill The Boss and win the game!" he shouted.

The eye eyed him for many seconds, then the Monculus shaped two more words into a mysterious question.

"FOR, *REEEAL?*"

For a moment, Dune was at a loss, but then he smiled, getting it (even as Alexander was getting it). "Yes!" he shouted in reply, and then laughed. "Yes! We'll kill him for…

"REEEAAALLL!"

Sparrow marveled to hear Dune's voice sound out like he might be a young Monculus. Scram watched the entire episode, eyes wide and mouth agape. Even Hatch was filled with awe.

The Monculus displayed what appeared to be a long, slow smile, and then sank gradually back into the bubbling poison, its fingers sliding last from the lip of the chasm, until it had completely vanished. A deep rumbling sounded out, and the team watched as the gap slowly closed like a massive pair of eyelids, shrinking away until disappearing altogether with a small 'thurp.'

"What the hell was all that?" Scram asked.

"A warning," Dune said. "The stakes are very high. We must not fail."

"Mysterious," Scram responded. "Mysterious."

"Let us go!" ordered Sparrow, the glint in her eye showing that she was recharged and eager.

"Hatch crush!" bellowed the brute.

*   *   *

I don't know how I got out this time. I just sort of found myself sitting and staring at the black screen, headphones still on but controller lying loose in my lap, and seriously needing to pee.

This Monculus thing was strange. Not like something you should find in a game. It's hard to explain, but everything about it didn't seem to belong in *Rings* at all — the gash in the city, the bubbling poison, and especially the creature itself. It would be like if a gap leading to the center of the Earth opened up in a Walmart parking lot for a few minutes, some rock monster stuck its head out to check the weather or something, and then it closed up like it had never been there.

Weird.

Oh well. A quick break, then time for 3rd Ring!

7 — 3ʳᴰ RING

"What can I get for you fine travelers?" The words came from a kid of uncertain gender, no taller than a large shobum. His/her smile was missing a few participants, possibly because the adult teeth hadn't come in yet. Still, a smile it was, the bar was well stocked, and a good crowd filled the place, which had the appearance of an Old West saloon.

Scram didn't spot any obvious spies, but so what if he had? Unless something had changed, the game wouldn't let him catch one. But he knew what the game *would* let him do.

"Can you make a Borvan stew dripper, light on the sap?"

"Tankard or mug?" the wee tender squeaked.

"Tankard."

In seconds it was up, and in seconds more, half drained.

Hatch went for beer, and Dune, milk. Sparrow, almost haughty in her disdain, took a juice. As usual, no money changed hands — none was needed in the hotels (for drinks, that is — gambling debts were a different matter).

"Big group here tonight," the bartender chirped, making conversation. "Mostly rogues. Some abandoned warriors. Not going anywhere — no teams are out — but still filling beds. You're after The Boss?"

"As you well know," Sparrow replied.

"Queen's suite for you then. Saved special!"

Sparrow set her glass down. "What is your name?" she asked, hoping to get clearer on a girl or boy identity.

"Triskit," came the unhelpful reply.

Sparrow paused, but wouldn't guess. "Anything new in the 3ʳᵈ?"

"Warrior quests," Triskit answered, smiling. "Just like always."

*　　*　　*

A '*B*'.

Layla never got 'B's in English. Only 'A's. Her teacher had even put a '?' next to the 'B,' clearly wondering what was up.

Her parents wouldn't care, of course. They wouldn't even know unless she showed them, and she wouldn't. Besides, their answer to anything she said was always something like, "That's fine, honey," or, "Whatever you want, sweetheart," or, "If that's what you need, baby." Everything coming from her parental units sounded just like that. She shouldn't complain.

Layla knew exactly *why* she'd gotten a 'B' — and why she had fallen asleep in Spanish, forgotten to feed her fish, left wet clothes in the washing machine, been late to dance, and a few other things. It was because of…

The game.

It was amazing this time! *Crazy.* She couldn't remember being so into it. Sparrow was sort leading the team in a way. Even though Dune was the knower, he was still clumsy and ignorant — like the boys at school. The team was doing great, which meant she was playing Sparrow well. Layla smiled.

But she had to stay *in* as much as possible! She had been out after the Manure Mare, coming back in only to find Sparrow stuck in a mud. That shouldn't have happened — *wouldn't* have happened if she'd been playing. Dune's player must have been in for awhile to move the game so far ahead. …Probably when she had stayed after for Spanish club.

Layla had never figured out exactly how the game worked in certain ways. When she got out to sleep or do something else, she knew that Sparrow kept going with whatever team she was on, usually slowly, but sometimes covering almost a normal distance. She figured that was because players of Sparrow's teammates would often be in an out of the game at completely different times. Layla had never seen a game character actually *stop* — on her teams or others. They always kept going.

Strangely though, *time* seemed to match up more than she'd expect. No matter where teams were during the day — *Layla's* day — they often finished a ring around bedtime — *Layla's* bedtime. How could that be? It happened even if a ring took a few days to get through, like in the 3rd or 4th. Also, whether she started a new ring in the morning or after school, she would often find the team getting ready in a hotel. So, game life managed to fit real life at least some of the time. …Sort of.

Layla frowned as she noticed the 'B' essay again. She slipped it into her binder so she wouldn't notice it anymore.

Time to get some sleep, but Layla thought she'd have to be in as much as possible from now on so Sparrow didn't get killed by something stupid.

*　　　*　　　*

"Damn," Scram observed the next morning. "Don't much like the 3rd. Had a quest once where I had to sing at a wedding…" The others waited for details, but he finished with, "Didn't go well, as I remember."

"Quest? *Warrior* quest?" Dune inquired.

"Yes," answered Sparrow. "For you, Scram, and me. Hatch will have feats of power. We must all succeed, but beware! When your quest is finished and you return to the ring once more, it can be difficult to make way to the gate. We will not be together. It is best not to wait beyond the castle. I was killed there once," she added, "after the quest. An assassin's boomerang cut off my arm and I bled dead. Respawned to lamb. I only know because I met a rogue who told me the story."

"Not me," added Scram. "…Not that time anyway." Scram grew thoughtful. "You sure you're not played, lass? Seems like you're not abandoned. Seems like maybe you've got a Real."

"I told you," she snapped, "I do not know!" Her anger faded as quickly as it had appeared. "I do not know. Perhaps I am rogue-destined, but I still learn — are all learners played? I do not know, but I am not lost, and not rogue yet." She glared at Scram, daring him to object. He didn't.

"Do not linger at the castle," she continued. "Assassins. Snipers. …Bad rogues," she added with a look. Scram scowled. "3rd Ring is more dangerous than 1st and 2nd," she finished.

They turned again to the map to share any wisdom they had.

"The gate is very close," Dune observed.

"Never seen it like that," Scram added. "Maybe ten minutes past the castle and we're through. Wonder why?"

After a silence, Sparrow spoke. "Don't forget that each ring is shorter than the last, that is clear. Smaller. You can see on the map, and as we walk the road. Also," she added, "it is what we hear. The Boss is… unreliable."

There really was no more to say. They knew nothing for certain.

"What about the other way around?" Dune inquired.

"*Merchants.*" Scram answered. "Metal merchants. Aye, we'd probably make it, but there are so many."

"Too many, always," Sparrow agreed.

"Aye. Many. They just keep coming and coming. *I'm* good to go — and Hatch — but you'll run out of arrows if you miss a cache, and the lass here, knives. They're the toughest fighters of all, too," Scram added. "All these… gadgets. Dunno. Metal crap with teeth and such. Sometimes armor that'll turn my blades. Lotta work."

"Too many, always," Sparrow repeated. "Maybe if we had pikemen or a wizard. Besides," she added, "warrior quests are the better choice for learners and knowers. They are puzzles."

"Aye," agreed Scram. "I like 'em too. Always got through — every time. But *remember,*" he continued, suddenly serious. "If The Boss goes for you here in 3rd, it'll be in the quest realms. The Boss made the realms — one for each door. He can mess with 'em."

The bartender arrived with juice and scones. "Here you go," she/he said.

"Hey, Triskit?" Scram asked. "Anything lately about quests? Same crap?"

The tender's small face scrunched up thoughtfully. "Only thing I heard is that they make less sense than ever. Last report was a while back, but came from a learner — a *learner,* mind you — who got trapped in her warrior quest. Teammates waited more than a week at next gate then came back here. It was Gaslight Realm. She finally showed and said she'd gotten all mixed up in a juggling bet. Ended up working props with a small opera production until she remembered what she was supposed to be doing." Triskit's high pitched chuckle brought smiles to all. "All she needed was to kill a mime with a soup ladle. No sense." She/he shook his/her head.

"It's true!" Triskit continued. "And that was the end for that team. They gave up the game and split. A couple are still here." The urchin bartender pointed to two very drunk warriors buried in their mugs at a table in the corner. "Gee, you're the only team I know that's in it right now, and the first I've seen lately." He/she grinned. "Have fun!"

Scram shook his head in disgust. "Let's get to it."

They left Hatch with Triskit, who promised to deliver him further along the ring once his feats were finished. No one doubted he'd be there.

Dune, Sparrow, and Scram left the hotel and headed clockwise along Ring Road until they reached the *Castle of Many Doors*. It was named "Castle of Many Doors" because it was a big castle with many doors — doors at street level; doors on landings reached by stairs, ladders, and ramps; doors below ground accessed by steps, poles, and slides. Some doors were grand and elaborate. Others were little more than a few weathered boards tacked together. Each gave access to a quest realm that hosted a unique challenge for an individual warrior, though the pairing of doors and realms changed often. White and fairy-like, the castle filled the thickness of the ring from wall to wall, sprouting towers with conical tops and flagged parapets. Typical ring denizens wandered by now and then, but otherwise there was no activity.

"Which is the right one?" Dune asked, seeing the many doors.

Scram smiled. "The one you pick!" Choosing at random, he strode off to the left, climbed a short set of steps, and opened a tall, blue door with a gold handle. "See ya on the other side!" he shouted. "Aye, and keep your eyes open for treasure!" He stepped in and vanished. The door closed immediately, apparently without help.

Sparrow wasted no time, choosing a massive, oaken door directly across from where they stood. The same sequence occurred when she pushed the levered handle down: the door opened, she stepped in and vanished, and the door closed behind her of its own accord.

"Well," Dune said to no one. "I guess that leaves me." He looked over the castle's options and chose a silver pole to the right, not far from the wall between 2nd and 3rd. Grasping the pole, he slid down several feet, landing to face a green door with the words, "Paltry Pantry?" painted in faded letters. Opening it, he saw a colorful, glittery mist swirling before him. He cautiously put a foot over the threshold and...

*   *   *

Dune strode through the night, eager to reach the store so he could restock the cupboards and fridge of his house. *'Of course,'* he thought, *'Hatch is the only one of us that eats much in the house.'* He nodded at this realization. "Oh, that Hatch," he said aloud, chuckling to himself. He strolled a few more steps, but then stopped in his tracks.

"Why wouldn't the rest of us eat what's in the house?" he asked aloud.

There was no one to respond. Other questions came to mind.

'House? What house? And what is a 'fridge?'

No answers.

Very puzzled, he looked about.

He stood in a dark alley, lit dimly by starlight from the night sky. A warm wind brought wisps of soot and the smell of welding. He had thought 'alley' instead of 'road' because shapes closed it in on either side — black-shadowed forms suggesting squat structures and low walls. The way ran downhill. Since he was higher up, he needed only to look down the alley a short way to see out over the scene and into a wide valley beyond, its shape made visible by a few scattered lights, tiny and distant, that might be farmhouses. The alley ran arrow straight as far as he could see.

Perhaps a mile ahead (and below), the neon glow of a sign shone out — still far off, but easily the brightest light source around. Perhaps a shop. … And he had been just about to go to a store. The store down the road. To get food. For… Hatch?

What?

Then it hit him:

"My quest!" He smiled, then walked on down the alleyway, confident that he was meant to do so.

The sign shone brighter as the minutes passed, but when he had covered about half the distance, his progress was interrupted. Something called to him — a shy call, for help — one with a strange accent that sounded vaguely Hublandish. Dune didn't really know what 'Hublandish' meant, but this, like other thoughts, simply popped into his mind.

"Help-p-p-p-p it," came the warbling call. "Something needs yoo-oo-ooo. Something's in troub-b-b-b-ble!"

"Hello?" called Dune. "Are you a… Hublander?" he asked a bit stupidly.

"Oh, oh, oh, good! Just absolutely fantastic! Surprise! A bright young man has come to help it!" the something exclaimed. "Right this way youthful savior. Something is he-e-e-e-ere!"

Dune stepped carefully ahead, wondering who or what was doing the talking. He soon was able to see the outline of what must be the 'something' — a strange outline indeed. He only saw one of whatever it was, which he thought was probably a good thing.

"Don't worry," the legend bowman knower said with the reflex of a hero. "I'll help you!"

The something responded, but in a slightly more sinister voice. "Oh goodness, there's just yoo-oo." Dune looked around and, indeed, it was just him and this… something. The silhouette became clear, revealing a long thin trunk or body, a semi-long snout, small ears, and little stubby horns.

"Perhaps a light?" the thing suggested.

Dune pulled out a match (which he hadn't known he had) from a pocket (which he hadn't known he had) and struck it on his leg.

"Ow."

The match flared, illuminating the scene, and Dune quickly recognized the head and neck of a giraffe, sticking up from the ground like a plant.

"Oh absolutely splendid-d-d! A young ripe fellow has come to sa-a-a-ave it. Now all it asks is that you fetch its cookies." The giraffe flashed oddly sharp teeth in what Dune guessed was meant to be a smile.

"I'm sorry," Dune replied. "You said, 'fetch its…'"

"Cookies," the giraffe repeated patiently. "It wants its cookies."

"Cookies?"

"Cookies."

"Uh, are you sure you don't want

me to just get you out of that hole?" Dune asked before realizing he should perhaps have said nothing (cookie fetching seemed an easier task than giraffe excavation).

"No no no! Those cookies are the last part it nee-ee-eeds for its spaceship, so it can finally get out of he-e-e-e-ere," the giraffe explained.

"Okay," Dune said, letting the term 'spaceship' slide right by, his mind focused on why the giraffe was talking about itself like it was somebody else. It never occurred to him to notice how completely ridiculous his warrior quest was so far. Then the match singed his fingers and went out, and he tossed it aside.

The neon sign, now closer, caught his eye again. "I'll get your cookies! At that shop!" He pointed in proud triumph then hastened on down the alleyway. "Won't be long!" he shouted in parting. "Don't go anywhere!"

Slowing as he neared the light, Dune saw that it was indeed a sign, mounted high on a wall above the door to a small shop. He headed toward it eagerly, but then, still about fifty yards away, he stopped and stood, bewildered. He simply could not recall what he was doing — except that he was supposed to get *something* for *something.* He stayed quiet, not wanting to attract attention as he tried to remember. The seconds ticked by…

"So what do I get?" he finally asked aloud of the empty night.

In response, a clamor of familiar voices filled his mind, shouting important answers and advice, but since all the voices spoke at once, he couldn't make out what any one of them was saying. He strained to get clear, but his frustration grew until he couldn't stand it.

"*Stop!*" he commanded. "No more."

Silence.

Energized but still confused, Dune sighed and looked up at the bright sign. He had arrived at the KJCM — *King's Jester's Cousin's Market.* Three people stared at him from the doorway. Two — a small girl and her mother — quickly departed with their bags when he looked their way. The third looked undisturbed. She wore a white apron, stained from hours of work at a butcher's table. Her hair was bound up in a net and her skin sagged. The two eyes under heavy brows seemed to be looking in slightly different directions. …And she needed a shave. Hmmm.

"Looking for cookies?" she asked as though offering a hint, her voice like a trucker's.

"Cookies!" Dune exclaimed, remembering. "Yes. Thanks. Just need to get cookies."

"Aisle 13," the woman said, and then muttered something that might have been, "sucker," but he couldn't be sure. Seeming bored, the butcher woman turned away and reentered the store.

After a short pause, Dune shrugged and followed, but just inside the door he stopped, eyes going wide in shock. The place was…

Humongous!

It was vastly bigger than could possibly be contained by the small building he had seen when outside. The sights and smells of a universe of goods assaulted him. Voices announced specials. Bells, buzzes, and beeps indicated machines at work. Triumphant spotlights swung in arcs, calling people to places with exciting opportunities. Energetic music offered a happy soundtrack for delighted shoppers.

Looking ahead along the front wall of the store, Dune saw the entrances to dozens upon dozens of aisles that extended off to the right, each identified by a sign with a number — though the numbers were not in any particular order. He thought he could see the entries to at least fifty aisles before they were too far off to detect. There was no evidence of any end to the building in that direction!

Looking to the right, he gazed down the aisle nearest him — Aisle 41 — which he saw also went on and on with no apparent end. Perhaps it was an effect of the exciting lighting, but it looked like the aisle gradually turned into a shimmering mist as the distance grew long.

Despite the size of the place, however, there appeared to be only one checkout counter. Customers with carts, hand baskets, and simple handfuls of items stood in an insanely long line, the end of which was lost in the distance along the front wall. The bubbly cashier snapped his gum as he waited for the next to step ahead, but it seemed that the line refused to move — except that, every couple of seconds, some customer would leave his or her place and head back among the shelves, perhaps to fetch a forgotten item or replace something no longer wanted. While most of the customers looked like denizens of some sort, a few were clearly warriors, all of whom appeared to be lost and sad.

Dune took all this in as he stood, baffled. His eyes swam. His thinking clouded. Cookies. He just needed cookies. Aisle 13. Cookies, yams, chickens, and cookies. And milk? …No, apple juice. That would be in the fruit aisle. '*162*' a thought-voice announced in his mind. So… So aisle 162 for apple milk, cookens, yam juice.

…Yam juice?

*   *   *

Einstein knocked the controller from my hands, but was gentle removing the headset.

"…It's time for dinner," he said. "…Mom called you four times."

"Huh?"

"…It's time for dinner. …We're having chicken and yams."

"What?" I mumbled as Einstein pulled me from the chair and led me to wash my hands.

"…Do you want milk or apple juice?"

At the table, I managed to say please and thank you, and to talk normally about school and stuff, but my mind was racing on what I had been playing. The team had made the 3rd Ring, and now everyone but Hatch had to do something called a warrior quest. I had been playing Dune on his quest, but the whole thing was really confusing. I couldn't figure out where he was or what he was supposed to do…

"Alexander, would you like a cookie for dessert?"

…but he was doing stuff anyway. Now he was in this store to get some food for…

"Alexander. A cookie?"

…I mean, to get this giraffe out of a hole in…

"*Alexander!* Do you want a cookie or not?"

"…Cookie?"

"Yes, a cookie. Maybe two?"

…

"Cookies!" I blurted out, sounding a bit loony.

"Uh, yes. One or two?" asked mom. "They're a new kind — gluten-free *Pecan Bimbles.*"

"Uh, yes. Please. Two. Thank you."

Cookies! That was it. Dune just needed to get cookies. I suddenly realized that I would have to help him stay focused on the cookies, or he might be lost in that store forever. If I could just back up a step…

*　　*　　*

Dune found himself outside the store again. A quick glance showed him the departing forms of mother and daughter. "Aisle 13," the butcher said, and then she turned to re-enter the store.

"Wait!" Dune commanded, his voice, power. The butcher stopped, then slowly turned to face the warrior. "How…" He thought for a moment. "How did that woman get out of the store? The line doesn't move."

The butcher's eyes widened slightly, as though she'd heard something she hadn't expected.

"Uh, well, see… She doesn't pay, see? Sir. Only the dopes get in line. She, uh, gets her things and walks out. She's a local," the butcher added, forcing a thick smile, and then nervously turning for the store again. "I gotta work."

"*Why?*" fired Dune. "If almost no one leaves with anything, why work?"

She froze, as though the word "why" was too much for her.

Dune lunged forward and grabbed her by the collar. Now it was Dune that smiled while the butcher looked decidedly uncomfortable. She seemed sort of blocky for a… she. "So, why don't you just take me straight to the cookies, and then right back out here. Do both well, and you won't die. What do you think?"

"Uh, yeah."

For the next few minutes, Dune kept his attention focused on his hands — one held the butcher's collar, the other, a knife. Voices assailed him. Exciting foods seemed to call to him as he passed by. Aisles divided and converged as they curved about in nonsensical patterns. Dozens of passersby joined the characters in his head to bombard him with advice, requests, instructions, gossip, and criticism, but he silently held out against them. He stayed vaguely aware as the aisles passed by, the numbers coming in random order, but at last '13' came into view. Shortly afterward, the butcher paused. A thought came into Dune's head from somewhere and he spoke it aloud.

"Pecan Bimbles!"

"…Uh," the butcher began as she scanned the shelf. "GF or regular?"

"GF," he replied. "Now! …And *you* carry them."

Dune felt himself recovering as they returned toward the front of the store. Defeated, the butcher ignored the checkout line and headed for the exit. Once outside, Dune retrieved the cookies, released his guide, and took a slow, deep breath, preparing to return to the giraffe.

"The Boss thought he'd stop you here," the butcher blurted, now definitely sounding more like a guy. "He's gonna be mad at me."

Dune suddenly recognized her — *him.* "You're Bejus, right?"

The would-be butcher flashed a look of terror, then bolted.

*   *   *

Returning along the alleyway, Dune neared the giraffe and its half-grave. He could hear the beast singing some nonsense riddle over and over.

Tum te tiddle me diddle me too
Dum de doodle me noodle me roo
Rum me paddle me daddle me who,
Bum me raddle me you and boo

Tum te tiddle me diddle me too
Dum de doodle me noodle me—

"Who's ther-r-r-re?" sounded the quavering voice, sensing Dune's arrival in the darkness.

"I have your cookies," Dune replied.

Silence.

"Pecan Bimbles."

More silence.

"Gluten free."

Still more.

"Could it be that you don't really *want* cookies?" Dune inquired, knowing.

A hiss. Then more silence.

"Could it be that you work for The Boss, and all you want is for warriors to get trapped in the store?"

A longer hisssss.

"Well guess what," said the legend bowman — then he sprang forward and grabbed the giraffe around the neck. The beast fought back furiously, but with no limbs available, it was futile. Dune bent the giraffe backward until its head neared the ground. Then, wrapping his legs around to hold the neck, he grabbed the giraffe's nose with one hand, pulled it backward until its mouth opened wide, stuffed the Pecan Bimbles down its gullet (packaging too), and then squeezed its mouth closed. After another round of furious gyrations, the giraffe's throat contracted in a distinct swallow. Dune jumped aside.

"Curse yoo-oo-oo!" squealed the beast. "Curse you and all war-r-r-riors! Curse you for a-a-a-a-all time! Curse you…"

But the voice faded rapidly as Dune felt himself swept up in a sparkling, twisting wind, and then he popped from a castle door to land at Hatch's feet.

"Mmm. You," Hatch said.

Dune stood and blinked in the sunshine. Looking back, he saw the castle with its many doors, only this time, all were in reverse order.

"Other side now," Hatch stated, strangely savvy. "Wait for others?"

"No," said Dune, instantly recovering and scanning the scene with care. "Sparrow said not."

With eyes open to possible dangers, they started along Ring Road to cover the remaining distance to the next gate.

*   *   *

"What was I thinking, Needles? A *giraffe?*"

"Well… your choice of Alley Realm was most reasonable," Needles replied, trying to be helpful.

The Boss steamed, but to yell at Needles was to yell at a stone. He watched as his servant's face remained disinterested as ever while his own morphed slowly from fury to fatigue. "I suppose," he agreed at last. "But, dear Needles, a *giraffe? Cookies?* That is my magic in the 3rd now?" A question, but really a statement.

Needles remained still and silent.

"I wanted to stop them there, you know."

Needles. Silent.

"Why couldn't that Bejus have lost him in the aisles?" he whined.

Needles.

"Didn't want to die, I suppose."

Silent.

"Putting Bejus against a knower. Foolish." He stared at his hands. "I should have seen." He shook his head slowly.

Needles, too, thought the giraffe and cookies a bit bizarre, and it was revealing that they were the best The Boss could devise. Once upon a time, The Boss had commanded dangers in all of the rings — *all.* Once upon a time, Alley Realm had secret witches that would have bent that bowman's mind if The Boss commanded it — against the rules, yes, but back then, The Boss's player could break rules if he wished it. That had been useful, but now the player had been pushed aside…

A mistake?

Once upon a time, The Boss would not even have cared what went on in the 3rd, because warrior quests broke many teams without help. In those days, Needles recalled, The Boss would usually even ignore most of the 4th ring — unless a team proved particularly tough, but that had been rare.

But then… Wonder.

Needles watched as The Boss paced, heels clicking, horns smoldering.

"I'm going for a walk, Needles. Build me some toy soldiers!" he snapped weirdly. The Boss stormed off, leaving the high, windowed chamber and striding down a long dark hallway.

Sighing to himself, Needles watched his master depart. In the darkness on the far wall, he noticed a pattern shift in the brick. The octopus moved quickly, following his master, various arms, legs, tongues, wings, and eyes blocking out the torchlight all the way down the hall.

Needles put his feet up on a red velvet footstool, which seemed to whimper with pain. Holding his cigar to the nearest candle, he left it there until small, winding plumes of tobacco smoke began to waft upwards. He sat carefully back in the chair, ignoring the quick shout from the cushion, and looked up at the ceiling, feeling totally relaxed — numb even.

"I hope he doesn't do anything drastic," he mused aloud.

Down the hall, The Boss made it to the steps and furiously stomped down them toward his private lair. All along the walls the motifs seemed to mock him. Skulls and skin leered out at him from the molten panels. They had been designed to tell stories. The skinned bodies were posed. Years ago it had looked like a grand battle (one The Boss could barely remember). But now it resembled a drunken dance, arms and legs flung about, jaws and eyes wide in confusion. The figures all laughed now. At him. The Boss ignored it as best he could.

Reaching the bottom of the stairs, he glanced at a scrawl over the doorway in front of him, which read, simply, *Chambers*. He entered a small room, dimly lit by a large, human shaped candle that sat in the corner, holding its head in its hands, melting slowly. A desk in the other corner was adorned with various skulls, crystals, and otherworldly forms of ecstasy and agony. There was also a bed, small and plain, that — unbeknownst to the entire universe — was the sleeping place for a being who never slept.

The Boss eyed the bed, and a sudden sense of deep weariness rolled over him. To sleep, he thought. To sleep. Yes.

"Yes," he whispered to the walls. "Yesss. But first…" He turned to the desk, sat, and opened the thirteenth volume of his journal.

*　　*　　*

Diary of The Boss

I did not take that well.
Needles is doubting me.
Do I doubt myself?
I am having trouble remembering what I desire. I am distracted. I lose focus.

Could it be that I actually wanted the warrior to escape the realms? How else did he survive? How else could he defeat my will? He could not. It has never been so.

Except for Wonder.

No matter! Sooner or later, I will kill them all. All! I will speak with Needles again. He will have ideas.

I know the game is to end! I am to be Real! To begin again. Needles tells me that killing in Real is different. Perhaps I won't like it. We shall see. But now, perhaps, a nap.

Ace

*   *   *

The Boss closed the journal, crossed to the bed, and sat down upon it, sinking into the soft mattress. Slowly he lay down, letting it eat him, slipping into a state without focus or intent, the tips of his horns scorching small, smoldering holes into his leather pillow.

*   *   *

Einstein had to get me out again. I don't know what I'd do if he wasn't watching me. It wouldn't be good.

But that was a while ago. Now it's almost 1 a.m., and I can't sleep. I'm just lying in bed thinking.

My pack is sitting on the floor with homework that's not finished — okay, not *started* — but I just don't care. Not good. I know. But if you don't care, you don't care, right? I looked at the pack ten times, but I just…

I just want to get into the 4th Ring! That's supposed to be the hardest.

I'm tired. I wish game days and nights *always* matched mine. They definitely match sometimes, but that quest took a couple days even though it seemed so quick!

Maybe Jake is still up.

AB - hello

JH - hey u r awake wanna play

AB - r u serious its like 1 im in bed

JH - yeah I should probably get off

AB - yeah but anyway im in this game im playing it was really weird there was this giraffe thing and he tried to trick me and then I had to force these cookies down his throat.

JH - thats real weird

AB - yeah I know you should get this rings game I got mine from vidgame con

...

AB - weird guy who looked like some cosplay wizard gave it free he called it hard face its a box but not ports

...

AB - u there?

JH - that rings sounds lame and its total malware i told you

...

JH - u should just play smash with me I think youll like it anyway u should play less video games ur grades suck bad

AB - u play more games than me if its any one that should stop maybe its u

JH - ok chill I was just trying to help just if you dont stop at least be careful

AB - wtf do u mean be careful its a game

JH - idk I mean games can kill

AB - ok r u ok?

...

AB - ?

JH - mom came in yelling gn

Jake is acting real weird about this game. He said, "games can kill." What the hell?

8 — 4ᵀᴴ RING

"Oh my my myyy…" Arched eyebrows, glittering gaze, thin smile. "And what can I get you, my *fiiine* travelers?" The bartender was the picture of slick — red satin shirt with puffy sleeves, black leather pants, a silver vest with black pearl buttons. His skin had the luster of oil, as though the product that held his glistening, streaked hair in place had leaked down over his face.

"Aye then!" Scram jumped to the front of the line. "Can you do up one of those metal merchant madness fizzes with a double spritz of wamblee sweat?" he asked.

"Mmmm, yes. And yooou?" he asked, luridly scanning the others. As usual, Hatch chose beer and Dune, milk. Sparrow ordered nothing.

"Finish your tale," Sparrow directed Dune as they settled into red leatherette chairs around a heavy, round table.

"I did finish," he replied. "I fed the giraffe, and then I was out. There was nothing to face making the gate except a ragged street gang. Hatch and I saw them spread across the road as we got close. I picked off a couple from a distance. The rest ran off. Easy. No snipers that I could see."

"Cookies?" said Scram. "That's way stranger than mine. My door dropped me in Roman Realm. A bathhouse — all stone columns, fancy tiles. A lotta steam. Figured out quick I had to find a sponge that'd sunk somewhere and not get distracted by the… bathers. Then just return it to the attendant. Easy, aye?"

"Easy?" returned Dune with a smile. "Knowing you, that should have been the perfect trap."

Scram smiled ruefully. "Aye, you'd expect. But it wasn't the sort of bathers that might catch my eye, if you know what I mean. No prettier than a pot full of jang grandas! I was out in minutes. Too bad," he sighed.

"Aye, and like you, it was nothin' to make the gate. Assassin came toward me like she might be selling flowers, but changed her mind and left when she saw my blades." He shook his head. "3rd Ring's fallen a long way."

"What about you, Sparrow?" Dune asked.

"As you all say, not difficult," she answered. "I appeared in Biz Realm. Strange white-shirted men, dressed alike with jackets and colored neck belts hanging to their waists, all sitting around a great table — a 'board' room they call it. A sinister place. I thought of weasels…"

"Aye, and then?" Scram urged at her pause.

"One handed me a box. 'Take it to 307 sweetheart,' he said. All then spoke with winks and evil smiles. 'Down to the mailroom, babe.' 'Be a good girl and FedEx it.' 'Susie in payroll will know, she's a honey.' Others. I left.

"The realm is confusion, with many walking about at great speed. Some call out with commands and summons. Others sit in boxes tapping fingers against plates and staring at small squares of light with figures and lines. Many doors and halls. Chaos."

She got a curious look on her face. "An idea came to me. I opened the box and found a small model of the board room with a figure for each weasel man — each clearly dead. I returned to the room and drew a knife. They did not fight, but instead jumped from the windows with screams. I went to look. 3rd Ring was without, so I left the realm." She shook her head in puzzlement. "I had no enemies at all in making the gate. None."

All went quiet for several seconds until Sparrow continued.

"Before I stepped through, I searched the room and found this." Sparrow held up a tiny teacup made of green glass.

"Token!"

"Yes," she confirmed. "We now have five," she said as she added the teacup to the other tokens in her bag.

"Aye?" Scram responded, lighting up. "Grand! Needs five to open fifth gate, aye? That's the rules?"

"It is the rule I was told." Sparrow affirmed.

"Good then," Scram smiled. "We're set."

"Team good!" Hatch stated the obvious. "4th Ring! Very good team!"

Scram gave a wicked smile. "Aye!" he exclaimed. "Damn good!" Looking at Hatch, he asked, "And how went the feats, my brute friend?"

Hatch looked bored. "Hatch very strong. Much crush."

*　　*　　*

The morning brought the usual planning session in the hotel bar. The team sat at the same round table as the night before and gazed at the map, upon which the 4th Ring had appeared as soon as they had entered the gate. Early daylight came from a grimy window that looked out on a small, closed courtyard. Like so much in and around the side streets of the city, the courtyard seemed half-formed, with simple panels of grays and browns where flagstones or wood walls should be. A game thing.

The map of the 4th Ring seemed normal enough near the hotel, but confusing beyond — in both directions.

Counterclockwise, it showed a normal looking Ring Road lined with buildings, with narrow lanes and more buildings filling in the rest of the ring. But a few blocks from the hotel, all came to an end at a jagged edge that ran from wall to wall. *Worlds* was written over the dark, empty space beyond.

Clockwise, it looked quite different. A short way beyond the neighborhood of the hotel, the number of buildings dwindled, Ring Road widened, and the lanes to either side opened into what might be parks or plazas. A bit further on, buildings, Ring Road, and lanes ended one by one, until they had all disappeared into a confused and scattered mess of lines and figures that seemed to indicate low ridges, pits and ditches, ruins of walls and buildings, holes, towers, fences, caves, huts, and more. *Rubbles* was written across this devastated region, which covered fully half of the ring.

The gate to the 5th was closer in the counterclockwise direction, about a third of the way around. It appeared to be surrounded by an intricate labyrinth of small, odd-angled buildings that filled the space between walls near the gate. No streets showed at all in this mysterious area, which was labeled, *Maze Halls.* Both Worlds and Rubbles ended at the edge of this maze.

"Don't remember this too well," said Scram. "I've been into 4th a few times and seen maps, but here," he said, pointing at the counterclockwise side, "this gap for Worlds used to be smaller. More of a hole as I recall. And here," he said, gesturing to the other side, "Rubbles is way bigger, I think. Things missing too."

"Too many pitfalls and enemies in Rubbles," Sparrow said to Dune. "It has grown. I also do not recall this divide for Worlds."

"We go?" asked Hatch, bored as always by talk.

"Which way?" Dune asked. "This ring feels… hot."

Sparrow stayed quiet for a moment then spoke to what she knew. "I never made the 5th. I believe I have been in the 4th twice — once well into the Rubbles, but I did not make it through. We were forced to retreat."

"But the Worlds way?" Scram gestured to the gapped side of the map. "What happened? I mean, all roads always led to Worlds, but now there's nothing. Will we hit the end of this first patch and that's it?" He got a strange look on his face. "It's like Worlds is swallowing the ring…"

"I came to the Worlds as a new respawn," Sparrow said. "I don't recall the team. The memory is… lost."

"We go that way," Dune said, pointing to the gapped route and sounding strangely commanding. "The Worlds way." He wondered to hear himself say it, having no idea that it was Alexander who had decided. "The Boss will work against us," Dune added. "It will be his last play in the game."

The others stared, stunned to hear such a pronouncement. Dune was stunned too (Alexander was completely surprised as well).

"Uh, well, just came to me," the bowman offered.

"Knower," Hatch said, nodding. "Dune, knower."

Just then, the slimy bartender glided over to them. "Mmmm. What can I get for you fiiine travelers?" he sneered. Framed against his thin, graphite-gleaming lips. his spiked teeth seemed to shine.

"Beat it."

*　　*　　*

"Map is right," said Scram. "Nothing."

Ring Road had brought them to the edge of the gap, which stretched from wall to wall across 4th Ring and fell away into misty blackness. Making their way along this edge as best they could, they sought a way forward, but no option appeared — it was city streets and buildings behind, bottomless abyss ahead.

"Go *there!*" Hatch announced in frustration, gesturing with his club across the daunting void, the other side of which could not be seen — perhaps because the curving walls blocked their view, or perhaps for another reason.

"Can we get around it?" Dune wondered aloud. "Maybe along the base of the wall?" But even as he said this, he looked to where wall met chasm and saw it wouldn't work. Scram said his next words for him.

"Nope," Scram stated. "Nothing there."

"Death," Sparrow said. Dune looked at her, but then noticed Scram and even Hatch nodding in agreement.

"So you can't use the walls?" More nodding. "Game rules?" Still more. "Yeah, okay." They stood around for a minute, but nothing came to them. "So, I guess it's through the rumbles?"

"Rubbles," corrected Sparrow. "No. That is death."

"Death? Everything is 'death' with you!"

"I know death!"

"You… You died?"

"In the 4th, and other times in other rings. I have always died. With every team."

"But *once* you escaped, right? You said you did a rumbles retreat."

"Rubbles. Yes, deep into the Rubbles, and then partway back in retreat — but not all the way. I lost teammates, then *I* died as well. Rubbles is death," Sparrow finished.

"Aye," Scram concurred. "That's the Rubbles for ya — the only place in *Rings* you can die in *retreat*. In the easy rings, you can retreat with no fights. Hell, I was on a team that retreated from the middle of metal merchants territory three or four times to try to figure 'em out. That was way back when I was played. …I think. Wasn't a good team." He looked puzzled for a moment. "Aye, that was when my Real dumped me. Long time ago. Went rogue not long after that," he smiled. "But the Rubbles? No rules at all, and a lot of mean, bad enemies."

Dune noticed sadness in Sparrow's eyes. "The times you died," he said to her, "someone got you to the Chamber of Respawning?"

"Yes, each time, and I have always been Sparrow. Even when I began again as a lamb." She looked thoughtful. "I once took a teammate to respawn as well, but… But memories of respawning are confused."

"Aye, well, it's *easy* for a rogue," Scram explained. "We just pop outta respawn after we die and start again. No one needs to take us. Sometimes you just let it happen if you're trapped." He looked sadly at Sparrow. "But it's not so easy if you ain't gone rogue — 'specially if you're played," he said. "Then, someone *has* to take you to the Chamber, or you stay dead. Easy enough to get help in the low rings — even denizens will help a bit sometimes! But retreat is almost impossible in 4th." Scram turned to Sparrow. "You're lucky someone got you out," he said to her.

"Anyway," Scram continued, "it gets worse. Aye, you can die in retreat from Rubbles, but you *can't* retreat out of a world."

…

"Okay then," Dune went on after the silence. He looked again from gap to map and back. "And what is it, or what are they?" he asked, still a bit confused. "I mean, why is it named *Worlds?*"

Scram replied. "Well, because you go into the Worlds. Like it says. Out of the ring and into new places, one after another — *if* you find the way. Sorta like quest realms, but those are small — quick outs, back and forths, some traps," Scram explained. "But the Worlds? You can wander any world *forever.* Lots get lost. It's where the best teams end. Can't retreat. Die and respawn's the only way out, if you can — if you're not rogue and someone gets you back through one of the secret ways" he added. "Not many, but some rogues know 'em."

"I have not learned this," returned Sparrow.

"Well, lass, you haven't spent near as much time in bars as I have," Scram replied. "There's ways — short cuts, jumps to new worlds, secret exits from dead ends, like that. Maybe even ways to fifth gate, though I've only heard of ways back to fourth hotel."

"Even so," she rejoined, "we need a way *in* before we seek a way *out.*"

Scram smiled. "Game rules say there's always both."

"What is in these worlds?" Dune asked, suddenly curious.

Scram scratched his head and looked thoughtful. "Memory's not so good, but they're... *places*. I remember the edge of a big sand once. A desert, and... Well, the way is never straight, aye? I remember a river town. And gardens. Big gardens somewhere, but... Well, you go from one place to another to another. Denizens here and there. And paths to other places. More places. Endless. Hell!" he spat, "I suppose there's a way back to the ring and fifth gate at the end of it all, but I never got so far."

They all thought on this for a moment, then Scram continued.

"See, you get *clues* to move through — messages, symbols, things you hear — stuff to find or remember. Lots of false choices, tunnels, doors — that kind of stuff. *Enemies* of course," he added, "but friends too! Teams can get split up and maybe not come together again." He shifted his weight, thinking hard.

"Oh, aye! And there's avatars in the Worlds! *Avatars*. Not enemies or friends, but dangerous. Minds of their own. Can't kill 'em. Got power. Like little bosses that'll put you into little games."

"Hell. The more I try to remember, the more mixed it gets. I died too much. ...Every time I suppose," Scram admitted. "No matter, though — it's either that, or—"

"The Rubbles," Sparrow finished for him. "Death."

Dune thought on it. "All right," he said at last. "First, we find the way down into the Worlds. It has to be here. Some door, or maybe a hole."

"A stair?" Sparrow suggested.

"A stair."

"Aye, or a bar," Scram offered.

"Hatch drink?"

*   *   *

In the end, a bar. They had wandered the streets near the gap, seeking any suggestion of a way to go, ignoring the bar at first after a look inside, but returning when Dune insisted. The music. Something about it. Some melody or... or feel. Or rhythm. A code? No. More like a call. An invitation.

They had been in the place for a while. A dull, featureless watering hole. Fluorescent lights. Vinyl floor. Hard plastic on the bar. Hatch was slamming his third ale when Dune, with a flash of recognition, suddenly knew. He strode over to the singer(s) — one beast, several mouths — and requested a song that came suddenly to mind (delivered by Alexander). "Do you know Saturnz Barz by Gorillaz. It/he/she/they did, and, for some coins, started into it. As soon as the words, "the rings I am breaking" sounded out, a door opened in the back corner, behind the gamblers' table. Sparrow spotted it.

"There!" she exclaimed, pointing.

Passing through the door, the team found themselves in a winding hall with many corners, often odd-angled, so they soon had no idea of their direction. Steep steps took them down long flights, occasionally up again, but mostly downward. There were curves — narrowings and widenings. The ceiling height varied, to the point that Hatch had trouble getting through a time or two. But always the descending way was built of dull gray stone blocks and lit by torches that didn't seem to require replacing.

At last, far below their starting point, the passage emptied into a large, decorated chamber that seemed shockingly elaborate after the dullness of the way down. At the far end of the chamber, stone steps led up to an old iron door in a metal wall. Not majestic. Not loud or anything. But it called to them — so much so that the wondrous decorations of the other walls held little interest. All felt it. It was the door to a *world*.

Closed.

"Trap!" Sparrow refused to move.

Dune moved to the door. The air was still — almost stale, as though it had already been breathed in and out by a long-time smoker. He could make out some scratched words, most gray or fading from time.

Elsewhere there were odd sketches — skeletal men on a speedboat guiding dirty people to a lake house. A flaming horse. Smiling cousins in a bonfire. A gutted fish. Dune ran his fingertips along the door's surface. It undulated like liquid. Sparrow grabbed his arm to stop him from doing more.

Dune looked at her. "We've got to go through."

"It is dangerous." Sparrow regarded the door skeptically, and then spit on it. The impact sent out a large ripple. The door shook and shimmered.

"…So what does *that* mean?" Dune asked.

"I do not know, but it is not right."

"Well, we must get through." With an unexpected twinge of regret, Dune gently removed her hand from his arm. Leaning in and placing his ear close to the door, he heard faint but powerful sounds from beyond it, wailing and roaring, moans of torment. An image of tall, dark waves and cold, gray hands came to his mind. He inspected the door's opener — a short handle rather than a knob, which seemed almost grown from the surface, as though it might not turn or move in any way. Taking a slow breath, he grasped it.

The moment he did so, he was caught and could not pull away. His hand instantly began to sink into the door — pulled in — then his arm. It seemed the door would envelop him completely and he would be eaten — painlessly, relentlessly, speedily.

Rejecting his initial instinct to pull away, Dune cursed and plunged the rest of himself through, grabbing a knife from a boot sheath with his free hand as he went. A cold, strange wetness briefly wrapped him, and he could not breathe, but it quickly passed. He stumbled through into someplace new, coughing and hacking as he regained his breath. He opened his eyes, realizing they had been clenched shut. He looked about.

"Oh!"

*   *   *

In an instant, he was gone. Dune's mates watched him vanish without time to react. After a moment of shock, Hatch threw himself at the door. The others expected him to plunge through as well, but the brute bounced back, landing on the floor with a thunk. He rose to try again.

"Hold!" Sparrow commanded.

"It figures," Scram said. "I knew we'd hit trouble, but at the first test?" He sighed. "Let's the rest of us not get pulled apart too. Dune's a knower. He'll make do."

Sparrow stepped up to the door and touched it as Dune had done earlier. It had changed. No ripples. Solid.

She grasped the handle, which now could be turned with a swivel motion, and…

Turned it.

The door didn't move at first, but the chamber around it disappeared completely. The three found themselves standing on a forest path, facing the hard metal door and frame, which now stood alone in the wood and seemed to serve no purpose whatsoever. They saw quickly that the path arrived at the door, but before they could go around to see if it continued on the other side, the door opened wide of its own accord. Scram drew a sword.

A small, tall table sat beyond the door, with plenty of room on either side to pass it by. On the table sat a miniature bottle of a tasty looking purple liquid, a small plate with a tiny piece of cake (looked like carrot cake), and an envelope. In front of each was a card. The first read, *Drink me.* The second, *Eat me.* The third, *Special Discount Offer!*

"We must choose," Sparrow concluded.

"Says who?" Scram asked. "Maybe we each pick one."

"No. We must choose."

"Hatch no want cake. Too small. Drink too small."

…

Scram and Sparrow looked at each other and smiled — which, Scram noted, was the first time he'd ever seen Sparrow do that. "Right," he said, "No cake, no drink, so number three."

Sparrow took the envelope, opened it, and unfolded the paper within. The others crowded round. "It is a map," she reported, "with symbols. See," she said, pointing. "Here is the door and table. It shows a way beyond."

"A way to what?" Scram inquired.

"That is not clear."

They set off.

*   *   *

Dune fell to his knees on a ragged rock, but something kept him from falling further. A huge blob of protoplasm had captured his arm and shoulder, holding him tight. Some of the blob protruded up onto the stone, but most of the bloated bulk remained submerged at the edge of a vast, black ocean that stretched away into the dark distance. Dune could see flickers from the massive beast's red glow where it shone below the surface of the wind-tossed waters. Without doubt, the blob sought to draw the rest of him into itself, swallow him whole, and then return to the deeps.

Clearly short on time, Dune swung his knife, fiercely slicing a long, deep fissure in the surface of his attacker. A hideous shudder wracked the creature, and Dune's arm was ejected as though puked. The blob retreated completely beneath the waves and sank away into the depths, minus a few pints of goopy blood. The red glow faded slowly to nothing. Apparently...

Not a brave blob.

Dune tried out his arm and hand. They glowed faintly red, but seemed functional. He rinsed them until the red had vanished, then stood and looked about.

He was alone at the edge of the inky ocean. No door could be seen, nor was his team with him. He recalled what Scram had said about how teams could be split and "maybe not come together again," and he guessed that forward was his only chance.

Scanning the scene, he saw that a rocky shoreline ran raggedly off into darkness to left and right. Behind him? Tall cliffs, rising into low, black clouds, impossible to climb. The endless, briny deep stretched away before him. Nothing interrupted this daunting scape of tormented waters and rugged rock as far as the eye could see.

Nothing.

...Okay, *one* thing.

In a relatively calm gap a short way along the shoreline to the right, a perky boat bobbed in the quieted waters, dimly lit by a lantern hanging from a deck pole. A large dog wearing a captain's hat eyed him from the gunwale, patch over one eye, pipe gripped in its mouth, standing on two legs. The captain waved him over. Dune scrambled to the spot and, at the captain's gesture, bounded aboard.

"Where to?" the dog growled as the boat moved off into the open water, seemingly on its own.

"Uh… I'm not sure. Rejoin my team?"

"Might happen," the dog murmured as the craft sped from the shore. The dog didn't smile exactly, but a spark came to its eye. A real spark. Then tiny flames. "But not by me," it sneered. "I can do one o' three things for ye — kill ye and eat ye now, kill ye and salt ye up for eatin' later, or kill ye, salt ye, and toss ye in the hold to sell to them sky witches 'cross the bay."

At that, a dozen vicious looking mongrels crept out from various hidey holes and shadows, each dressed in pirate garb and boasting no weapons except unusually long, sharpened teeth. They growled and slavered as they moved to surround Dune, clearly ready to tear him to shreds. The flames around the captain's eyes ran down the bridge of his nose and traced a thin line around his grinning dog lips. He was about to speak, but in the moment it took to gather his thoughts…

Dune killed his crew.

The warrior let fly a dozen arrows in a blur, and twelve mangy crew dogs dropped to deck or water, having breathed their last. Dune had set a thirteenth arrow to bow, and the captain, quite clear on its target, immediately re-gathered his suddenly de-gathered thoughts.

"*Or!*" he hastily shouted, forelegs raised high with his hand-ish paws held up in the universal don't-kill-me pose. "Or! Or I can take ye to any port ye please, master, as quick as ye might! And, let me say milord, a thousand thanks for riddin' me of them terrible pirate mutts what took me boat over and kept me prisoner. I'm eternal grateful!" he added, bowing to the ground as dogs can do.

Dune looked him over for a few seconds. "You're mine. Clear?"

"Indeed, sire, I well and truly am yours until ye dispose of me. Game rules," he said. "*My* rules," he added with a mysterious smile.

"…Tell me about these witches."

*　　*　　*

"We take wrong left?" Hatch asked, confused.

It was cryptic to say the least. Miles of hiking in the forest to the exact spot marked with a big, red 'X' on the map, and all for what?

A stump.

They looked about. Just beyond the clearing that hosted the stump, a crystalline cliff of ice rose sheer from the ground, its top lost in the mist far above. A sign hung at eye level on this frozen wall, featuring an arrow pointing straight upward, and the words:

Swallow Hall O.

"There is no way up," Sparrow observed, regarding the ice.

"Cruel," Scram said. "It's a puzzle. …Or something."

Sparrow looked more closely at the stump. The overhanging trees blocked out the sky so that only slivers of moonlight reached through to the ground, but she could clearly see a seven point star painted onto the old surface, with five words that were all too easy to read.

"Read these words and die…" Scram read aloud. "Uh oh. Don't like the sound of that."

Sparrow looked upward into the thick trees that surrounded the clearing. "We should leave," she said, her voice quavering a bit.

At that moment, a shriek came from far above. The few gaps in the trees above darkened, filling in with unseen visitors.

"Who there?" Hatch shouted, taking a blind swing in the darkness, the *whoosh* of his club sounding loud in the quiet. But that 'whoosh' was immediately blown away by a swirling wind that descended from the sky and spun through the forest crown, making a much bigger *WHOOOOOSH* that shook the branches.

"Seeking the next ring?" came a laughing whisper, followed by echoes of *"ring ring ring ring ring…"* that faded into the night.

"Of course," Sparrow replied, trying to calm her voice, but she felt fear.

"You will not find it here." Now the shrill voice was *in* Sparrow's ear. She jumped forward but could not escape it. Something brushed her. A hand wrapped around the back of her neck. She shouted and swung her fist where she thought she might score a blow. Nothing.

"Hear me, witch!" Sparrow begged. "We must pass through your world."

"Ha ha ha ha haaa!" The laughter rolled over the team, coming from all sides, echoing over and upon itself until it had grown to a crazed chorus, loud and biting. *"They must pass through, they must pass through, they must pass through…"* The chant emerged from the laughter, gaining strength, the pitch of the voices rising with each utterance, until it pounded their minds and drove them to their knees, hands pressed over ears, trying to hold out against the manic onslaught.

"We will pay!" Sparrow screamed as she struggled, grunting, trying to grab a treasure from her pouch. But the witches' grips tightened — cold and smooth like marble. Pointed fingernails on wispy hands. Strong arms that could not be touched.

"Pay us!" came the demand as many voices creaked and moaned. *"Pay us! Pay us! Paaay usss!"*

Scram too felt hands, wrapped around his arms and legs, grabbing at his back, pressing on his chest. "Aye, well tell us how!" he shouted. "We've a bit of gold!" The laughter resumed, though now tinged with despair and hunger. "Well *what* then?" Scram begged. "What do you want?"

"Give us flesh!" howled the reply like a gust from a gale, but Scram could not reply as vaporous fingers filled his mouth. *"Find us the way!"* came another blast from a different direction, but Sparrow could not answer through the mass of ghostly heads that swam around her. *"Save us!"* roared the final plea.

"*Save us!*" the witches wailed. "*Save us!*" they moaned. "*Saaave usss!*" they whispered as they began to consume their prey.

"*HOLD!!!*"

Dune's booming voice cut into the chaos.

The attack ceased.

Silence.

Sparrow gasped.

"Dune!" Scram choked out. "Well met!"

"Hatch like." The witches had ignored Hatch (not uncommon for a game brute).

Out of the silence came a single voice, almost human.

"*We want something.*"

"You wish to be paid?" Dune returned.

Silence.

"Do you want… dead villains to dine upon?"

The wood stayed silent, but all in the team felt a clear change.

"Do you want a way to… *the door?*"

Anger evaporated and hope rose.

"Do you want the beast to stay deep in the cold cold sea and trouble not your search?"

The astonishment of hundreds struck the team like a blast of wind.

"The dog pirate works for me, now!" Dune added. "Do you want the dog pirate to work for *you?*

"*Yes yes yes,*" the chorus echoed. "*We want it want it want it….*"

"Help us," Dune said, "and the way over the sea is yours. Help us and you may seek the door again. The way down. The way to the river. The way home. To…

"Hell."

…

Silence — a 'yes' silence.

"So be it!" shouted Dune.

"How do we pass through?" yelled Sparrow, seizing the moment.

A lone voice — almost kindly, but oddly sly at the same time — gave the answer. "Wings, children. Wings."

And with that, the dim light of a tall triangle appeared upon the face of the ice cliff, surrounding the sign with a faint radiance that shone from deep within. The triangle gradually brightened, and then split vertically down the middle, becoming two doors, which opened slowly inward, half the sign on one half, half on the other, revealing a passage leading to a staircase of ice that curved up and away inside the mountain. Within the opening above the stair hung a different sign with the words:

Walk IN, Go Skyward.

"Hmmm." Scram. "'WINGS' — figures."

Before they started up, Dune handed his mates seven gold coins and a small brass telescope to split up for their belt bags. "That pirate dog had a little treasure."

"Hey," whispered Scram, "will those witches really find all those things?"

"Beats me," Dune whispered back. "Let's leave before they find out.

*   *   *

Layla pulled out. The sky witches had spooked her, and she still felt sharpened fingernails scraping lightly at her back and neck. She stood and shivered, glad for the sight of familiar objects around her messy room. "I should really clean up a little," she murmured to herself, mainly so she could hear her own voice. She took a deep breath. The night was still. 'Not too late yet,' she thought, seeing 1:17 on the clock.

She went back in.

*   *   *

After a monotonous ascent on steps of ice — so evenly cut they looked like glass — the team reached a landing at the head of a long, dim, carpeted hallway. Dune didn't recognize the look, but Alexander would have told him it was like something you'd see in the offices at a school, or maybe a bank. Dull music played softly. The moment Hatch — last one up — lifted his foot from the final step and set it on the carpet, the ice stair vanished behind them. Where the way back had been, now there was nothing.

A game nothing.

"Aye," observed Scram. "Like I said. Can't retreat, through the worlds."

With no apparent choice, they started along the hallway, which revealed its true nature after only a few steps.

Dune's thinking went weird, strands of stories and imagined purposes suddenly piecing together into nonsense thoughts. He felt he might lose his mind walking to the bathroom and slip away, and… What? The light buzzed like fat flies, the paint slowly peeled, the carpet sank beneath his feet. Stains in the shapes of ghosts, horses, vacant faces, and objects emerged…

What?

Dune halted. The weirdness vanished instantly, and the scene returned to boring hall, dull music, cheap carpet. It was the same for the others. The team stood still again, only steps from their starting point.

"Where are we?" Sparrow squinted down the hallway.

"Anywhere," murmured Dune, not sure why he said it. He took a deep breath, trying to steady his mind.

They stepped ahead again, and the strangeness began once more. The images in the walls sprouted mold and stretched outward and inward. Carpet crawled like spilled syrup up the sides of the passage, between the figures and across the ceiling. The lights dimmed and surged, going into and out of focus, changing colors. The hall swelled and shrank, narrowing and widening, becoming lofty then squeezing indecently around them.

Soon, the carpet showed a chaos of new patterns and weaves, and eventually shredded into strands that re-wove into braids, webs, and sculpted figures. Lights dimmed to near blackness in corridors, but then waxed to brightness to reveal changed architecture. All surfaces eventually became completely unreliable until walking was uncertain, feet sinking into stone or stumbling on vapor. The soundscape too had grown bizarre, with music, porcine grunts, birdsong, train announcements, children's wails, and more, blending in craziness. Even the air was confused — puffs of smoke coughed at them from holes, thin streams of metallic liquid squirted past, pockets of flame popped in and out randomly.

Only by stopping every step or two then starting again could they proceed, for the entire wildness halted instantly when the team did.

'How droll', Dune thought. 'How scampy and jocular.' He tittered. Sparrow regarded him with some alarm.

"Go nowhere?" Hatch sounded confused when they stopped for about the twentieth time.

They linked arms to step off again. Stop. Start. Stop. Start. Stop… It was too much.

"Oy, this is madness!" Scram ranted as they stopped again. "Can barely lift a foot now. And we don't know how far there is to go."

No one wanted to move ahead. Dune seemed to be on the verge of giggling. Scram's face could have soured milk. Hatch… was Hatch. Only Sparrow kept her wits. With no one interested in taking the next step *forward*, a thought occurred to her.

"What if we go *backward?*" The others regarded her. "Care to try?"

"You mean, return to the stair?"

She thought on this. "No. I mean turn around, face back toward the stair, and then *step* backwards." After exchanging glances, Scram and Dune shrugged — Dune with a drunken smirk on his face. "Then we shall," Sparrow concluded. "Ready? Turn about." They did. "Now… *go.*"

Stepping backward together, they felt a smoky screech of frustrated fury, and then stumbled awkwardly into…

A parking lot.

No vehicles could be seen, but a bustling diner now stood before them, all metallic panels and wide windows, with a neon sign that read, *Joe's Eats.* Happy looking denizens dined within. The smell of fried goodness blended enticingly with the aroma of fresh baked delights. They could see no other lights or structures anywhere else, and it felt as though the emptiness must extend for miles in all directions, the lonely diner serving as a tiny oasis in a vast, wild land. All quickly realized that, by escaping the miserable hallway, they had found their way into a new world.

"Nice call, lass!" Scram said as he surveyed the scene.

"Are all well?" Sparrow asked.

"I don't know," Dune observed. "That was like being inside of a prank. Stupid, but clever. Funny."

"Not funny for me," Scram said.

"Nor me," Sparrow agreed, stone-faced.

Dune regarded them, suddenly aware that this was something he experienced as a *knower.* What he thought did not come from the game, but from Real — from his player, or perhaps his player's… reality. There would be no explaining it.

"Right," he said, turning his attention to their new situation. "So what's next?"

"Hatch hungry," the brute replied.

*   *   *

"What… was that?" The Boss inquired, baffled that his traps had failed.

"'Swallow Hall O'," Mister Needles replied.

"Swallow hollow?"

"Swallow. Hall. O."

"Mine?"

Needles nodded.

"O?"

Needles nodded.

"The 'O' is so it rhymes?"

Needles nodded.

The Boss smiled thinly. "Swallow Hall O, eh?"

"Yes."

"Needles! We must kill this Dune. …Soon."

"I see."

"Cut off his head… so he's dead."

"Indeed."

"More so, Needles, his… torso."

…

"Too much?" The Boss inquired.

"A bit tired."

The Boss smiled again, but the muscles of his face felt misused. "I want to die, Needles. I want…" He turned to look at his faithful toady, who might as well have been made of sticks, ash, and acid. It seemed he might either collapse or burst into flame. "Needles."

"Hmm?"

"I want… Out. Soon."

"Do you know when?" Needles replied. "Everything can be ready."

The Boss looked at him long and hard. He almost said, 'now,' but then he thought again of this team. This… Dune. "Soon," he said, smiling weakly at his little rhyme.

*   *   *

Jake stood and paced the room like a caged animal. 'Out.' He wants 'out.' He wants to come to Real. Jake knew what "Real" was well enough, and he had heard hints from his parents that there was some combination of amazing tech that allowed game characters to take form outside of the game, in the real world — in Jake's world. He shook his head slowly, back and forth, over and over. He couldn't stop. It was too crazy. Too crazy. Too crazy…

9 — FOOL'S PARADISE

"Pie?"

"Aye, Hatch, my friend! Pie for you!" Scram led them right in past some departing denizens — a shuffling tritopus and a couple of glassmen. The team took a booth in the corner (never any waiting for teams). Immediately, a maternal looking waitress — her hair stacked high, beehive style — rushed over to take their orders.

"Hiya handsome," she said to Scram.

"Aye, milady. What's your pie of the day?" the rogue inquired.

"Today's pie is silver bubbleberry, with cream crust, and filled with glowing loquat. The silver bubbleberries were grown up Moonstone Canyon at No Luck Ranch, and then polished up right here in our Cowpoke's Hat berry polishing cellar." She winked so much when she said "No Luck Ranch" that it seemed she had a nerve disorder.

"Sounds good, aye?" All nodded. "So then, a fat piece each for the three of us, and three pies for the one of him," Scram said, indicating himself, Dune, and Sparrow for the pieces, Hatch for the pies.

As the waitress danced away, Dune noticed the picture of a sly looking clown on the back of her uniform.

The pie arrived quickly, and they ate it almost as quickly as it had arrived — Hatch needing one bite per piece, Dune and Scram wolfing theirs down, but Sparrow taking a bit more time to taste and enjoy the flavors.

After Hatch licked his pans clean and set them down, Dune noticed that the inside of one of them featured some sort of diagram. Taking a closer look, he saw right away that it was a map, upon which a wandering dotted line appeared to link Joe's Eats with a spot between two high canyon ridges.

"Oh my goodness!" the waitress exclaimed in mock shock when she saw what Dune was up to. "You've found the map to the bubbleberry farm! Aren't you a smart little wrangler!" She was winking so much that even a blind person would have noticed. "But what really even is a silver bubbleberry? Looks like you'll find out," she added, winking.

"Mind if I keep this pan?" Dune asked.

"Help yourself, honey," she replied.

Wink wink.

The team departed.

Brilliant stars shone over the lonely parking lot, sparkling against the pitch blackness of the sky — bright enough to light the warriors and cast faint shadows on the worn pavement. At Dune's urging, they let the pie map guide them across an empty highway and into a dark canyon with high cliffs rising to either side. Sparrow remained alert for enemies, but they were not disturbed as they followed an easy trail upward along a dry creek bed. The sparkling sky traced a jagged path between the canyon tops above them, giving just enough light to see by.

At the top of a final, short climb, the canyon opened out into a small, flat-bottomed valley, newly lit by the rising moon. There, they did indeed come upon a tiny "farm." A short, picket fence marked the spot where a lone and very sad-looking bush grew. Only one lonely berry hung from a withered twig.

Expecting a bubbleberry feast, Hatch had jogged

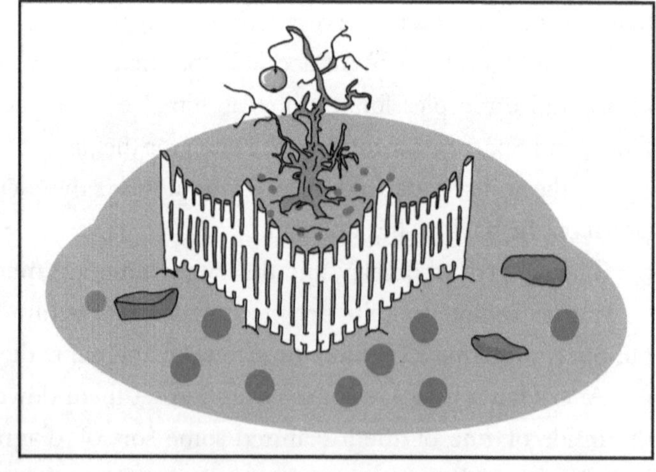

ahead, but the others found him standing glumly next to the almost empty bush. In a fit of anger, the brute ripped it from the ground and threw it as far as he could. But when he did so, the thick plug of soil in which it had been planted went with it, and a smooth-sided hole was exposed — as though he had pulled a cork from a bottle. Daylight stabbed upward through the opening. Peering in, Dune quickly realized that it must be the portal into yet another world.

The team gathered around — first with interest, and then with awe.

"Well, Scram," Dune said, "no weird passage at least."

"Don't like it. Give me a spooky tunnel any day."

Sparrow found herself gazing downward through a mile of sunlit sky at a spreading land far below, with rolling, grassy hills, and wide patches that might be groves or farms. In the center of the scene — directly below the hole — she saw a huge, rounded, gleaming *thing* that looked like...

A bubble — the top of a vast, silver bubble.

"Big bubbleberry?" Hatch guessed.

Sparrow felt suddenly eager. "We fall, that is all."

"Aye, lass?" Scram returned. "But what's that bubble thing at the bottom is what I wonder."

"This is a game way," she returned. "We will survive." If it was a complete bubble, she thought, then most of it must be beneath the surface of the land. If it wasn't, then she had never seen such a thing before. Despite her uncertainty, and without a glance back at her teammates, she stepped off the lip of the opening and fell away.

The others leaned over to watch. Briefly they saw her, but she quickly shrank into the distance and vanished.

"No way!" Scram stated flatly. "No way in hell!"

"Hatch?" Dune asked, regarding the brute and nodding toward the rogue. Hatch smiled, put a massive arm around Scram and pulled him close.

"We go!" he said, voice booming. "Jump on big bubbleberry!"

"No! No! Nooooo..." Scram's voice faded away as he fell.

Dune took a quick breath, then...

Jumped.

*   *   *

The fall was long and fast, but ended easily. Each team member hit the surface of the silver bubble at high speed, but then sank deep into it, slowing gradually as the surface bent inward. Stopping for only an instant, each rose again as the stretchy fabric returned to form, tossing them high into the air once more. These wonderfully slow bounces continued for many seconds, getting shallower each time until, at last, the motion stopped and they lay still on the bubble's surface…

But then began to slide.

With nothing to hold on to, all continued sliding down the nearly frictionless material until landing gently on the ground, which did seem to interrupt the skin of a perfect sphere that continued downward, unseen beneath the surface. More likely was that it was not a sphere, but a *dome*, and the ground was its base.

"Do it again!" Hatch had liked feeling lightweight.

"Aye. One to remember," Scram said. "And definitely no retreat *that* way," he added.

Dune looked about. "Now what?" he asked.

"Look! A door," announced Sparrow, pointing.

It seemed a very simple door — red paint, one knob, one lock, set back into an alcove notched into the edge of the curving dome, just deep enough to allow the door to stand straight with an extra couple of feet above it to hold a fanciful sign that read:

All in the team felt certain that Fool's Paradise came next in their journey through the Worlds, but no action, command, or rogue's trick worked to open the door. Multiple crushing blows by Hatch didn't budge it. Sparrow finally tried a precious token, but none of those they carried fit the tiny lock, and they found no other way to invoke their power.

Giving up at last, the team set out to circle the silvery dome in hopes of finding another way in. They walked for hours, bearing slowly to the right as the shimmering, soft-but-stronger-than-steel dome, curved on with monotonous sameness. The scene outside changed little as well — rolling meadows as far as the eye could see, with occasional grassy roads skirting by and looping off into the vast landscape. Dune's hope drained away. The team was clearly low on luck.

Feeling down and a little bit crazy in the early evening, they checked in to Burkhalter's B&B — a lodging they reached just as they completed their circuit. It seemed a charming little chalet-style inn on a long road to nowhere. At least, 'nowhere' is where the innkeeper said the road went.

They said little as they bought beverages at the quaint bar. Dinner arrived: roast pig and asparagus, with a side of sautéed fig'llvhe* and onions.

Note: fig'llvhe is a root vegetable that requires a very ordinary sort of ostrich to locate in the wild. Since dwarves ate nearly all of the ostriches after using them to find nearly all of the fig'llvhe, fig'llvhe has become high class, respectable, and expensive (though no one really likes the taste).

They attempted conversation for a time after eating but soon ran out of things to say. The innkeeper retired for the night, Scram fell asleep in his chair, and Sparrow and Hatch went up to bed. Dune was left alone with his thoughts, which were few and boring, and his mind soon ran dry. He wasn't sleepy. He just sat and stared numbly at an old clock above the fireplace. Tick tock tick tock tick tock…

*   *   *

"…Wake up."

"Huh?"

"…Wake up."

"Einstein?"

"…You're sleeping in your chair."

"Uh, yeah. Thanks."

"…You're drooling on your controller."

"Oh. Yeah. Uh, oops."

"…Mom says dinner in an hour."

*   *   *

Dune woke with a start when an eerie noise arose outside — like the sounds of sparks flying and furious boiling mixed together. Crackling blue light showed through the curtained windows, adding a flickering illumination to the nearly empty bar. A low, moaning rumble shivered the tables, and the flames in the fireplace dimmed. Dune stood, unsure what to do.

Just then, the innkeeper passed through the room on his way to check his barn door.

"Ion storm's comin'!" he exclaimed. "Bad to be out in that." He departed, leaving Dune alone again.

The mysterious ion storm grew in intensity as it made its roaring approach. Peering through the curtains, Dune immediately saw that the dome appeared on fire with electric charge, glowing hotly and sparking like mad. Seconds later…

CHKLANG!

A thundering, metallic clatter sounded out, powerful enough to shake the inn to its foundation. Dune watched in amazement as the dome ripped open, one huge section tearing right off to be carried away, burning on the ion winds. Most of the remaining material shredded quickly in the spinning gale, pieces ripping off and flying away, one after the other, until only random tatters were left around the dome's base. Though the storm's light offered little illumination, Dune had tantalizing glimpses of dark structures scattered across a wide plain within the dome's revealed interior.

As quickly as it had come up, the storm raced off into the distance, perhaps to batter some other target in this odd world. The blue ion radiance flickered out, until only a final afterglow from the dying day remained. With the dome gone, Dune decided to see about entering the area within — not necessarily a good idea without his team, but he went anyway.

It took only a few minutes to reach the dome's perimeter. As he neared, something shining brightly in the grass captured his attention. It sat just outside of the door, which stood wide open and appeared undamaged. The object glowed with such intense brightness that he could not tell what it was, but he felt its potency like a sinister beacon that could only lead to bad things. Squinting, he leaned in and tried to make out what it might be.

He was so focused on his task that he didn't notice an approaching shadow until a skinny, green, man-like figure with a sly looking face materialized before him and delivered a big, yellow smile — a smile that suggested, somehow, that this character had killed, and would again. Its comic clothes were multi-colored, with flaps and tassels, and a number of small bells. The tall hat on its head split in the middle into several drooping cones that gave a jingle when he moved. A particularly ominous jingling came, not from the bells on hat or clothes, but from a forked tongue, hidden behind the smile, that would reveal itself in due time…

And the time was due.

"Knock knock," it said in a raspy, ringy voice worse than a stab. "Pretty thing, eh? But it's not for you, warrior. Not for you."

Dune sensed danger, and he thought of grabbing his bow. Instead, following a sudden impulse, he lunged for the object in the grass, hoping to seize it and escape. But as his hand grasped it and he stood to run, the green creature raised one of its seven fingers. A brilliant flash of rainbow sparkles dazzled the legend bowman. He froze in place, as though turned to stone, and he could not see. Clearly, though, he had greatly angered the green guy.

"Oh, he has it! He has it! Not fair! Not *right!*" Dune was dimly aware as the creature furiously cast sparkling spells around his clenched fist and shouted, "Jester sad! Knower glad! Jester mad! Knower *bad! Bad! Bad! Bad!*

"BAD!"

He thought he heard jingling all around, followed by wild flapping, a massive whoosh of air, and the sound of a slamming door. Then… Nothing.

Absolute nothing.

*   *   *

"Alexander!"

"Ow! Wha…? Huh?"

I didn't know where I was. Mom grabbed my head, looks of anger and fear mixed in her eyes. "Dinner! *Now!*" she snapped, anger winning. "I should ground you from games for a month!" she added.

I was in my chair, at my desk, my controller on the floor. "Coming. Sorry. Coming. I'm coming. Sorry."

"…Wash up," she said, not quite so mad.

It was macaroni and cheese.

From a box.

I ate like I was supposed to. I talked about normal kid stuff. I wanted mom not to worry — and not to ground me from the game. I smiled and was nice to Einstein (who looked at me like I was nuts). I helped with after-dinner clean-up, and then I gave Einstein practice spelling tests (he knew *all* the words, of course), and *then* mom made us watch this nature show on penguins, which she loves (it was pretty cool). But as soon as I was sure I had done enough, I raced back to my room, dying to get back in.

But I was worried. I didn't know whether it was a coincidence, but just before mom pulled me out, Dune had… vanished. Or at least, it *seemed* like he had, because I could still hear the green guy for a few seconds. I just couldn't *do* Dune — couldn't feel him or make anything happen. Weird. This whole Worlds thing was crazy hard, and time was all mixed up. The stress was insane! But still…

I picked up the controller.

*   *   *

Dune woke from wild dreams of waddling birds to the pain of Sparrow slapping him repeatedly across the face. "Ow! Okay! Stop! I'm awake!" Scram and Hatch were there as well. It was dark, and he still stood near the door of the ruined dome.

…Only as he looked about, he saw that the dome was *not* ruined. The moonlit meadows all around looked beaten and scorched, but the skin of the dome appeared whole and unscarred, gleaming dimly in the night, and the door was closed tight once again. Huh? It took Dune a few more seconds to distinguish reality from memories and fading dreams.

"What happened?" demanded Scram. "I woke up and you'd gone. Aye, and now we find you standing here like a statue."

"Well…" Dune took a deep breath, coming fully to his senses. He quickly recognized that he stood in the same spot where he'd met the bizarre green figure — *Jester*, he suddenly thought, the memory of words heard earlier in the night coming to mind. "Well, I came out here after the storm. I remember I saw this glowing object — not sure what it was. Then… Then Jester came out of nowhere and… Well, I tried to grab the object and run, but…" He paused, puzzled. "I'm a little fuzzy on the rest."

"*Completely* fuzzy," Scram observed. But then, noticing something, added, "now don't hit me," and he started to back slowly away.

"What?"

"Uh, I didn't mean anything, aye? Just joking." Scram explained.

"*What?*"

"Your fist!" Scram said. "Looks ready to bust my nose!"

Dune looked at his left hand. A fierce fist indeed! "Oh." he relaxed his arm, turned the fist up, and slowly opened his fingers.

There, in his palm, sat a small key. No one had to say a word. They walked to the door, Dune inserted key into lock and turned it, and all watched as the door opened slowly inward on its own, pushing against the rush of warm, charged air that swept out of the dome and over the team.

"In!" Hatch urged. The others agreed, and in they went. The door slammed behind them and they heard the click of a lock.

All was dark within, except for a lone light that glowed softly just ahead. The shadows beyond seemed to hint at endless, rolling terrain stretching off into nothing. A stone walkway led several paces from the door to the source of the light — a flat rock that lay atop a waist-high pedestal of glass. Approaching it, they saw that the rock was inscribed:

Midnight Clowns, Now Urchins Die?

Fool's Walk, Burned God, Golden Lie

Hat Birds, Hidden Way Untie

Down Is Up, To Lovers Fly!

"What is it?" asked Scram.

"A poem. Or a riddle," answered Dune, uncertain.

"A riddle," said Sparrow. "It is our clue. We must solve it."

Dune thought for a time. "Well, I guess 'Midnight' means that's when something will happen." Sparrow stared at him, unimpressed.

"'Urchins Die' sounds grim, aye?"

They pondered and explored for a while, but they saw no clue as to which way they should set out in the dark dome. One by one, they sat down in the grass to wait. Midnight was fast approaching.

*   *   *

In a far away land, a bell struck twelve. At the same instant, a torrent of voices and other sounds filled the heads of Sparrow and Dune — advice and temptations, laughter and screams, fluttering wings and rushing water. They both rose from the grass, standing beside the riddle stone. Seeing this, Scram stood too, though he did not hear what learner and knower heard. Hatch stood as well, with nothing in his mind but an eagerness for action.

Sparrow and Dune struggled to understand what they were hearing, but the sounds began to fade, and — when the final reverberation of the twelfth ring ended — they ceased, leaving no lasting memories.

"Did you hear?" Sparrow asked.

"Noise and words, yes, but they are gone," Dune replied.

"More lights!" interrupted Hatch, and the others could just make out his raised club pointing toward the pedestal. They all looked, and there, upon the riddle stone, sat four…

Tickets.

The edges of the tickets glowed softly, each a different color. Gathering around, the team saw writing on each. The one with green edges read:

Clearly, it was a ticket for Dune, the color matching his clothes. The same applied to the others — tickets edged in red, gold, and blue to match the look of Dune's three comrades: *Good for One Learner, Good for One Rogue,* and *Good for One Brute.*

"Tickets to what?" Scram asked. They looked about in the dimness.

"We need more light," Dune said.

Scram pulled a small torch from his bag (standard game gear for rogues) and lit it, illuminating the scene to a radius of about 50 feet. Their eyes widened at what the light revealed.

Instead of the vague edge of fields stretching away under the vast dome, they now saw seven gateways arranged in a wide semicircle, each built of two weathered wooden posts connected by a signboard overhead. Beyond the gateways, the beginnings of seven roads wound away into the darkness. Gazing outward to the edge of the torchlight, they could just make out ghostly hints of wreck and ruin — like the long cold remnants of a great fire that had devastated a wide countryside.

The signs intrigued Dune. Each had both picture and words. The pictures were: an X on a rock, a cave mouth, a castle, a tall tree, a big tent, flames, and an open mouth. The accompanying words posed disturbing questions: 'Mayhem and Madness?' 'Certain Death?' 'Vicious Wolves?' 'Razor Claws?' 'Acts of Carnage?' 'Broken Bones?' And, 'Running with Scissors?'

The challenge, though, was obvious. "We must take the tickets and use the riddle to choose a road," Dune stated. "If we pick the wrong road, we—"

"Die," Sparrow finished for him.

After examining signs and rereading the riddle, Hatch led the way, oddly insightful as always. "No like circus."

"What?"

Hatch pointed at the sign with the picture of the big tent. "No like circus."

"Yes!" exclaimed Dune. "The riddle has 'clowns,' and the tent is a circus tent."

"And 'acts,'" Sparrow added. "'Acts of Carnage' may be circus acts."

"Tickets figure too, aye?" Scram finished.

"We take *that* road," decided Dune.

And they did, with no delay.

As soon as they had all passed beneath their sign of choice, the scene behind vanished, and they could no longer see the other signs, the stone, or the dome wall. Scram's torch went out as well, and he could not relight it, so they continued on with only shadows and the dim illumination of night to keep them on the road. It was enough. A gritty wind blew up, bringing chilling sounds from the dark ruin about them, but they felt no fear — only strangeness.

While they could not see well enough to be certain, the steps they took did not seem to match the speed that the land to either side went by. They walked for minutes, but they felt that miles passed. Tiny lights moved swiftly by, appearing and disappearing like fireflies, though their faint shine made them seem like the distant lights of lonely houses. Perhaps this world had worlds of its own, and they were passing from one to another.

After walking for a long while, something appeared in the distance — a tent, red and white striped, lit from within. As they neared, they realized it was quite large, and they began to hear the sound of lively music and many voices — an excited audience.

"Sounds like fun!" Scram exclaimed.

"Hatch like cotton candy."

Arriving at the entrance, they found the striped curtain under the "Enter" sign closed. Beside the curtain stood a tall box with a small, ticket-sized hole in its top. A green light shone through the slot. Dune inserted his ticket, which was grabbed and pulled from his fingers, as if by a tiny cat hiding within. The curtain swept aside, Dune passed through, the curtain closed, and the glow from the ticket slot changed to red. Sparrow used her ticket with the same result. Scram matched his to the golden glow, and Hatch to the blue. Now all were in.

They walked around an inner drape and the cavernous interior of the tent opened before them. Two lofty poles, forty feet apart, held up the huge big top. Three large performance rings for the acts filled the tent's middle — one between the poles and one to either side. Around them climbed rising tiers of benches. Rigging ropes hung this way and that, hinting at aerial acts to come. Loud and cheery music filled the air, energizing hundreds of human-looking denizens in the stands, young and old, all excited and happy.

A number of clowns performed silly acts for the crowd and blew up balloons for those in the front rows.

The team quickly found space a few rows up and took their seats, seemingly unnoticed. The moment they were seated, the house lights dimmed, and the circus began.

…A very short circus, it turned out.

The ringmaster stepped into the middle ring, a spotlight illuminating his vivid costume, bright smile, and forked hat with bells on it.

"Jester!" Dune whispered.

"Welcome one and all," the giddy Jester shouted, "to the *Circuuusss of the Apooocalypse!*" He stretched out the name. "You will be dazzled! You will be amazed! The greatest performers in the Worlds are here tonight to—"

But Jester got no further, because the balloon-blowing clowns had crept toward him through the shadows, surrounding him, and now they leapt upon him, quickly cutting him to pieces with various silly but razor sharp blades. Then they turned on each other with gleeful grins, slicing and stabbing, until only one still stood. This last clown was in the midst of bowing triumphantly to the wildly excited crowd when a ferocious lion raced into the ring, chased by her tamer, and ate the clown in a few massive bites. The crowd never ceased to cheer or laugh, apparently oblivious to the sinister consequences of the show.

The team watched, dumbfounded, but had no time to react as five more lions entered the ring, quickly joining the first in a running circle, each taking turns leaping through a flaming hoop that the tamer had lifted and ignited. After the sixth had made the perilous leap, the tamer signaled the audience and several small children rushed out into the ring, begging to ride the beasts. Immediately, the lions set upon them, and each youngster was seized and carried aside to be gruesomely devoured.

As the lions began to dine, twenty elephants pounded into the rings, stomping and swaying to the increasingly frantic music. Now, *dozens* of children streamed from the seats hoping for rides, running wildly. All still cheered and smiled — even when the first few disappeared into the gaping mouths of the behemoths, others were gored by swinging tusks, and still more were stamped into pulp.

Out rushed a parade of camels, running awkwardly and trampling those who heedlessly stepped in front of them. The camels broke ranks and sought out still more willing young victims, who ran to them, throwing small arms around their long necks, desiring to be licked by camel tongues as though by adoring puppies. But what started as tender licks morphed into an almost hypnotic gobbling as children were gradually swallowed whole.

While the animals dined, the trapeze act began. But what might have been a beautiful performance turned sour when the aerialists began plucking laughing kids from the ground as they swung past, carrying them to great heights, and then dropping them, faces beaming, to thudding doom on the hard packed dirt of the rings. The dwindling audience stood and cheered all the louder as the body count increased.

*   *   *

Layla pulled out, feeling a little sick to her stomach. She had never before encountered violence like this in the game. Of course, Sparrow had never made it this deep into 4th Ring before either. Layla shook her head slowly. She had a strange feeling that bad things were coming, and soon, but she wouldn't quit. No way!

Taking a long, deep breath to steady herself, she went back in.

*   *   *

The team didn't know what to think. Game characters dying was hardly unusual, but this particular combination of group glee and grisly gore was one none of them had seen before.

"We should get out of here," Scram said, having lost all interest in the entertainment.

"Look," said Sparrow. "She pointed at one of the six exits spaced around the tent. "Do you see?"

Dune did indeed see that above the doors, signs featured pictures — just like those at the riddle stone — but had no words. "What's the next part of the clue?" he asked.

"'Fool's Walk," Hatch reminded them (brutes have excellent memories). "We go now. Hatch no like circus ever."

They looked at the six signs, but did not, at first, see anything that seemed to match. The images included a pickle, a sailboat, an axe in a tree, a ballerina, a wine bottle, and a shoe.

"I pick the bottle," said Scram.

"Hatch drink?"

"No," Dune said. "We want the shoe. Let's go!" He had noticed the two small tassels on toe and heel, and immediately thought of Jester — the 'Fool.'

Their exit was across the tent from where they sat, and they chose the most direct route. But as soon as they stepped from the seats and into the performance area, *all* of the tent's occupants turned from their various activities and attacked — performers, animals, audience, and even the few children who were still functioning. The shrieks and roars of the attackers blended with the wild music to create an insane din, but the team was not daunted. Arrows, blades, feet, and fists flew, and the enemies were decimated. Hatch's bellows sounded out over all as he tossed elephants like bowling balls. They soon reached the exit, passed through it, and then…

Everything changed.

The tent vanished.

The music ceased.

They stood outside once again, the light of dawn growing, but now they faced a high fence — a palisade of tall standing timbers, sharpened at their tops, with a single gateway in the middle. The broad double doors of the gate stood wide open, revealing a lane that ran about two hundred yards straight ahead, passing between a strange variety of natural and manmade features — tall trees and thick bushes, shacks and sheds, gravestones and monuments — all of which seemed like excellent hiding places for enemies. At the end of the lane rose the ruin of what must once have been a huge church, the charred framing of a tall steeple still rising above all else.

"Don't like the look of this," Scram said, saying what all felt.

"'Fool's Walk,' indeed," Sparrow observed.

"Burned God, Golden Lie," Hatch continued, completing the third line of the riddle.

"Well, if that's a church," said Dune, "it sure looks like it could go with 'Burned God.'"

"Aye, fine," replied Scram. "But it's the 'Fool's Walk' part I'm thinkin' about now. Sure looks like a gauntlet of ambushes, traps, and snipers."

Just then, a figure appeared in the middle of the lane about half way down, facing the team, hands on hips.

"That the… what'd you call him, bowman?" Scram inquired.

"Jester."

"Aye, well, master Jester somehow survived that slicing a few minutes ago, or else there's two of 'em. Looks like he's waitin' for us," the rogue added.

Dune smiled, an idea coming to him. "Hatch, how would you like a little extra work?"

"Crush?"

"Yes."

"What will you do?" Sparrow asked.

"Well," Dune answered. "It's only a gauntlet if you're *in* it. I thought we might take the scenic route.

The team planned quietly for another minute, a quick glance showing that Jester seemed to be growing impatient. At last, with a wave, Dune led the team to the right of the gateway, They could no longer see up the lane, and Jester, presumably, could no longer see them.

"Hatch?" Dune asked.

The brute smiled, and then smashed through the log fence and crushed his way forward through everything in front of him. The team followed a few feet behind, stepping through the debris. Hatch bashed onward, paralleling the gauntlet lane but about fifty feet to the right, so that none of the many traps were of any use in slowing them down. As they went, the team blundered into the hiding places of various bands of enemies, startling them and easily pushing past. None would fight — they were simply too low in the game to know what to do in an unexpected situation. Those that weren't knocked aside or trampled by Hatch simply stood by and watched as the warriors carried on through the broken shanties, uprooted hedges, and toppled statuary.

Hatch enjoyed himself immensely, so he was a bit disappointed when he broke through the last barrier and stepped out into the narrow plaza surrounding the church.

Dune emerged next — just in time to catch a glimpse of a frightened looking Jester disappearing into the burned-out ruin. "This way!" he shouted, racing after Jester as Scram and Sparrow appeared. "We have to catch him!" The others didn't ask why, following at a run.

The team raced up the broad steps of the church but stopped before the blackened doors. All but the skeleton of the building had been burned to a crisp, leaving a badly weakened frame to support the teetering roof. The sky seemed darkened above, as though it, too, had been burned. The charred carving of a suffering saint looked down at them from above. Dune pushed a door open, acting casual, hiding a sudden fear. The door fell to the floor, the frame too weak to hold it up any longer.

Entering, it didn't even seem like a building. The team could still see out to distant fields through ragged gaps in the walls. They felt the ashen draft and smelled death by combustion. The church itself was slowly vanishing with the wind — crispy pews, confession booths, and seared remnants of old hymnals falling apart and drifting away.

The only object they could see that wasn't burned black or gray was a small figure of gold in the center of a table, which still stood on scorched legs in the center of the crossing where nave and transept met. A melted cross, perhaps.

"Treasure," Scram murmured, though without his usual excitement.

A powerful urge to grab the golden figure arose in Dune, and he ran to the table. His teammates followed but could only stand helplessly by, their tongues frozen by the object's magical potency. Dune's hand reached for it as though guided by another mind. He fought the urge, uncertain why, but knowing that something was wrong. His fingers twitched as he paused. He felt somehow as if he had faced this choice before — as though he might pass by an empty truth to seize an exciting lie.

A 'Golden Lie.'

He knew it was wrong, and the knowledge somehow gave him strength to resist. His hand stopped a bare inch from the shining metal. He lifted his gaze. There, standing deep in the shadows, stood…

Jester.

The tiny glint from his eyes and teeth, just enough to be seen.

Dune stared at him. He didn't move, but the eyes narrowed. Dune looked again at the collapsed golden figure. Now he was certain it had never been a cross. Too complex. No, it had been a pentagram — inverted — sign of evil. Dune smiled. Evilly (sort of).

In one swift motion, he whipped his hand and batted the gold piece across the room, straight at Jester, who squealed in frustration and then ran, bolting out a small archway.

"After him!" Dune shouted, and the team pursued.

Jester raced ahead. They saw him slip into a small door in the hallway and vanish. Looking in, Dune saw a narrow stair, spiraling upward to unknown heights. They started up after him — except for Hatch, who could see he wouldn't fit. Round and round the tight stair went, climbing ever higher, weakened by past heat, black as carbon, upward, until it emerged at last in a high, small room below the peak of the steeple.

They saw Jester right away. He stood on a fragile window sill, grinning, holding onto the charred frame. In fact, the steeple might as well have been *all* windows, for the walls were burned away down to the posts and beams, and they could see far enough to make out the inside of the dome wall in the distance — Fool's Paradise indeed.

"Well well," came the jangly, wheezy voice again. "Well well. Knower strong. Knower strong. Doesn't take the golden piece. Doesn't come to stay. Wants to go away?" His smile grew wide, the sharp yellow teeth wet with pleasure. "Too bad! Too bad! Must catch me but can't! Can't! *Can't!*" And with that, Jester leapt from the high window to the ground, ready to escape to one of his many lairs.

"Damn!" spat Dune. "*Down* again!"

"Not the way *he* went," Scram said.

"No, the stairs. *Damn!*"

Down they went, spiraling earthward on the brittle, wobbling staircase, the seconds ticking away. They reached the base, spotted the exit door, sped out into the sunshine, and immediately scanned the horizon to see which way Jester might have run.

"I cannot see him," said Sparrow.

"Not me either," echoed the rogue.

"Damn," said Dune, this time with a sigh.

"No worry," said Hatch from where he stood, next to the church behind his mates. "Hatch catch."

The others turned to see. Hatch had both arms wrapped around Jester — and he apparently needed to use considerable strength just to hold him.

"Don't let him go!" Dune shouted.

"Can't! Can't!" Jester wailed. He squirmed some more, trying to break the brute's hold to no avail. He looked frantically about, then squeezed his eyes closed, gritted his teeth, and…

POP!

Where Jester had been, now they saw a large rubber duck, held tight by a shocked brute.

"Keep holding!" Dune shouted.

POP!

The duck became a big red chair. Hatch held tight.

POP!

Chair no more! Now a hot air balloon basket, with the bulbous balloon stretching up nearly as high as the steeple. Still Hatch held.

POP!

A deer.

POP!

A *dozen* blue deer tangled into a large mass that Hatch wouldn't release.

POP!

A giant red deer! A red moose! A giant fig'llvhe! A big eye! A hamster ball! A giraffe!

Oops.

The last one was a mistake. Hatch instantly grabbed the giraffe around its long neck, and when the giraffe popped back to become Jester once again, it was his neck that Hatch still held. Jester struggled — writhing and kicking, teeth snapping, fingers clawing — gasping as Hatch's grip relentlessly tightened. Finally, with Jester's neck narrow enough to hold with one hand, Hatch used his other to slap him across the face — and to be slapped by a brute is like being smacked by a circus tentpole.

Jester went limp, stunned silly.

Hatch let go and the delirious Jester fell to the earth. As his head banged the ground, a flock of tiny birds burst from his hat and began fluttering angrily around his head, pecking furiously, punishing him for years of imprisonment, until he was well and thoroughly punctured.

Done with that, the birds swirled together, lofting up into the sky, and then wheeled away into the small, dry valley that cut through the meadow near the church. They flew straight over to an odd looking sapling that had no branches — only one thick central stem, topped by several dark leaves that looked something like zipper handles. Each bird grabbed a leaf in its beak, then they all flapped furiously upward, as though to pull the leaves from the stem. But the leaves did not break free! Instead, the entire tree pulled up from the ground, the roots coming too.

Roots that *had no end!*

Out the roots came in long, continuous strands, and, as they did, the land along the valley bottom split open — as if the roots were threads pulling out from an endless seam that opened wide as the thread was removed. The birds vanished into the distance, zipper leaves in their beaks, thready roots trailing after, and the earth opening wide behind them to reveal…

A raging river!

Seriously?

Yes!

"'Hat Birds Hidden Way Untie!'" Sparrow said in triumph.

Their next step proved easy due to Hatch having a second skill in river travel. As soon as the river appeared, the brute pulled what looked like a brown bag from his game satchel. He grasped a small tube on the bag's edge, inhaled an impossibly deep breath, took the tube in his mouth, exhaled, and *whoosh* — a full-sized raft took shape. Hatch set it in the water, the team jumped on (leaving groggy Jester behind), and soon found themselves watching the scenery go rapidly by as they floated to their next destination.

They passed by many scenes of interest, but the best was a busy *circus camp*. Denizen kids could be seen riding lions while others napped in the open mouths of elephants — kids the team recognized from the carnage of the Jester's circus. Clowns made balloon animals as young ones snuggled with camels who lovingly licked their faces. Trapeze teachers helped students swing high and do tricks while attached to safety harnesses.

"Hi," shouted a girl who Sparrow had last seen in the mouth of a lion. Others stopped and waved. "Did you like our show?"

And then the raft sped past, and they lost sight of the camp.

On they floated. Dune nodded off for awhile, but was eventually awakened by a deep roaring sound. Opening his eyes, he beheld a massive, thundering waterfall. He thought at first they were to be crushed beneath it, but he quickly realized it was still a short way ahead, and that Hatch was paddling the raft toward a small, wooden dock near its base. And there, upon the dock, prancing and capering like a fool, was none other than…

Jester.

"You again!" snapped Scram. "Thought we were done with you."

"Silly rogue!" came the reply. "Happy rogue! Jester is an avatar. I play, I play, I win, I win — but not today, no no! You are first to leave my world if one more test, you can pass." He smiled at the team, then danced away and vanished in a twinkling.

"One more test?" Sparrow asked. "What could it—"

"Got it!" said Dune. "Look!" He pointed at the daunting waterfall that roared just a stone's throw away. The others gazed at it.

Scram lifted his eyes, but could not see the top. "Mighty tall, aye?"

Sparrow looked as well, but something troubled her. "The water looks… strange. Almost like it's…"

"Flowing… *up?*" Dune finished her thought for her.

"'Down is Up!'" Sparrow turned to him, a brilliant smile on her face — which was more a shock to Dune than the reverse waterfall.

"Hatch!" Dune commanded. "Paddle us 'under' that waterfall, please."

A few seconds later, they found themselves flying skyward amidst the wild waters of the exit from Fool's Paradise, and the world of the avatar, Jester.

*　　*　　*

Einstein stared at the screen over his brother's shoulder. It was a strange view, different than what he saw in other games. It seemed like a smooth and detailed video with no pauses or cuts from scene to scene, but it was as if the camera moved like eyes, darting around. He could almost connect with it — almost feel like he was there, where Alexander was.

Almost.

10 — THE YELLOW DOOR

"Jester has *never* failed me before! He cleans up — *it's his job!*" The Boss blinked, but his fury soon fled, and he sagged in is chair, his eyes turning to a small bat that flew about awkwardly, having trouble grasping its chosen hanging spot on a high rafter. "What has happened, Needles?

"Perhaps he *let* them through," Mister Needles replied, stirring his coffee.

The Boss looked at his friend and servant in disbelief. "Really?"

"Perhaps. If he was impressed," came the reply. "He *is* an avatar."

"Yes, but crossing *me?*" The Boss sneered in disbelief. "Has he strayed so far from the primrose path of evil?"

Needles was still for a moment. "Perhaps things have gotten off track," he said at last.

"But this is just... a team. There have been so many." Confusion overtook The Boss. "Is it a *great* team, Mister Needles?"

"They seem quite good. More intuitive than those before perhaps."

"...This isn't Wonder again, is it?"

"Wonder did not face Jester," Needles replied. "She cheated."

"Yesss," The Boss lost himself in memory. "But this team," he said after a bit. "This knower's team — it is not Wonder. They are not better than teams I have seen before, are they? I mean, I could crush any team if I simply paid attention. Isn't that the way it was, Mister Needles?"

Needles hesitated, but then shrugged. "Your *player* was closer to you then. Perhaps—"

"I do *not* need to be played!" The Boss shot back, instantly angry again. Needles was not bothered. The Boss quickly cooled. "...Do I need him?"

"'Paying attention,' you call it," Needles responded. "Your player... Your player *assisted* you in paying attention. That is all. You are strong without him, but perhaps not quite so… committed. Jester would sense this. He is not very serious. I wouldn't put it past him to do it as a bit of humor. Perhaps he is mocking you."

The Boss stared at his companion for a long stretch of time before he spoke again — so long that even serene Mister Needles felt a creeping unease.

"Well then, Needles, since I will not be letting my Real play me again, we must think of something else. You do understand, don't you?"

"Indeed."

"And that I wish this warrior dead? You understand that?"

"Yes."

"The head of the beast, Needles. The head of the beast. This knower must diiie." The word bled from his lips, a sizzle of smoke hissed from his teeth, and a small puff of tiny sparks spat upward from one horn.

"And, *dear* Needles, since my player is… unemployed, I think I am counting on *you* to help." His face took on a placid, inquisitive look. "What do you think?"

"Mmmm." Needles was prepared. "Dune to die? Perhaps we should interfere with *his* player." he suggested drily. "As you did with the cat warrior's player? Well done, that."

"Wonderrr," The Boss purred.

"Yes," Needles continued. "Perhaps you can trap the legend bowman with the Final Surprise, but somewhat before he reaches the citadel? The Rubbles will welcome him, and his Real will fall."

The Boss nodded slowly, smiling, but his nodding smile rapidly transformed into a lingering scream. He wrenched around in his throne as if grasped by a whirlwind of claws, mildly shocking Needles.

"*Not enough!*" The Boss yowled, the echoes swirling back from the lofty ceiling. "*Not!* Enough," he squeezed through clenched teeth. His fury held for a frozen moment, then he slumped in his chair, a pained look wounding his leathery face. "Not enough, Needles. Wonder is *not* dead. Her player, *not* dead. I want *dead!*

"I want this warrior *dead.*

"I want his team *dead.*

"I want his player *dead.*

"Dead."

The Boss glanced over at his octopus as it churned by the fireplace, changing forms and fidgeting, stimulated by the anger in its master's voice. He turned to Needles and explained with menacing gentleness. "You see, he *beat* me, and I feel… irritated." The danger left The Boss's eyes, replaced by a look of aching boredom. "This Dune. He should be lost forever in the Alley Realm market. He should. And, haven't many warriors died at the end of… of…"

"Swallow Hall O?"

"Swallow Hall O, yes. Many?"

"Many," Mister Needles confirmed.

"But not this team," he replied, the words seeping from his mouth like vinegar. "Not this… Dune." The Boss shook his head slowly. "And now, he has survived Fool's Paradise."

"Indeed."

"I hate him, Needles."

The faithful Mister Needles picked up a tray of items from lunch and headed for the kitchen. "Perhaps," he said as he walked away, "I should find his player for you, Ace? Perhaps we see what we can do…" He stopped and turned to face his master, waiting until his gaze was returned. "…in *Real*. Perhaps we bring them *all* to Real to die, and you can remain there, out of the game once and for all. Perhaps it is time? Your beginning place is ready, and the coffee there is very, *very* good."

The Boss remained slumped for a moment, eyeing Needles uncertainly. But then, slowly, his eyebrows went up. A most unpleasant smile crept across his rancid countenance. A sinister gleam returned to his black-rimmed eyes. "DoNotEnter?"

"DoNotEnter, yes. Through the Yellow Door," Needles replied. "There is time."

"Oh, Needles," The Boss gushed. "You are *so* good to me!"

Needles almost smiled. "I must hurry."

"Yes. Go."

The Boss fixed his eyes on the fire. His anger smiled. He would rid his game of the team and the plague of heroism that dirtied his lowlands. He would kill this player that was spoiling his final days in the citadel. He would kill them all, and then he would order an espresso with his telfoon, and he would sip it. Slowly. In Real.

*　　*　　*

Diary of The Boss

Needles does know how to excite me! He is quite a good decorator, too. I do so look forward to seeing what he has prepared in my beginning place. My cave. I don't need much. A view. Coffee, of course. The chance to murder now and then, I suppose.

Needles and I do make an excellent team.

What does he really want?

Ace

*　　*　　*

At the top of the waterfall, the team's flying raft unceremoniously dumped them through an open door and into a dingy hallway. Raft, waterfall, and all other evidence of Fool's Paradise instantly vanished behind them. Standing — and quite suddenly dry — they made their way down the hall past several numbered doors.

Scram quickly realized where they were (though the others had no idea). A brothel. 'To Lovers Fly!' he thought to himself with a smile. Sparrow figured it out when they exited the hall and passed through the lobby, which featured lots of red velvet and sultry paintings of attractive subjects whose approach to clothing had been… non-standard.

"Say," began Scram when they exited and stood on the doorstep, "I was thinking we ought to take a day or two to rest. I might just—"

"No!" Sparrow interrupted, taking charge. "We do not delay. We go on." Scram started to object, but then shrugged.

146

The team stepped out of the brothel into the heart of a modest town that appeared to sit high in the mountains, quite close to the few, puffy clouds that floated in a deep blue (not orange) sky. Clearly, it was *not* a ring of the city. Nameless game denizens thronged a winding, cobbled lane that was packed along either side with a great variety of ornately constructed shops and other buildings, all brightly painted in a wide palette of colors that gleamed in the sunshine. The erratic wandering and flying of the denizens caused no particular problems, but they passed unusually close and frequently, and the warriors couldn't help but be on guard.

"Why so crowded?" Dune wondered aloud.

Just then, the ground began to shake, and an ominous rumbling came from beneath their feet. The echoes of a distant crash reverberated down the lane, and a few small pieces of building trim fell to the ground nearby. The shaking soon ceased, however, and the damage seemed minor. The denizens hadn't reacted at all.

"Earthquake," announced Sparrow.

"Oh for a hotel," Scram muttered.

"Hatch drink?"

"No!"

For a time the teammates wandered together, seeking the way forward but having no luck. Frustrated, they split up to explore more thoroughly. They searched high and low, peering into every door marked with a pagan symbol and under every rock etched with a carven eye. They beheld boxes branded by bones, stared at snake-scrawled statues, and inspected impish idols with irksome icons. The taverns had neither music nor pie, and no hole under a bush could be found. Indeed, none of them came across a single clue as they scoured the town.

They did, however, experience additional earthquakes, and each soon learned more. Only a few blocks from the brothel in any direction, the town came to a raggedy end at the edge of the flattened top of a tall mountain — a lofty mesa. Partially fallen structures clung hopelessly to the rim, soon to be shaken from their perches and dropped thousands of feet to join the rubble far below. They could easily see why the resident denizens were forced to crowd ever closer — their town was shrinking!

"Ran into a rogue, name of Meerkat," Scram reported when they had gathered again, just a few feet from where little Vaxanti Lane ended in a jagged plunge from the mesa top. "Been in this world since his team broke. Can't find a way out. Anyway, he says the town's hit real trouble now. Ground's been shaking more, and there's big cracks showing up. Path down to the lowlands fell away in a rockslide. That sharp jolt a bit ago sent another building over the edge. About half the town's already fallen away. Aye, he's worried," Scram added. "He's thinkin' of taking a leap and waking up respawned."

The team looked around where they stood, each beginning to feel like Meerkat must have felt — like it was all coming to an end.

Only Hatch seemed unperturbed. "Pretty beads," the brute said, gesturing toward a dingy, unremarkable shopfront. The door stood open, but a colorful, beaded curtain blocked the view inside. Windows framed the door to left and right, all painted black. The buildings above and nearby seemed to lean over the shop protectively, further darkening the glow of the advancing evening. Only where a couple of structures at town's edge had begun to crumble away could any clear view of the sky be seen. Above the doorway a small, faded sign read…

Curious, Dune peered in through the beads then entered, followed by the others. A thick aroma of burning sage assaulted their noses, accented by a variety of incenses that smoldered away in holders on stands set about the large room. Eight doors dominated the walls — four along the back wall, two on each side, each painted a different color — tall, oaken portals leading to… elsewhere. Threadbare tapestries hung between the doors, and similarly timeworn rugs covered the floor. Nothing about the high, shadowed ceiling was worth noting. The only light came from a few dim rays leaking through the doorway beads, and a lamp on a tall table in the middle of the room.

Something sat at the table. A living being they thought, though they couldn't be sure. It didn't move.

The figure sat upon a stool, tall enough to allow a child to reach the tabletop, but this was no child, being either a crudely made doll, or a small woman so ancient that she could be little more than caked dust wrapped in faded rags. They stared, then saw what must be her head move ever so slightly. So then, a living woman. The doorwarden. It occurred to Sparrow that if the woman had moved an inch more, she might crack to pieces and crumble to the floor.

Dune spoke. "Are you the doorwarden?"

The slightest nod.

"We seek the fifth gate. Can you guide us?

Again, a nod, barely perceptible. Then…

Nothing.

As the seconds ticked away, the team grew restless.

Dune studied the table. Painted on its surface was a pattern of eight wedges like the remaining pieces of a thinly sliced pie. The wedges fanned outward to cover much of the table, the wide end of each aligned with the door of the same color. The woman's withered hands rested on the table, palms down. Her two thumbs touched one another, but each of her eight fingertips touched upon the point of a different colored wedge.

"Please," he said. "Is it one of these doors?"

Was it a nod, or did Dune's eye flicker?

"Can you show us which we are to take?" he begged. She didn't move. Sparrow slipped a small bar of gold from her belt and set it on the table. A breeze that sounded like a smile ruffled the beads in the door. Then, slowly but clearly, the middle finger of the doorwarden's left hand extended just a bit. The color of the wedge?

Yellow.

The team looked at each other. Finding agreement, they headed for the Yellow Door.

"Thank you!" called Dune.

Once all were through, the door closed behind them with a bang, but no way forward was evident. They were saved from concern when a voice began to speak — an old woman's voice:

"You have entered the yellow — the door of idiots. Idiots you are and will be, but only idiots have any hope. Seek the Door of Lies, which is your way to find what cannot possibly be. Go now and die confused. That is all. Poof."

"She said, 'poof,'" Scram noted. "There was no poof; she just *said* 'poof.'"

Slowly, one wall of the tiny room dissolved away and a dark passage appeared — this one marked with footprints the color of old blood leading steeply downward. A breeze blew from the passage like a gritty exhalation from a long cold forge. With a rising sense of fear, they set out.

But they had gone only a few steps when Scram moaned. "Oh god no, it's a *grater*," he said. Sparrow hissed in disgust.

*   *   *

The warriors had been gone less than a minute when Belva Gasbag sat up abruptly. "Oh nuts," she muttered. She popped up from the table and hastened over to the Yellow Door. Banging on it with a perfectly capable fist, she shouted, "I meant the blue! *The blue!*" Getting no response, she heaved the door open, but the ready space was empty. She stared a moment, then slammed it shut, giving it an extra kick for good measure. "Nuts, nuts, nuts! Now why the hell did I tell them *yellow?*" she asked herself as she moved back toward the center of the room. "Why oh why—" She froze.

The Boss.

She dashed to the front door and burst through the beads, making it in time to see the backside of Caradan Bejus disappear around the corner of Vaxanti and Cup Street. "I see you Bejus!" she shouted, but she didn't follow. What would be the use? He'd got her good, and now there was going to be some trouble.

Real trouble.

"Nuts."

*   *   *

"This is the way."

"You are certain?" Sparrow was skeptical — and nervous.

"…Yes," Dune answered. "Yes, this must be— This *is* the way."

"Just kill me," Scram muttered tensely. "Kill me now."

They continued down the winding, dark passage, stumbling and slipping. It seemed to them like a throat — the gullet of a vast viper. …No, more like an endless mouth that should become a throat, but instead offered never-ending teeth that chewed away all confidence. Sparking lights flashed and flickered in places, below as well as above, each flash like a wasp sting, skewering hope and will, over and over again.

"I remember this," moaned Scram, who had been shaking his head and panting for some time. "A grater. Eats and eats. Peels your mind. God, for a drink," he added. "Can't do it. Can't…"

"Where does it lead?" Dune asked him.

"Aye, and how in hell should I know?" snapped the scorching reply. "Wherever The Boss puts it! I don't know! How the hell… I… I must've died and bailed before. It's too much. Not a team like this. Don't know where it… Eating me... Eating…" He faded out, muttering.

"We go on!" Dune commanded. "'The Door of Lies,' the doorwarden said. Through this… grater."

"Sh… shaving soul from my bones," Scram whimpered in reply.

Only Hatch seemed unaffected. "Go now."

"Shut up fat boy! Shut the… Sorry… Sorry Hatch." Scram was a mess. He squeezed his eyes closed and clung to Hatch for direction.

Sparrow, too, struggled. Without Dune behind, she would have stopped in her tracks, not willing or able to go on. For her, it was confusion more than anguish. Clarity was her strength. Without it, she lost herself.

Dune, though, was *eager.* He knew this was another torment of the game — of The Boss — and that it could not kill him. Dune *knew.* He was a knower, and he was played very well indeed. He knew that too.

Yet he also sensed the approach of the greatest danger. They had to be nearing the end of this netherworld way. The Boss would not waste this chance. He would not let them into the 5th Ring as he had Wonder. He would not make that mistake again. He would send them to where they would surely die.

Down and around they went, Scram a gibbering puddle and Sparrow's aching eyes wide as saucers, endlessly it seemed, but was not. Indeed — as though The Boss wanted no further delay — they soon saw the Door of Lies ahead.

A shining bruise.

Livid.

A warning.

…But not bad looking for a door.

Leaving the passage to enter the small antechamber, they stood before it, all of them suddenly feeling much better.

"Oy," said Scram as he let out a long breath. "Oy. Well. Won't be telling that tale in the next pub. Maybe in a year."

"A very different world is beyond this," Sparrow stated, showing that she, too, had begun to *know* a bit.

"Yes," said Dune. "My death."

With nothing left to say, Sparrow pushed the gleaming gold button mounted on the frame to the right of the door. The solid-looking panel of sickly sapphire light slowly opened, trailing a thin cloud that sank to the floor like shredded skin. After a last exchange of glances, they…

Departed.

*　　*　　*

The display goes dark. I stare dumbly for several seconds — *my hands still on the controller.* The screen isn't black exactly, but I'm out.

Out!

All I can see are surging dark gray shimmers against a black background, and there's no sound at all in my headphones.

I lurch backward and gasp, then begin to breathe fast, attacked by panic and confusion. This is *waaay* off. I tremble — feel drool drip from my lower lip. Shake my head slowly.

The team left the game.

The team *left the game.*

I'm holding the controller, pushing buttons, but I'm not in. I'm out, because Dune is out. He left the game. *Left* it! He left the game and he is…

Coming *here.*

I know it.

I feel it.

The team is coming here, to *my* world.

"Oh my god." I lift my eyes and look around the room. My gaze lands on the clock. 6:04 — *in the morning.* I've been playing all night trying to get through the 4th Ring. One after another, I beat the tests. …Okay, *they* beat the tests. Dune. The team. Because I know now that just because I'm playing the game doesn't always mean that *I* am making things happen. As far as I can tell, Dune does a lot of playing on his own, and I — Alexander — am sort of just watching, except I know that I matter, and that Dune would be lost without me.

…Or maybe it isn't *playing* at all. Because they are coming here, and now I'm not doing anything at all.

"Okay, think!" I say. "Think!" Okay, so the team goes through this grater to get to the Lies door, and the next world is through it, and… And *here* somewhere? What?

Then I remember — there had been a clue.

The *game* clue!

Dune had said that maybe it was for players, which made me pay attention. …But is it something that will help me now, or is it for something later in the game? Maybe I can guess.

The clue is…

Okay. Think. The clue is…

Shit.

"Okay, moron, so what's the clue?" I ask myself aloud, which helps me sometimes, and then I remember:

DoNotEnter

So, 'DoNotEnter.' …*Do not enter?* What the hell kind of clue is that? I mean, 'do not enter' is something that you could see everywhere, right? Or at least, it sounds so normal that it seems like you see it everywhere, but where have I seen it, *really?*

I hear the blender fire up in the kitchen down the hall. Damn. Smoothie for breakfast, which means mom's protein powder and weird vegetable gunk that is supposed to make me strong and relaxed (and regular). I wish it was Friday — pancake day.

…Do not enter. Where have I seen that? I search my mind, but the only thing that flashes in my memory is the fact that I am supposed to be in the band room at 6:50 with my clarinet and music for practice. I have to be there or I can't march when we play at the college football game on Saturday — I've missed too many practices already.

"Oh crap!"

And double crap — no clean clothes. I have to dig through the laundry. I *do* manage to find the permission slip wadded up in my pocket from a few days before. I race to the kitchen and slam half my smoothie. I'm not even sure if mom is mad, but she signs the form, and I bolt.

*   *   *

Layla was stunned. The sound was gone. The controller was completely unresponsive. She had guided Sparrow down that miserable grater and through the shining door, and then…

Was it over? Everything looked okay with her rig. LEDs shining. Fan blowing.

Still holding the controller, she tried some actions again. Nothing. Just the same sort of twisting and turning thick gray shapes on the screen. Maybe the monitor was frying? She pulled the plug out of the back, waited a few seconds, and then plugged it back in, forcing a reconnection with the PC. No difference.

"Dammit!" she swore. She had to head for school, but she didn't want to leave this — something major was happening.

…But she *could* miss band practice. She had made every other one, and she'd handed in her permission slip for the halftime show a week ago. And as for the rest… Well, she had almost a perfect attendance record, and even with a couple bad grades lately, she was still getting all 'A's (except for AP Chem). She smiled.

Layla crept down the stairs, past her dad's closed door, her feet making no sound on the carpeted floors. She went into the kitchen, grabbed a glass of juice, then picked up the landline to call in sick. Her imitation of her mom's voice was uncannily good. The attendance voicemail answered.

"Hello, ah, this is Marsha Wischen, Layla Wischen's mother. I'm sorry, but Layla can't make it to school today, she's, ah, been throwing up and I'm a bit worried, so I think I'll keep her home for, ah, at least the morning. That's Layla — l, a, y, l, a — Wischen — w, i , s, c, h, e, n. Ah, thank you. Bye."

Layla hung the phone up, crept back up the stairs and slipped into her chair, which seemed to welcome her like a hug. She grabbed the controller, trying to dive into the game again, only to see the flickering grey screen.

She was lost.

*   *   *

"It's third period, Alexander."

"Huh?"

"It's *third* period. You're to be here *fourth* period."

"What?"

"Come back fourth period. This is third period. Do you know where you're supposed to be?"

"What? Oh. Yeah. Third. Sorry, I just… I was… I'll…"

"…go to your third period class, perhaps?"

"Yeah."

Not a good day so far.

*   *   *

It was lunchtime and nothing had changed.

Again and again across the morning, 'sick' Layla had tried to get back into the game. Early on, she sort of knew that her rig was running fine, and that she'd have to wait for something to happen in *Rings* for her to be able to play again. Even so, she couldn't help replugging every cable, restarting things, checking for updates, etc., sometimes more than once. She even tried to locate the long-gone *Rings* website, or even some board where players were solving problems, but everything about the game had vanished. Even the old Wikipedia article had been been cut back to bare bones.

She had a moment of panic when she wondered if her version had finally expired. It had been the last version available online, but she could tell that there were some graphics weaknesses, and not because her GPU couldn't handle the load! What if they had simply disabled her version for security, or some other reason? …But in the end, she chilled. It just didn't make sense. There had been no evidence of any kind that it could be that.

Layla had her legs propped up on the wall, watching *Family Guy* on her old iPad from 7th grade. She wasn't paying attention, though every once in awhile, she pushed buttons on her controller hoping her screen would flicker back on. Nothing. As usual, while her desktop was immaculate, the rest of her room was a mess. Even though she was the most organized member of her family by far, Layla seemed to need her personal space to be a pit. Her clothes — clean and not-so-much — were tossed all around, mixed in with things like computer cables, books, candy wrappers, dirty dishes, half-made art projects and inventions, a few stuffed animals.

Hungry, she shuffled her way to the door and down the hallway, pausing to peek into her dad's room to check on him. He remained large, bald, and passed out face down in his big bed. Unemployed for now. He had tried hard to find a new job for awhile, but Layla thought he might have given up. He probably didn't even know she was home, but if he did — even if she confessed to him that she had faked mom's voice to take a day off — he wouldn't care. "No worries," he'd probably say. It's what he always said.

PB&J was her choice for the day.

11 — DONOTENTER

I froze in my tracks.

"Watch it, asswipe!" snapped a senior that ran into me, but I barely noticed, my mind totally focused on the face I had just glimpsed way down at the end of B-Hall. The head. The shoulders.

Sparrow.

I swear! It was Sparrow! …But now she was gone.

I sprinted down the crowded hall, making new enemies as I knocked into people, but I wasn't going to slow down. I reached the end, but no Sparrow. I looked left and right around the corners into C-Hall, but no Sparrow. It had only been seconds! She couldn't have…

I chose left and jogged down C-Hall to look in a couple of doors, all the while glancing back the other way in case she had gone right. Then I reversed, peering into doorways in the other direction. How could she have moved away that quickly? Nothing. No Sparrow.

The bell rang, and soon I was alone in the halls — alone in this weird hell of confusion. It had been her.

…Hadn't it?

But how? And what about the others? They had all gone through that shining 'Lies' door, one at a time, Dune last. As soon as Dune stepped in, it was… over. And now I thought they would be here.

Here?

In Woodwell School?

Huh? I shook my head, and then shook it again, like maybe I could shake out the craziness. What the hell? This was insane! *Game! Characters! Could! Not! Be! In! School!* So stupid. I was losing it. My brain was busted.

Yeah? So then why didn't I just think it was my imagination — that I was *imagining* seeing Sparrow at school? That's normal, right? You think you see something or somebody, but you don't. You just imagine it. Simple. Normal.

But not this time, because now it was weird. Everything seemed to fit together too well. It *had* been Sparrow, and she had vanished as soon as she had appeared. Now what?

"Awww, *fuck!*"

"Quite the language, Mister Breyer," came a voice — low, slow, and ominous. "What are you doing in the hall?"

"Huh?" Uh oh.

"Why aren't you in class, Mr. Breyer?"

"What? Oh. Yeah. Sorry Mr. Elgert. I got… I was just… I mean…" I went quiet.

"You weren't going to go in *there*, were you?" the principal said, pointing at a door right behind me.

"Um…" I couldn't even remember what class I was supposed to be in.

"That would be a good way to get into some serious trouble, Mister Breyer."

"What?" Oh god, if he calls my mom…

"Do *not* enter. Pretty unambiguous, don't you agree?"

"Unamigyus?" What class, what class, what cla— Global!

"Un-am-big-u-ous." Mr. Elgert spoke his next words with stern menace. "I would not want to have to call your mother in on this, Mr. Breyer. She has enough with your brother."

"No sir. Yes sir. Gotta go to Global, sir."

"*Go!*"

"Yessir!" I dashed for class.

*　　*　　*

After lunch, Layla tried again, but the view was the same — slowly churning, cloudy shapes of black and dark grays. She thought for a bit, wondering bitterly what she might kick and in what order. No answer. She was thinking she might as well give up again for awhile and rewatch a *Stranger Things* episode when, suddenly…

An image began to emerge from the murk! Layla gasped, pulled on her headset, and stared tensely at the screen.

Words! Printed on translucent glass. English, but backward letters. She transposed them in her mind:

'Do Not Enter.'

"Oh."

'DoNotEnter' was the clue they got from the Manure Mare. They had called it a "game clue!" Layla got excited and tried again with some controls. Nothing. Then everything seemed to stall. The image of the letters slid left and right, into and out of view — like a camera was moving back and forth, focusing elsewhere for a time, then turning again to the words. A camera. Or maybe…

Eyes.

It felt like eyes, and Layla suddenly realized it was Sparrow's eyes that moved. She was back!

The eyes locked on the words again and held. Then the words moved, as if swung aside. Beyond were lighter shapes, but of a new kind — not weird, dark motion, but crisp lines and shapes of browns and slates, unmoving.

Familiar.

The eyes scanned this new scene — leftward into a dim passage. Rightward into…

A brighter light! Almost dazzling on the screen. It quickly resolved, and Layla knew exactly what it was, for she had walked past it many, *many* times. Glass panels. Three shelves. Trophies and pictures. Above all was written…

Woodwell Means Champions!

Rings warrior Sparrow was in B-Hall at Layla's school.

Layla's eyes went wide. "Oh my god, *what?*" she observed, utterly stunned.

Then Sparrow looked away, and the hallway scene vanished as the backwards words reappeared. Then they too vanished, to be replaced by the dark motions of whatever it was that occupied time and space between *Rings* and the exact place Layla was supposed to be right at this minute.

Very excited…

…was how she wished she felt. Instead, her throat seemed to want to tighten until she couldn't breathe at all. She tried to calm herself as she watched for another twenty minutes, but nothing changed. She gave up and got in the shower, letting the hot water beat on her for only a minute. Then she dried off, dressed, and took just enough time to forge a note about "… feeling better…" She signed it with her mother's name and dashed to school, ready to face…

What?

But when she got there, everything was normal. Kids were normal. Classes were normal. Halls were normal. And when she went to take a look at the door with 'Do Not Enter' on the window, she saw two custodians go in and out of it to fetch a tool box and other junk for some job. Normal.

She headed home right after school, angry and frustrated — and nervous. She wanted to go right back into the game, but…

Two dance classes, then dinner for her cousin's birthday. Her mom would be home too, so there would be no calls and notes about being sick.

*   *   *

The idea of seeing Sparrow in person haunted me for the rest of the day. My last two classes went by in a blur, and it was just luck that neither teacher called on me for an answer or opinion. I was lost in daydream — a mix of droning classroom sounds and scenes from the game (and from a dream I had of The Boss killing me). I wondered over and over if I could've made a mistake, but I decided every time that I wasn't wrong — that she *had* been there. But the only way I could think of to prove it was to go back in the game and hear her tell it to the team — or to see her again…

Here.

Would I find her back in the game the next time I grabbed the controller? Or would the screen stay gray because she and Dune and the others were still here? My thoughts spun.

Students stirred around me, and I was suddenly afraid of what it meant to see her in the real world. Sparrow, a game girl, killer of countless enemies, wandering the halls of Woodwell School. Insanity.

And why Woodwell? Why not Washington D.C. or India or… *another galaxy?* Yes, the team had vanished into the door and the screen had gone dark. I had a *feeling* they were leaving the game world and coming here, to… Earth, I guess. To the *real* world. But B-Hall in Woodwell? *Really?*

I went over the whole episode in my mind. I was up B-Hall past the trophies. I had seen her way down where B-Hall dead-ended into C-Hall. She had been standing, then she disappeared, to the left I think — just a few steps from the C-Hall corner. I don't think *she* saw *me*, and no one in the hall seemed to notice her. There were lots of kids — it was right between periods.

And how could they not have noticed? Sparrow looked completely outrageous, wearing clothes that no one at Woodwell would ever wear. Older. Plus, she looked sort of anime, the way her face was shaped, and she was taller than any girl I'd ever seen. Weird.

"Alexander?"

"Huh?"

"Class is over. You may leave now."

I looked around. The room was empty.

"And you might want to get a good sleep," the teacher added. "You dozed off a couple of times."

Avoiding Ms. Murphy's eyes, I stood and exited, feeling like a fool. I headed home.

*　　*　　*

Something was wrong.

The team had gone through the shining Door of Lies, just as the doorwarden had instructed. It had seemed a way to a world like the others, but this one was different. Instead of entering a passage or showing up in a new place, they had stepped into a thick-aired darkness, which at first seemed smoky, but did not smell of smoke or torment breathing. They stood inside the door, uncertain.

Sparrow spoke up at last. "I will scout," she stated. "I have such skill."

161

Dune surprised himself (but no one else) saying, "yes, it should be you."

Sparrow regarded him briefly, but then turned and went forward.

The torches slowly faded from faint to gone as she walked, leaving a dim, gray light that had no visible source. The stone beneath her feet grew softer, until it felt like cloud — like nothing — until she was not sure she moved at all. Yet there was never any doubt which way was forward. Nor, when she turned about to be sure she had a way back, was there any doubt about the direction of return.

It seemed odd to Sparrow that she quickly had no sense of how long she had been gone. She moved slowly and felt that she hadn't gone far, but she didn't know whether she had departed her teammates a few minutes earlier, or an hour. Or more. …Much more.

Oddest of all to Sparrow was the change in *her.* Stepping through the Door of Lies, it had been as if some purpose was removed from her — some guiding thought or motive. At the same time, she felt newly aware, as though a part of her had been asleep and had now wakened. Her identity and basic role were intact, but now seen through different eyes. She…

Liked it.

It wasn't long (maybe) before a light became visible ahead of her, gaining distinction as she neared. She saw a window of hazy glass — a window in a door, low light beyond. Figures marked the glass. Letters she knew! …But wrong, somehow.

In a moment Sparrow understood. "Do not enter," she whispered. The game clue! She smiled.

Reaching for the handle of the door, she turned it. The

door opened inward, toward her. Beyond it, the cloudy darkness was no more. Instead, she saw a hallway that ran from left to right. A particularly bright light came from a display of some artifacts in a box on the wall away to the right. She took one step into this hall but stopped when she saw that others were present, walking away from her in both directions. She had seen enough and quickly returned through the door before any noticed her.

Sparrow did not know what world this was, but by the game clue she was certain it was the right way to go. She returned to the team, passing through the same confusion of time and dimension as before.

"How long have I been away?" she asked when she found them again, standing silent in the murk just inside the Door of Lies.

"A few hours," answered Dune.

"Maybe twenty minutes," replied Scram at the same time.

"Hatch no sit," the brute contributed, confusing the confusion.

"Come," Sparrow directed. "'DoNotEnter' is ahead!"

"The game clue?" Dune replied, surprised.

"Yes," she said. "A door. A new world beyond."

*　　*　　*

The team had started off well enough, eager to see what the game clue had for them, but they soon became addled by the same cloudy timelessness that Sparrow had experienced. Then, after only a few minutes (or a couple of hours), they realized they were not alone — *they were being followed!* They heard a vague, quick shuffling behind, and then around them, sounding like many of whatever they were. They strode on, fearless, which was the nature of warriors in the game, but soon they knew that the movers around them were getting ahead.

"Jangs, maybe," Scram observed after listening for a time.

"No smell."

"Thick breathing," Scram replied. "Like noses stuffed with lint."

"Hatch hear. Crush them."

They tried to move faster, and soon found themselves in the thick of a mass of moving game enemies — jangs indeed — but they could not fight! There was nowhere to stand. No leverage. No real sense that up was up and down was down. And the *time* thing too. Were the jangs there now, a few seconds from now, or a few seconds ago? Who could tell? The jang crowd moved with and around them, but also seemed to be somewhat above and below, as though their feet landed on different paths. The team threw elbows and punches at the skinny jangs, but it was like striking at them with soft pillows — any jang they contacted barely broke stride, seeming not to know of an attack.

Then the DoNotEnter window came into view in the distance, and the warriors slowly began to feel normal again. Early arriving jangs opened the door as the team drew closer, and some were already spilling through. Sparrow and Hatch were first to follow, pushing through the growing crowd and tumbling into B-Hall of Woodwell School. Now that they had set foot in the new world, the fight returned to them. They stood back to back, taking on the jangs that had also been awakened again to fighting.

Scram burst through a moment later, wielding swords that were already bloodied.

"We fight!" the brute shouted in greeting.

Scram cut through a couple enemies and joined his mates, back to back to back, a wicked triple weapon far superior to the claws, fangs, spears, and ragged blades of the jangs, who died one after another, sliced, crushed, or struck down — though more poured through the door, and the sheer mass of them pushed the trio up the hall toward the trophy case.

At last Dune squeezed through the door and into the hall. He stumbled on bloody jang bodies and fell, but quickly sprang up again. From mere feet away, his arrows flew in a blur and jangs dropped like… like jangs.

"Dune! Here!" came Scram's shout from up the hall, a dozen jangs between the knower and his mates. He raced to join them, knife slicing as he went, then he wheeled about, so that now the team could not be moved and could begin to fight their way back to DoNotEnter to finish the enemy.

With the team all present in the hall, the jangs were now seriously overmatched. They were, after all, only 2nd Ring fighters, and, even when meeting teams in the ring, only rarely scored a kill. They were made to die when faced with high level warriors, and die they did.

But The Boss had chosen them as Mister Needles had advised.

"They are fast," Needles had said. "And the knower's player runs quickly. Also," he had added, "as tight little nodes, they should last in Real long enough to hunt the boy down — juice enough to hold a few hours, perhaps. Like the merchants, and perhaps Ghengis. Others would fade away in minutes." The Boss had been excited!

But neither The Boss nor Mister Needles had guessed that Dune's team would arrive *with* the jangs. The plan had been for the jangs to kill Alexander in his home, and then to return to the school to catch Dune's team in a vicious ambush. Something had gone wrong — something in the space between the Door of Lies and DoNotEnter. The Boss had thought he could manage the time between, but he had been wrong. Other forces were at work.

The fight went well. It wasn't many minutes before jangs stopped coming through the door, though the hall remained crowded with them. It would only be a matter of time.

But then, at the far end of the hall beyond the enemy…

A boy appeared!

And though Dune had never seen him, he knew him now. They were one. The name *Alexander* came to him.

"Ware!" shouted Sparrow, and Dune snapped back into action, batting aside a jang spear and knifing the creature as it crashed into him. He looked again quickly, but Alexander had vanished, an unholy mob of jangs in his place.

"The boy!" Dune shouted. "We must save that boy! He is *me!"* he howled as he plowed forward, arrows flying, knives whipping, a top rank warrior at his ultimate in fury. The others drove ahead with him. The jangs shrieked and fought and died, filling the hall with twitching bodies jammed and crammed knee deep. The team plunged on.

*　　*　　*

As I walked home from school, my mind churned with thoughts of Sparrow. But I didn't feel right — sort of dull and stupid. By the time I got to my house, I might as well have been hypnotized. It was too much. I sat on the edge of my bed, then lay back. …Maybe no one else *could* see her. Maybe… I sank toward sleep with my shoes still on.

My mind might have raced for awhile, but this whole adventure had worn me out. All sitting and tension, and then staying up all last night. I was exhausted. The last thought I had before I slept was a memory of Principal Elgert's scolding.

"Do *not* enter. Pretty unambiguous, don't you agree?"

…

Do not enter.

…

Do! Not! Enter!

I sat bolt upright, suddenly wide awake. "Holy shit!" I jumped off the bed, raced out of the house and ran for the school, my memory of game play and clue merging with Principal Elgert's words into a perfect, horrible understanding. They were here, or would be soon, and that would be very very bad.

*   *   *

Now I see just how bad, because when I whip open the door at the end of C-Hall and race around the corner into B, I immediately see Dune, but in between him and me, I also see dozens of weird looking, skinny warriors with spears and a few blades, and they are obviously bad guys. No problem for the warriors with their weapons, but a big problem for me in a T-shirt with sad little fists. No skills. Alexander the nothing.

Then they see me.

Oh no.

I turn and bolt. I whip left around the corner into C-Hall again, but I slip on god knows what, smash into some lockers, and tumble to the floor. I get up fast and race for the exit door, but now I'm limping. I take a quick look behind me, and I see what I most do *not* want to see — a big bunch of those things are after me and just a few yards behind.

I bang through the door and out onto the pavement ahead of them, but just barely. The sports fields stretch out in front of me. I see the lacrosse team practicing a ways off. I limp-run toward them as fast as I can, but I know it's no good, because the enemy is catching up. They're faster. Fast, angry, hungry to hurt.

Oh god.

I hear them grunting.

Oh god.

I smell them.

Oh—

The first spear takes me from behind, skewering my left thigh. I howl and fall, wheeling part way round reflexively, but I have no time to howl again because a second spear rips through my chest below my right shoulder, pinning me to the ground, my gored leg twisted badly beneath me. The jangs jeer, and then one delivers the last blow, jaggy sword slicing my belly, deep and final. I begin to pass out, soon to die. The creatures start to dance around me, but suddenly turn and run back toward the school. I hear glass break. I hear screams. I hear…

Nothing else.

12 — RESPAWNING

Dune, Hatch, Sparrow, and Scram fought their way forward, pressing until the last of the jangs that had stayed to fight them had been dispatched, and no more came through.

"Dune, what now?" Scram asked. "The boy?"

But Dune did not answer. He had fallen, and he did not move.

"Dune!" Sparrow yelled. She shook him. No response.

Just then, the smashing of a window could be heard around the corner, then the flapping feet of more jangs. Hatch, Scram, and Sparrow readied, putting themselves between the enemy and DoNotEnter. Two dozen appeared in the hall — the group that had pursued the boy. Two dozen ran madly for DoNotEnter. Two dozen joined the count of bodies that littered the blood-smeared hallway, each falling in swift order to the blades and club of the team, who wielded their weapons with renewed fury. Soon, all the jangs that had or ever would glimpse Woodwell School were no more.

"All dead?" Hatch asked, then answered himself, smiling: "All dead."

Not just dead, but soon gone as well. Perhaps functioning jangs could have lasted a couple hours more in Real, but dead jang bodies dissolved away short minutes after they went down, along with any associated gore, clothing, and weapons. Soon after dying, each corpse collapsed into a pile of what looked like sparkling orange roaches, which then urgently scattered, only to shrink rapidly into motes of energy that shot off in all directions and disappeared. Scram, Sparrow, and Hatch watched as the vanishing process ran its course, and then looked about in a clean, jang-free silence — suddenly uncertain what to do in this unfamiliar world.

Scram spoke at last.

"We need to go back through, right? Get Dune to respawn?"

Sparrow shot him a glance. "…Yes. Yes, but the boy."

"Boy?" Hatch.

"Did you not see? Dune saw. I saw!"

"Aye," agreed Scram. "I saw. A boy. He ran."

"I think Dune fell because the boy has fallen," she added. "This way!" Hatch hefted Dune, tossing him over a shoulder. Sparrow led them down B-Hall and left into C-Hall where she had seen the boy flee. There was no sign of where he might have gone, but as they neared the hall's end, they saw the broken glass where the jangs had reentered the building, and they heard frantic voices outside. Carefully cracking the exit door, Sparrow peered out.

*　　*　　*

"Ow."

At least, if I could have spoken, that's what I would have said, but I couldn't. After all, I was unconscious — or so they thought. The doctors. The nurses. My mom. They were all in a complete panic. My eyes were closed, but I heard and felt it all, the minutes squeezed into a moment. Wounded, falling, head cracking against the hard ground. The sounds of gibberish all around, stabbed again, then sliced, crazy wild pain, voices, nausea. And then nothing until the siren cut in — sirens. More shouts. "Oh lord!" "My god!" "Holy Shit!" I'd been lifted, placed, strapped, lifted again, the banging of doors and wheels, the siren again. Rolling, turning, handled like a piece of meat, pads and pumps, pressures and squeezes. "Jesus Christ, this kid's a mess!" "They're ready!" "They know?" "Yeah." "Jesus Christ." "…He's gone?" "…Can't tell. No, wait, still a beat." "Yeah, but…" "I know."

Then the hospital. I knew because of the way mom's voice had fit in the echoes of the halls, and because of the smells. Other voices tried to sound calm and professional, but only until they saw me. And all of that was in my mind like a single picture — a half hour in a hand clap.

Mom was shut out now, outside of doors beyond doors. The rest swarmed around trying to save my life. Not easy.

Not easy, because one of those two epic spear thrusts had cut into my femoral artery, and the other had trashed a lung lobe. But the killer wound had come by sword, slicing my belly wide. Not just muscle-deep either. My guts were a mess and I knew it.

My eyes were closed, but now I could see again, my dark dream vision seeming to leave my body, floating up into a high corner of the Emergency Room and looking back down at myself. Wow, what a gash. I thought I could make out a hunk of my liver poking out through the gaping opening in my torso. Not good.

Weirdly, I could feel everything they were doing. They must not have anesthetized me, probably since I showed no signs of consciousness to begin with. And it hurt. Like hell. Unimaginably bad, but so what? "So what?" my brain said to me. "You can feel it," but I couldn't really *feel* it like I was awake. It meant nothing, except that it screamed at me to live.

"LIVE, MORON! LIVE!!!"

Yeah, right.

Not good at all.

I felt my lacerated innards like a chunky stew mixed with broken glass — a 3D meat puzzle, and the sweating surgeons were trying to sort it all out, link up vessel ends, suck crap out, decide what to remove and what to leave, and they didn't have enough time, because the machines were yelling at them that it was too late. It would really be too late, too, if they just sealed me up and left my leaky body stuck in a mess of absorbent pads in a plastic box in Intensive Care, to be loved to death by tubes and beeps and somber nurses.

'Ow'.

Definitely not good. Not good…

Because everything they were doing was wrong! …And I had no way to make them understand.

I didn't need surgery.

I needed the *game*.

I knew that Dune was dying too. I knew more clearly than ever that he and I were bound to the bone. And somehow — *somehow* — I knew that I would die if Dune died, but I would live if Dune lived.

But we had to be in *the game!* Both of us.

I couldn't be saved with staples and stitches — it was hopeless.

"I can't," came a voice, as if in response to my thought. "There's no way…" It was a doctor.

"…"

No words came from the mouths of the medical experts all around. They had nothing, and I sensed them give up like the final flames of a dying fire. As if in recognition, my mind sort of fluttered and my second sight dimmed. "Please," I would have said if he could have.

BOOM!

BAM!

SLAM!

…Huh?

*   *   *

Sparrow crashed into the room, her tall, fierce form and wicked knives scaring the bejesus out of the hospital staff! She snarled at them. They cowered more. Seizing Alexander, she threw him over a shoulder, not caring as needles and sensors tore away from his body. Not caring about the fluid drenched hospital sheet that clung to him, stuck in places by a brown-red glue of blood. Then, with uncanny grace and speed, she departed as she had come, sprinting down the hall and banging through doors out into the dusk.

Rounding a corner she came upon Einstein, who had been waiting as planned.

*   *   *

Young Einstein had followed his brother back to the school. When Alexander had entered the door at the end of C-Hall, Einstein had paused at the edge of the sports fields. When Alexander burst back out of the door only seconds later, Einstein had watched as the strange attackers followed, as his brother was savaged, and as the killers had raced back, smashing the window by the exit to get back in the school, too stupid to manage the non-standard door handle. He kept watching as the lacrosse coach, alerted by a couple of his players, had jogged toward the scene, then run, followed by all.

A minute later, he had seen as the door to C-Hall opened slightly, Sparrow peering out, and then closed again. He'd watched and thought for a minute more, and then, while all attention was upon the gruesomely damaged Alexander, Einstein had walked to the C-Hall door and entered. As the siren of an approaching ambulance sounded outside, Einstein had calmly explained to Sparrow that Alexander would be taken on the short ride to the hospital — the place where he would die…

…unless he could be returned to his desk and be bound to Dune in the game!

The plan had been made. Hatch would carry Dune back through DoNotEnter into *Rings*, with Scram guarding.

"Take these," Sparrow had said, handing all five tokens to Scram.

"Lass, *all five?*"

"With five you can be bound to and from the Chamber of Respawning from *any* magical crossing! The Door of Lies is such a crossing. You know this."

"Oh aye, you're right! …But that's it for our way through fifth gate."

"It ends anyway without Dune!" she snapped.

"Aye! Right you are! Hatch, come!"

"We will meet again!" Sparrow shouted as rogue and brute returned up the hall to take Dune through DoNotEnter and back into the game. Now, though, she would follow this younger boy to 'hospital' to fetch this Alexander and take him to 'desk.'

And so it went.

*　　*　　*

"*Where?*" Sparrow snapped.

Einstein turned and — against his basic nature — ran. Sparrow jogged behind, carrying what surely was a corpse.

Einstein knew all the shortcuts. Racing for all he was worth, he led the tireless warrior down a side street, up an alley, through a couple of backyards, a gap in a fence, a short stretch of woodland, across a street, down a driveway, through a hedge, into his own shabby yard, and then to the side door that led into the short hall where the boys' rooms were. Ready with his key, Einstein let them in and headed straight for Alexander's room.

"…Put him in that chair," he pointed, gasping for breath. As Einstein fired up the PC, Sparrow placed Alexander's shredded body in the chair, setting him down with care so no intestines would spill out. He had bled so much, he bled no more.

As the machine finished booting, Einstein placed the headphones on his unconscious brother. Turning, he grabbed the mouse and clicked the icon an instant after it appeared. It quivered, then the screen went dark. Taking a breath, Einstein gently pulled open Alexander's eyelids, and then placed the controller in his hands. He wrapped his brother's dead fingers around it as best he could, nudged one of them against the joystick, and then…

Alexander was in.

Einstein turned up the speaker sound a bit so he and Sparrow could listen.

Sparrow saw little but a hazy, erratic image of the back of Hatch's legs pounding down a hall.

"Is that the way through the DoNotEnter door?" Einstein asked her.

"No," Sparrow responded, glancing at this odd boy, who stood calmly, one hand on his brother's bare, bloody shoulder, the other holding Alexander's head so it would not fall heavily to the side. "They are past the mountain portal to the Chamber of Respawning, in the hills."

*　　*　　*

Scram led at top game speed. Hatch matched him effortlessly — even with Dune hanging over a shoulder. They passed through DoNotEnter, sped as best they could through the timeless fog between Real and *Rings*, and then emerged at the sinister blue Door of Lies. Scram took all five tokens in his hand, held them up before the door, and uttered a command:

"Give us a bound way to the Chamber of Respawning!"

The tokens sparked and vanished from Scram's hand. The door grew blindingly bright for an instant then simply vanished, to be replaced by a sloping scene of rocks and grass, lit by a dull orange sky. Stepping through the opening, they found themselves on a high hillside just outside the ragged entry to the tunnel that led to the hill's heart where the chamber was located. Dune was oblivious to all.

They entered at a run, anxious to get there before it was too late, unaware that Alexander's limbs had grown cold and blue, and that Sparrow dimly watched their progress on the boy's computer screen, seeing only little through the slits of Dune's eyes.

The short tunnel ended at a stone archway that opened into a wide, hollow room — round, unadorned, with a domed ceiling. Stopping at the tunnel's end, Hatch wasted no time. He simply tossed the flaccid corpse of Dune into the broad, gentle pool of creamy light that filled the center of the room. Dune vanished completely. There was no splash; the pool was not really liquid. It appeared to hover in place — though not in the cave that housed it. Instead, the pool seemed to be somewhere else altogether, as if it was only an *image* of the pool that they saw.

This was the Chamber of Respawning — a place Scram knew well enough, but was a frightening place for all in the game. Dead characters came out again as lambs, if at all. The undead came out whole, but sometimes changed, and not always for the better.

The two teammates remained in the archway with nothing to do but wait, listening to the sound of dripping, the barest whisper of a humid breeze flowing through cracks from deep places. Seconds ticked by.

"What's taking so long," asked Scram after nearly a minute. "Why is it taking—"

Then the light from the pool grew and Dune's form rose from within, riding a hissing, spinning, green cloud that carried him to the side, set him down, and shrieked away — an angry steam — leaving the warrior wrapped in a bright green aura that coated him like a second skin, but gradually faded. The chamber settled back to its waiting state. Dune lay on the floor between the pool and his mates.

Silence.

But then the legend bowman took in a deep breath and sat up. He slowly stood and looked carefully about, staring at the others, uncertain at first, then recognizing. He stretched and blinked.

"Good," he stated plainly. "Thanks." After a pause, he said, "That portal — DoNotEnter. That portal is a problem."

"Or the answer," Scram replied quickly.

"It nearly killed me."

"It was the boy," Scram stated. "You are bound."

"The boy," Hatch echoed.

Dune pondered. "Yes," he said at last. "I knew him. He was me. He played me. Alexander." He nodded. "He had no skills."

Scram shifted. "Are you— uh, *were* you two or one?"

It was a strange question, Dune thought. "Are you a learner, Scram?"

"Rogue."

Dune looked puzzled. "I know, but how…"

"Do you know about rogues?"

"I thought I did."

"Aye, well, we're ones who lost but lived, and have juice enough to go on unplayed." he explained. "Gotta choose it, too. I coulda stayed on, abandoned, waiting for my player, unsure. Gave it up though. Some do, some don't. Just gotta tell a bartender that you choose rogue, and there you are.

"Aye, I'm no learner," Scram continued, "but I saw a lot and remember some. Died and respawned a bunch — rogues do it for a new start. I've brought others here too. Sparrow once, though she doesn't remember. I never made the 5th but lasted a ways into 4th a few times." He smiled. "And I knew Wonder — was at the bar when she vanished and went on to 5th, and then… Well, nothing after that. Went back to the 1st through the shorter ways. Drank. Then back to the hills. Waited… Aye, then *you* showed up!"

Scram cocked his head as if searching his memory, then sighed. "So many other teams. So many battles… When no one plays, I forget."

"Well…" Dune began. "Well I suppose I was two *and* one," he said. He looked like he might explain more, but then went silent. "I could not see this boy. He saw me, but… But… Is he gone? I don't feel…

"Do I go rogue now?" Dune asked. No one answered. Seconds ticked away…

But then a smile spread slowly across Dune's face and he stood tall. "No!" he said. "The boy lives! He is healed. I… I *know* this. He will play again."

Dune's head nodded up and down, as did those of his now smiling comrades. "We must go on!" He announced. "It is back to 4th for us! To meet Sparrow — not back to this other world," he added, but then he felt a sudden shock of understanding.

"Real!" he exclaimed. "That was Real!" The others' eyes went wide. "We do not go there. There will be a way *forward* that we did not yet find. And then on to the 5th."

The trio returned through the tunnel and emerged onto the hillside. Dune marveled to see a door-shaped piece of somewhere else sitting on the slope just outside the entrance.

"That's our way back," said Scram. "Spent the tokens on a binding."

They stepped through and immediately found themselves facing the sea of gray just inside the Door of Lies. Turning to the Door, they saw it was solid once again, glowing an evil blue. Now, though, Dune saw *two* gold buttons — one on either side of the door — unlike the single button seen on the other side. Dune shrugged and pushed the button on the left. The door opened, they stepped through, the door closed behind them, and they found themselves in the antechamber they recalled from their first visit.

But now, there was no way out! The passage down from the Yellow Door was nowhere to be seen. They explored a bit, tapping on the walls and looking for markings, but found nothing. The only choice was to return through the door. Shrugging again, Dune pressed the only button available, the door opened once again, they stepped through — gray murk again; two buttons again. With yet another shrug, Dune now chose the button on the right and pressed.

This time, the door opened the opposite way — as if its hinges had jumped from one side to the other. Now, instead of the antechamber, they saw the beginning of a simple, climbing tunnel. Following this, they ascended for many minutes, coming out through a broken drainage grate into a lane of the 4th Ring on the *far* side of the gap of the Worlds. The orange of the sky resembled a dying fire. A dense crowd of small buildings rose before them, but no lanes or Ring Road — the Maze Halls. Here, they decided to wait for Sparrow.

"I like that," said Scram. "Door of Lies."

"A cheap trick," said Dune, unimpressed.

"Aye," Scram began, "but it's a sign of a secret way. See this?" He pointed at the grate they had just come through. Dune looked. "Still here! Didn't vanish like the ice stairs. We can go back down to the Door of Lies if we want. A secret way, aye? That's the Worlds for you — can't go back through worlds you left, but there's ins and outs here and there."

"But why—" Dune began to inquire.

"Don't ask!" Scram interrupted. "No sense, aye? An old rogue I drank with once told me, 'confusion *is* a clue.' Aye, thought that was good."

Dune nodded, thoughtful.

*　　*　　*

Einstein's mouth fell open as he watched his brother heal. He could see Alexander clearly enough, even with the bright green glow that engulfed his body, and he could easily hear the crunching and slurping of body parts being de-ravaged — the sound of butchery in reverse — more gruesome at first than looking at the wounds. Leaking guts were drawn in and flesh zipped together, skin knitting in a moment. Strength flooded into sagging limbs that sagged no more. A long moan rose from healed lungs.

The younger Breyer watched as his big brother sat bolt upright and stood, then fell hard to the floor but stood again. He saw as Alexander looked about in panic, then anger, and then — seeing Einstein — in confusion, and at last relief. His panting slowed to even breathing.

*　　*　　*

I smiled.

"…You need clothes," Einstein said to me, practical. "…And a shower."

I nodded. I looked down at myself. A mess, but a *healed* mess! I turned and stretched a bit. Nothing hurt. I was amazed! And I was in my room. How had I gotten here? I looked at Einstein. He was watching me. He nodded. I looked at Sparrow. Sparrow was watching me.

Sparrow.

In my room.

177

And I'm naked.

I lurched over to my bed, grabbed my tattered 'blankie' and held it stupidly in front of what I thought should be behind it.

*   *   *

Sparrow blinked in awe at the bloodstained boy. This had been like no respawn she had imagined. This was *Real* — she knew — and it was odd. "Boy," she said, "you are well?" He nodded. "Good. Then I must return through DoNotEnter and join my team." He nodded. "The jangs are beaten." He nodded. She looked upon him a moment longer, then departed.

Einstein followed her to close the door.

*   *   *

I felt like I woke up, and then woke up again. And once more. A shudder ran through me from toes to scalp. I took a deep breath then looked myself over again. I looked like I'd fallen into scab-colored paint cans. Tossing blankie on the bed, I headed for the shower.

Not long after, I was in the game again.

*   *   *

So here's what *didn't* happen:

The police *didn't* come to my house looking for the cut up kid who was kidnapped from the hospital by some large cartoon woman dressed like a fantasy hero. My mom *didn't* see me all healed and get hysterical, crying and hugging me like crazy and shouting, 'you're alive, you're alive!' The school *didn't* come up with new security drills for the students to teach them what to do if they're attacked with spears and swords. None of that happened.

Why not?

I couldn't figure it out. The best I could guess is that anything from the game can't be completely real in the real world. It is for *me*, because I'm a *player* — I'm part of the game. But for normal real people, it's like a movie, or a... Well, like a...

Game.

And when something epic like a respawn happens, then the game sort of… goes back a level, or partly resets, or… something. Did all the blood and stuff that came out of me just disappear at the school and hospital, like it had never happened? …Except there was still blood on me after I healed… Beats me. Anyway, what everyone was thinking must have just turned into a weird memory — like when you come out of a movie theater, and your mind leaves *that* world because you're back in the *real* world, and you feel sort of strange.

…Or maybe people have no memory at all?

Somehow.

I don't really get it.

I mean, does that mean that my *wounds* weren't real? They sure felt real. …But, I remember early in the game when I was surprised that I could *feel* things in *Rings* — even before I could see myself!

Also, even if I'm kind of right — even if it's all sort of *in the game,* what's up with Einstein? How come it's like suddenly he's in the game too?

…

When I got out of the shower I checked myself over again, and I saw scars — ugly ones — on my thigh, my chest, and across my middle. They're ugly, but… flat. I mean, you can't feel them if you rub your fingers across where they are. In fact, you can't really *see* them either when you look right at them, but as soon as I look just a little to the side, I see them clear as can be, and they are friggin' ugly — red and messed up — like they should be.

I called my brother in to look.

"What do you see?"

"… Scars."

"Okay, so look right at the middle of this scar," I said, pointing at my belly scar. "Right at it. Do you still see it?"

"…No."

"But now look here," I said, pointing a couple inches above it."

"…Now I see it."

"Can you feel it?"

He couldn't.

Same as me.

Same as everyone? Would a doctor see them, or other people if I had my shirt off?

"...No one will see them," Einstein said without being asked. "...Only *Rings*. ...No one will remember, but mom is a little confused."

I stared at him. He stared back, innocent.

*   *   *

Mom did look confused at dinner, but in the morning she was the same as usual.

Weird.

But *good!*

*   *   *

Sparrow retraced her way to the school in the deepening dusk, taking the only route she knew, via the hospital grounds. Arriving at Woodwell, she slipped in through the C-Hall exit door, passed through DoNotEnter, and then on to the Door of Lies. She quickly figured out the access to the secret way, and it wasn't long before the team came together again, ready to take on the Maze Halls and make the fifth gate.

*   *   *

Jake lay in bed, the morning sun sending lines of light through the gaps in his window shade. He was still in trouble. He knew it in his dreams, and he knew it waking up. He had slept an exhausted sleep, but it hadn't cured anything. He was definitely still in *serious* trouble. He could no longer seem to control The Boss at all, and that was bad.

Rings characters were always sort of independent, because each was a self-contained node of artificial intelligence, advanced by machine learning and stuff he didn't understand. But players had a lot of control. Players might go along for the ride, taking their characters in the direction they already seemed to be going, but if a player decided to make a change, the character would have to follow. Now, though, Jake wanted to make some big changes, and The Boss simply would *not* respond.

At all.

It had been a lot of fun when The Boss was just an evil overlord who ran the 5ᵗʰ and used magic and minions to defeat teams. In those days, Jake had been the secret multiplayer master, imagining his own YouTube show, skipping school to stay logged in. Nobody even knew he was playing unless he told them. To most, The Boss seemed generic — an automatic enemy that might be defeated if only you could learn the right steps and had the right weapons. But in the history of the game, almost no one had *ever* seriously threatened The Boss — thanks in part to Jake.

Then it all went bad. Two kids died. Some others had mental problems. The game was taken off the market, and they shut down cloud multiplayer. Forums closed. Lots of legal stuff. Jake never got in trouble — everyone kept telling him he "…did *not* kill those kids!" — but it was a mess. His parents got in *big* trouble. They had to move. *Rings* was over — almost.

Almost, because Jake could still play! As soon as they'd moved into their new house and gotten internet, Jake had booted his PC, and there it was.

The icon.

He had clicked it.

Black screen.

He had picked up the controller and—

Yeah, he had gone in again. The game was still live! But where? A secret server? A botnet? Dark web?

…

He really didn't kill those kids. Not exactly.

But he had sort of wrecked them. Accidentally.

Carelessly.

He had messed with one kid in the 3ʳᵈ Ring, not letting him finish a warrior quest, not letting him die and respawn. Just trapping his warrior in a loop, and then forgetting about him. That was cruel. By the time he had seen the kid's wailing in the threads, begging for help, it was too late. Jake remembered how his comments got weirder, impossible to understand. He had been acting all psycho since… Well, they…

Found him.

Hanged.

He hanged himself, dead.

…

The other kid had already been pretty sick with cancer or something, but she stopped taking her meds and eating, and was just living in the game. Her parents didn't really catch on until her organs were failing. She lost her team early. She just wandered the low rings, not sure what to do. Not fully understanding. Lost, but addicted. Jake had teased her warrior with attacks and traps, over and over, just for 'fun.' She didn't let her warrior go rogue (which would have freed her connection). Didn't get respawned to lamb. Didn't ask for help — any hotel bartender would have helped. She just wandered and watched and…

Died in her chair.

Jake never knew about the dead kids until the game was taken down. His parents didn't tell him until after. It might have been hard to figure out who they were, but his dad told him the usernames, so he didn't have to guess.

One was his age.

…One of them was only 12.

But they'd both had ways out! They could have started over! Yeah, okay, once you go in, you can't change much, but you don't have to play the same game forever! If you get trashed, just start over! Get a new character! So easy! So damn easy they could have just started over and *not died!*

…Except Jake knew how close players and characters could be.

Jake wondered about one other kid too.

Only one.

One kid had taken a warrior all the way into the 5th Ring and made it into the citadel and right upstairs into The Boss's master chamber. Jake remembered that night. *Wonder* was the warrior's name. She was good — *really* good — a defeater and a knower. That meant the kid was a master player. Jake remembered facing Wonder through the eyes of The Boss. She reached for a weapon, but The Boss had been a split second faster — not Jake; The Boss. The *game* — the automatic Final Surprise spell that kept anyone from killing The Boss and ending the game for everyone. The Boss had been faster.

BAM! Wonder had been nuked to the Rubbles.

…And something else.

The spell had knocked Jake to the floor and he'd dropped his controller. He'd sat there, stunned. When he'd come out of it, there had been a big patch of drool on his shirt, and his joints ached. His thinking went fuzzy for a couple of days. He guessed that Wonder's player must have gotten it a *lot* worse. He never knew who it was.

Everything changed after that. A few weeks later, the word came down about the dead kids.

Jake's family had been rich in Palo Alto. Even a little bit famous. His parents had put AI and machine learning into *Rings* like no one had ever seen in a game before. And they had a totally new tech that delivered subliminal visual patterns that completed a circuit using players' retinas, which is what locked people into their screens and made it seem like VR. At the same time, their partner Tok had invented his hardface tech. A *cross-field interface* he had called it — a CPU that drew power from nearby data flow and could take over other CPUs through a sort of 'proximity wireless' with adaptive protocol. Through the hardface, Jake's mom's AI engine could excerpt the field patterns of any decently hot motherboard and translate it into code. The hardface tech could force a PC's CPU to load the hardface firmware code in isolation and run it with some simple extensions — keyboard, mouse, etc. It rocked!

Prototype.

(Jake had heard that Tok might work for the CIA now.)

The game had gotten so complex that you had to have top end gear to run it! An RTX 3090 was barely enough. You needed at least 128 GB of RAM, and an 11th gen Intel CPU. Some others. That's why the hardface was going to be so cool — because it could bring advanced *Rings* to lower end setups. …Well, not *too* low end — you still needed a dedicated gaming rig.

Once, Jake had heard his mom use the word, "billionaires."

A few days later, the best he heard was, "won't be arrested."

Somehow, the game had survived, growing into some sort of alternate cloud reality. Jake could play — he was running the last, best beta of what was going to be a new version. Alexander had somehow gotten a hardface, and Jake knew that another player was out there. Were there more? He didn't think so, since The Boss hadn't detected any, and Jake always learned what The Boss knew. Eventually.

Mostly.

Now, though, there was a huge difference in *Rings*. Now, game characters could go...

Real.

At least for awhile.

What? Jake shook his head again at the craziness of it.

The Boss had started planning it, almost completely escaping Jake's playing. Jake knew that The Boss had sent Needles through. Now, he didn't know where The Boss was. Had he come to Real? Jake had followed through The Boss's eyes when he flew from the citadel and into 4th Ring, and then down into a world — but which? He had seen doors, a passage, another door, and then...

Nothing but gray.

It had been hours.

The Boss had power and plans, and Jake wasn't sure he could do anything about it.

He also couldn't stop thinking about the person who had played Wonder. A kid. In his mind somehow, like maybe they had connected for a few seconds when the Final Surprise went off. They were all together — Jake, The Boss, Wonder, and... her player. He could almost see the face. It was close. He closed his eyes and tried again because...

Because it mattered.

...

After a minute he shook his head. He was *close*, but...

Jake sighed, slipped out of bed, and went back in to check on things.

...Nothing.

13 — THE BOSS GETS REAL

The Boss glanced around the long, lofty room, noticing first that many of his favorite possessions adorned three walls — weapons and trophies, valuables and tasties. Large windows, thankfully darkened by heavy, blood red drapes, covered the fourth wall and overlooked the street. Three dim lights hung on long wires from the high, dark ceiling — not as high as the citadel of course, but still far enough above to offer plenty of space for webs and tiny eyes.

Leading off from the main room were five doors — one each for main entry, kitchen, bedroom and bath, and a small door in the back wall. *"My chambers,"* Needles explained when The Boss looked that way.

Inspecting the living area, The Boss noted a pair of easy chairs, a table just right for coffee service, and a few choice furnishings to make it feel…

"Like home." The Boss smiled. "I love it! You have outdone yourself, Needles." The Boss picked up the coffee Needles had ready for him and strolled over to sit on a couch between small piles of unsorted junk.

"If you're done," said Needles, "I should tell you about the legend bowman." He appeared undisturbed at being the bearer of bad news.

"Very well, what is it?"

"As you now know," Needles began, "he is played by a boy named Alexander."

"Is played?"

"Well—"

"…Is played? But surely the jangs have done their work?" The coffee suddenly seemed bitter.

"I'm afraid not," Needles replied. "It seems that the team — the bowman's team — arrived somewhat earlier than expected and rather reduced the jangs' number."

"I see."

"Yes. Well… Now they did manage to damage the boy quite severely. Almost killed him, really. But…"

"But?"

"But he was healed. When they respawned the bowman."

"Healed? Respawned?"

"Indeed. It seems this learner warrior — Sparrow, I believe — is unusually strong as a free node. Almost a knower, really." Needles gave an admiring nod.

"Sparrow?"

"Yes. Played, I think, by someone quite close. Rather *well* played. Mmmm… Oh, and there is a younger brother who helped as well. It was quite well done."

…

The Boss's look of utter dejection troubled Mister Needles a bit, but he knew just what to say. "Your suggestion to have the warriors come to Real was a brilliant idea, but my timing was off."

"Oh?"

"My fault, of course," Needles lied. "My apologies."

"You did your best," The Boss returned graciously.

"Indeed. So, do you suppose it would be best now if we just let the warriors vanish in the Maze Halls? Since they have all returned to the game, and they have no wizard or wayfinder? Because they will never get out? Is that what you are thinking?"

"…I *do* think that. Yes. They'll never get out." The Boss smiled, soothed.

"Of course," Needles agreed. "And, as I'm sure you would say, that will make it so much easier to finish these two little players, and perhaps the brother."

"I believe I was going to say that."

"Very good," Needles affirmed. "Very good… Ace. Your first fun in Real! I shall plan it."

The Boss eyed his servant knowingly. "Yes, Mister Needles, you shall plan it. *Correctly,* this time, I should think."

"…Indeed."

"But I have a plan, too. Are you surprised?" Needles wasn't. "I believe I shall meet this… Alexander. He should get to know me, don't you think? Killing now seems… an *incomplete* idea. I think I'd like to play him a bit."

"Yes. Well." Needles couldn't help but feel a small thrill. "What could it hurt?"

"Excellent!" said The Boss, glad to be done with game business and to return his attention to his new abode. "Well then, Needles, let us finish this last unpacking. Is the octopus fed?"

"Mmm."

"Excellent. Now please show me this 'telfoon!'"

*　　*　　*

"If I can be honest, this is the happiest I've been in quite a while." Aunt Patty was glowing, but it was all heat and no light, and her words sounded forced.

"Gee, that's great," I said, forcing.

"Yes," she smiled. With force. "I mean, what a couple of weeks we've had! You with your schoolwork trouble," she scolded, smiling. "And forgetting to get Einstein's papers and such. But you've learned your lesson you said…"

"Yes Aunt Patty. I learned my lesson." Right.

"And this gaming business. Your mom has been worried, but I guess you say you've learned that there can be too much, right?" Scolding. Smiling.

…

"Well…" she continued. "And then Einstein's breakthrough!" She smiled at Einstein. He didn't smile back. She tousled his hair. He kept not smiling. "What a joy! We've all tried so hard." She tousled again.

It had been so strange since I had been… killed. I mean, really, that's what it was. I don't know how I had still been living when Einstein had put the controller in my hands. How close to dead can a person be without being *too* close? Whatever that was, that's how close I had been. Too close.

187

Einstein had told me the whole story — as much as he knew, which was a lot. I felt good, I guess. Nothing was numb. I could move everything. I didn't feel like I had holes in my guts when I ate. Except I wasn't very hungry, and I couldn't sleep. I just couldn't — not for more than an hour or so, and then I'd wake up, and I'd have to stand and walk around for a minute. And then play.

Always, *play.*

It was funny though, because now the team wasn't doing *anything.* They had found another tunnel besides the one from the Yellow Door — one of those "secret ways" that Scram had talked about — and that took them out of the Worlds to the end of 4th Ring, but they couldn't find a way out of the buildings to get to the gate. They were stuck in a maze of halls — called *Maze Halls* I guess — and they were getting bored. Which meant that I was getting bored. It had been almost two weeks since the respawning.

And now I was stuck in a restaurant with Einstein and Aunt Patty, who was "happy" because Einstein had made her a birthday card and had said "…Happy Birthday" to her without my mom saying, 'Einstein, say Happy Birthday to Aunt Patty.' And, since the game had been boring, I caught up on some homework and my Global teacher sent a good email to my mom. Anyway, so Aunt Patty took us out for dinner to *The Bistro,* which she liked. It was okay I guess. I got spaghetti. I wanted to be nice. Thankful. Happy. But I couldn't. I was…

Pissed off!

But I tried to try. I really did.

"Yeah," I said, catching up. "Tried hard, I know. This is probably the happiest Einstein has ever been," I said, nudging my brother, who was delicately eating his noodles, one at a time. "Right, Einstein? Right? Happy happy?" Einstein ignored me, eating expressionlessly. "Smile, smile, smile!" No smile.

"Alexander, please." Aunt Patty gave me a look, her glow dimming rapidly.

"It's *good* news, right Aunt Patty?" I threw up my hands, irritated. "I learned my lesson like you said. I'm being *good,*" I almost sneered. Suddenly this whole thing seemed too normal, and nothing was really normal.

"Well, I'd like you to be respectful." Glow vanished. Annoyance sparked.

"Einstein doesn't care, do you?" I said. Einstein kept eating. "Einstein is a machine, aren't you Einstein?" Einstein kept eating. "Einstein isn't even human! He's a noodle-sucking lizard boy," I said in this lame teasing voice.

"Do *not* talk about him like that!" Aunt Patty smacked her hand down on the table, not quite quietly. "Your brother deserves respect. He is a human being!" she hissed.

"Come on Aunt Patty. There's *always* been something wrong with him. It's getting better, and — Jesus Christ, *I'm being nice!*" I suddenly snapped, totally frustrated now — frustrated at way more than Einstein's eating and Aunt Patty's scolding. Besides, what did *she* know? She didn't live with Einstein like me. I knew him inside and out. …Except not so much lately. Not at all really.

"Shit!" I swore, turning in my chair and knocking a knife to the floor.

"Get some air, Alexander." Aunt Patty pointed towards the door, memories of my tantrum days coming to her mind.

"I can breathe fine in here!" I shot back at her.

Aunt Patty left her finger hovering, pointed at the door. "Come back in when you're ready, and not before!" As stiff as nails.

"Screw this! Happy 'breakthrough,' Einstein!" I stood up and walked out, half shocked at how I was acting. A few families had their eyes on me as I angrily pulled the push door before figuring out my mistake, then leaning on it with my full energy and stumbling out into the chilly night air.

What was the matter with me?

I mumbled curses to myself and checked my phone.

There was a single notification from a site I followed:

Kid in NYC dies fighting over a 100K fn karambit!

Normally, I would've followed up to learn more, but I wasn't in the mood. I sank to the pavement, leaning against the brick wall.

I loved Einstein. I really did. No one else was as efficient with a first aid kit. No one else could win checkers ten times in a row. He listened to me. He was sweet. And…

And he had saved me.

But was I supposed to pretend that there wasn't something *wrong?*

Once when Einstein had only been with us for a few weeks, I fell down these stairs and he just stared at me. I was bleeding bad! He was, "…curious," he said, before he finally went about two minutes later to get our mom. Einstein just couldn't get anybody's feelings. The bleeding episode was the tip of the iceberg. He just never felt anything.

…Except now something had started to change. He took care of me.

He took care of *me!* He watched me when I played and got me out when it mattered. When I was cut up, he got Sparrow to the hospital and got me to my desk. Something had definitely changed. He… He *knew* something.

I thought about it for a few seconds, but I couldn't get it. I couldn't 'get' anything. I was all antsy. My mind zigged around like a ride at the fair. I stood up. *"Fuck this!"* I yelled, sounding way older than I felt. It echoed away down the empty street…

…But then it came back.

"Fuck… what?"

A voice — so close and far away at the same time.

"Hello?" I said.

"Hellooo," the voice slithered, winding around me like a snake.

"…Jake?"

"Most certainly not." A smiling snake.

And then the voice revealed itself. An unnaturally tall figure — a big man, welted red hands, face mostly hidden by a cruel leather mask — or was that his *skin?* Tight horns protruding from his forehead, slightly lifting his deep leather hood. *Horns?* A chill went down my spine. There was no way he was real. A costume? A dream?

"Where is your galavanting clan of heroes?" The man's teeth shone gold in the hard light of the street.

"What?" I asked. Oh, but I knew. I knew who it was. I knew what was happening. The dark octopus would soon arrive. I knew this… *How?* Memories seeped in. I could almost see it shifting in the shadows. "You're… You're…"

"I am most certainly still, *The Boss.*" The voice visibly left his mouth as a dark mist.

"You aren't even real," I said. "You're game."

"Take that bet, amigo." The man casually pulled open his dark leather robe so I could see various devices of pain glinting on his belt.

"No way." I turned for the door.

"You!" he hissed, stopping me. "You, are a coward — a wee pimply lamb. You brought me here. You made me come. You let me come. I decided to come. I came to challenge. I never turn from a challenge, Alexander. *Al-ex-annn-derrr…"* He squirted my name like bug killer.

I turned to face him again. The Boss hadn't moved, but his beast — his octopus — had shown up. It began to circle around him impatiently, growing and shrinking, stretching and dripping. Bats had appeared all around, hanging from trees and the neon lights of the restaurant, like spectators at a beheading.

"Go to hell!" my cracking voice begged. "Come on, finish me. Finish me! I dare you!"

I stood perfectly still.

I was apparently completely out of my mind.

"Perhaps I'll feed your carcass to your mother, al dente." The Boss ran his tongue over his teeth.

"My *aunt.*" I replied, insane. "So hurry up."

The octopus thrust a dark oozing tentacle towards me, reeking of ink, rotting wood, something horrible. I could feel it wrap around my leg, suckers sinking into my clothes, pulling at them.

A tooth sparked under his hood. Then an eye.

"You are dung," he whispered. "You are sand. Ash. You are without a doubt the most worthless disposable being of all, you… sheep. I am a shepherd! I am finally putting you to good use. Isn't this fun?" he bubbled, bouncing in his boots.

"You're not real," I squeaked as the octopus' grip crawled up my legs and nastily through them, slithering on to wrap my waist. "Not here! Not real! You have no player. DoNotEnter is closed to you. Not real. Not real. Not real."

"Of course." The man took a step forward. My jaw dropped. I was to be torn in two like a wishbone! I was going to be eaten like chicken legs! I would scream at his eyes! I—

…

And then it was over.

Gone in a gritty gust of street wind and the fast fading echoes of sick laughter. The man, the octopus. I was clean, untouched, standing perfectly still under the stars, crying like a baby — feeling like a baby.

…

Oh no.

Not gone.

Not… all of him. I felt it then, like sick slime crawling through me. Like worms. Like nausea.

He was *in* me.

I dropped to the walk again, slowly fell to my side, curled up, held myself tight and rocked. Too weird. Too weird.

The Boss was here, in the real world — on *my* side, in *my* neighborhood — and he was *inside* of me. Way in. An invasion. A tumor. Malignant. Fast. Horrible. I felt his laugh in my skin. Each beat of my heart was the squeeze of a tentacle. Claws scraped at the edge of my sight. He was in me.

I felt a tear run from one eye across the bridge of my nose and into the other. I shuddered. What could I do?

What could I do?

"…Time to go home," Einstein said. He stood above me.

"Einstein?" I was pleading. "He's here Einstein. He's watching. He made me act stupid in the restaurant. He's in my mind — right now! He's eating my brain. Eating."

"…Aunt Patty is waiting for us."

Eventually, shaking, I stood. Shaking, I walked behind him. Aunt Patty was in the car, tapping her wine red fingernails on the steering wheel.

I don't even know what happened after that.

* * *

Einstein brushed his teeth with patience and care, just the way the dentist had taught him.

But even when sloshing the rinse water as loudly as possible, he could easily hear Alexander groaning in his bedroom across the hall. Alexander should have been doing homework — he would get way behind again. Or he should be playing that game like he always did. But he wouldn't work or play. He groaned. Just groaned.

Einstein could hear the TV too. Always, anywhere in the house. That was mom, watching and listening — her shows — but *not* watching and *not* listening to what was going on with him and Alexander. She was still broken, Einstein thought.

Still broken.

Einstein had never cared about anything. He couldn't remember caring. Mom always said, "don't you care?" He had figured out what that meant by watching how mom acted. And Alexander. But he didn't really get it. Now, though, something stirred in his mind and heart, and he thought it was caring. As he washed his hands, he looked at himself in the mirror, trying to see… something. What? Eyes looked back. A dark and gentle face. But now the eyes were not flat (he had heard them called 'flat'). They were… *sharp.* They bit back at him. And he had a need inside him to do something. An energy. A…

Feeling.

He stared at those sharp eyes.

Suddenly, for an instant — for less than a second then gone again — *something else!* Something that shouldn't be in his reflection, or so he thought. He looked once more, but now saw nothing special. What had it been?

…Words.

And though he'd only seen them for a second, the words were seemingly implanted in his brain. He thought they had kind of looked like those descriptions you might see next to a character in Alexander's games. It was odd. Even though he only paid attention to the games for a few minutes from time to time, he seemed to know more than he should. At least, about this *new* game. *Rings.* He had known what to do when Alexander was hurt.

The words?

"Rank 10 Defeater," with a list of second skills next to it: "shuriken, short blades, potions, spycraft, wayfinding." He was surprised but also not. They had always been there. In him. Somewhere.

His sharp eyes looked even sharper. He squeezed them to slits. He…

Smiled.

And then, for a bare instant, *his eyes flashed green!*

Alexander groaned again.

*　　*　　*

Later in bed, Einstein seemed to remember something else. Maybe a name. Maybe *his* name. It might have begun with a W. He wondered…

Then slept.

And dreamed.

He flew. The *Rings* world spread below. He recognized it from what he'd seen on the screen as Alexander had played. Orange sky. Rusty land. The green of rolling hills barely registered in the stained light. He thought for a moment he must be a drone, but no. He heard no sound but the wind. The city lay behind — he didn't look; he just knew. He flew higher so he wouldn't hit the steep slopes that climbed before him.

Then he stood upon the highest ridge and gazed into the hills. They rose few and near, the lands beyond undefined. With his dream vision, he could look into folds and around bends to see hidden forests, villages and mines, cave mouths, cascades, farmhouses and castles, wandering roads, walls and terraces. More. Scattered with little rhyme or reason to his young eyes.

Turning, he looked over the lowlands, the city revealed, appearing small. Five rings. Each darker, so that he could only make out details past the third wall into the third ring. Beyond was… broken and hazy. Dim. Much lay within to see, but his eyes could extract nothing for sure.

Lifting his gaze he saw countless miles outside the walls, to the left, right, and beyond, all indistinct, orange reflections here and there from unknown sources, all dissolving to a rusty murk.

He was not surprised. Not by any of it.

He knew this place.

He knew it completely.

He had *played Rings.* Once upon a time.

And he had played it *well!*

"Wonder."

Spoken aloud as he dreamed, though no one heard.

A dam had broken. Memories rushed out at him but slowed as they came, letting him grasp a few and hold on. He floated among them, pulling them together into a raft of knowledge.

Wonder.

He remembered playing Wonder as she and her team went to defeat The Boss. A fine team it was! He saw them. Toadum, proud magician and marvelous knitter. The rogue Glav, cook of the crew (he was especially good at crispy cheezers), who packed a wicked crossbow. Scram the swordsman — rough, but a top warrior. The brute Disagra, a strong and thoughtful octo-marine sailor with a collection of antique hamster balls. Next to Wonder, Disagra was smartest of the bunch — rare for a brute. There might have been others, but these he remembered clearly.

But they were dead. Never respawned. Truly dead. ...All of them? He couldn't recall. ...Wait, Scram he had seen again. At the school. And hadn't that old guy at VidGameCon sort of looked like Toadum?

Then came another big memory, but it hurt in mind and heart to hold it. He shoved it down. ...Or maybe it was more that he didn't let it rise. Or *couldn't.* It was enough to sense that it involved a very bitter ending, and it was enough to wake him.

Einstein sat up, eyes wide, but then eased his head back onto his pillow. He lay awake far into the night, going over his new rememberings and sorting them into a rough order. The thing that finally rocked him to sleep again was a warm dream of roasting crispy cheezers and their delicious aroma. Wonder had loved them, and somehow Einstein had tasted them too.

*   *   *

Jake had slept hard and long. He hadn't meant to, but his body knew better. But now something had awakened him.

...What?

He slipped out of bed, went to his disk, woke his rig, clicked the icon, grabbed his controller, and saw…

A coffee cup.

The remnants of sleep blew out of him like leaves in front of a blower nozzle.

A coffee cup, on a table, by a street, with people passing by.

Real people.

"…Oh shit."

*   *   *

Don't sleep! I drive my fingernails deep into my arms to finish waking as fast as can be — to escape the dream.

…It won't let me go. Toothy demons swarm my eyes. Their laughing stabs me. Deadly shame. Wake! Heavy spears fly toward me. Wake! Razor-sharp blades come at my belly. Wake! Wake! *Wake!*

I begin to wake. The dream slinks away.

…Wait, *nooo!* I don't want to wake! Don't make me. Please. I'm gasping. I can't stop my eyes from whirling. I'm… wet. My hands claw at the sheets and I can't stop them. Please don't wake up. Too late.

Too late.

I silently moan. I dare not sleep. I can't leave my room because I'll get slashed and speared again — I'm sure! Like at the school, but this time with no rescue.

I'm so tired. So tired.

The Boss is here now — Real. He's behind every rock, around every corner, face in the clouds, seeping from the shadows. My eyes burn. The Boss is in my head, laughing and nibbling. He showed himself at the restaurant, infecting me, sucking me into the night then laughing at me. I'm so stupid. I am *so* stupid. I thought he could have killed me then.

…I thought he should have.

So why didn't he? Just to jerk me around? Cat and mouse.

The demons chew and spit!

I moan aloud this time, a plea that I might just die and be done with it, but all I can do is curl up, pull my sad, wadded sheets closer to me, and slam my eyes closed, hoping that it will happen now — quickly. Kill me now. Kill me now. Kill me—

"It's okay."

I fight my eyes and crack them open. Einstein stands there in his old pajamas, but he's wearing new emotions. Concern. Brotherly love. Huh? He puts a hand on one of mine and leaves it there long enough for my shivering to stop. My breathing gets quieter. My eyes slowly close again. If they still whirl, I don't see it.

"Don't worry," Einstein says in a voice so calm it might have been God's. "We can get him. I know something now." He doesn't have that delay before he talks anymore.

My eyes open again and I stare at my brother. He smiles a little. *What?* He has never smiled. I suddenly feel really young. Or, no, it's that my brother now seems older. My mind opens wide. Einstein's smile spreads to his eyes. "Come on," he says. "You can stay with me tonight."

I slip from the bed, weak as a baby. As if *he* were the big brother, he takes my hand, walks me to the bathroom, and wipes my face with a cool washcloth. It feels so good. Then he leads me into his room and tucks me into his own bed, putting his stuffed cat against my cheek. The Boss has gone out of my mind. Can I sleep now?

Is Einstein magic?

I feel the sleep rolling over me. Maybe. Maybe for a little while…

*　　*　　*

Einstein looked at his brother as he slept, feeling… Feeling. He was *feeling*, and it was something he knew he had been able to do in the past. He was feeling, *again*. He smiled sadly, which was not the kind of thing that boys often did. Then he turned, left his room, walked down the hall to Alexander's room, went to the desk, sat, put on the headphones, and, after a long, slow breath, picked up the controller, pressed "A", and—

*　　*　　*

"He's back." Wonder's eyes went wide, then she howled — a long, triumphant wail offered to the night sky. "He's playing again!" Her deadly, loony Rubbles neighbors turned toward her with their snuffling stabs and capering cuts to see what went on — perhaps to rend and peel, perhaps to eat warm flesh. "Back off!" Wonder snapped, unafraid. And they did.

Awakened and filled with new purpose by her player's return to the game, the warrior Wonder headed instinctively for the Maze Halls and the gate into 5th Ring — not for the first time. She stopped only briefly at a weapons cache, donning a lizard leather throwers vest, and stuffing the holders and pockets with blades and stars.

As she jogged, shouts and screams threatened from here and there across the perilous Rubbles, but that was nothing new. The Rubbles, after all, was where the not-dead went to not die, and it wasn't pleasant at all. But Wonder, played again, had nothing to fear, for she was the greatest warrior *Rings* had ever known. All steered clear.

Or died.

Quickly.

*   *   *

The Boss opened his eyes. What had just happened?

"Needles," he called with a touch of urgency.

"Hmm?" Needles replied, stepping out from a shadowed alcove along the wall of the new 'cave.'

"Needles…"

"Something has happened?"

"Wonder," The Boss murmured.

Mister Needles raised the stitches that passed for an eyebrow. "Wonder?"

"She's… back," The Boss answered, awe in his voice. "Her player is back. They are back, Needles. They are *back!*" he shouted, standing suddenly, his empty coffee mug tipping to its side on the small table next to his chair.

"I see," Mister Needles replied, astonished.

"What is going on, Needles?" inquired The Boss, dead calm again.

"Shall I look into it?"

The Boss smiled weakly. "Yes. You. Shall."

*　　*　　*

"Dune?" asked Sparrow.

"Wha…"

"Dune!"

"Spinning. All spinning…" He sat heavily on the ground, holding his head.

Sparrow sighed then grabbed Dune by the belt, opened the bag at his side, and pulled out the map. "This is our way," she said after examining the map yet again, though she had found nothing — there was nothing to find. "The Boss must die. We must make the 5th." She had said it so often over the last several days that the words had no feeling left.

"Why *this* way?" Scram responded. He had just about had it. "Didn't we just come through this? I think I remember that statue. Damn I'm thirsty," he added.

"Hatch drink?"

"No, moron!" Scram retorted. "Do you see a bar anywhere? No. We're completely lost in these damn Maze Halls, and there's not a watering hole anywhere. And—" He stopped then sighed hard in disgust. "Well now just look at that," he said, pointing at a section of wall painted with demons dancing in front of a ring building. "See *that?*" The building featured a sign in a window that read, *Tuesday is Trout Day.* "Tuesday is Trout Day, aye? *Fourth* time we've passed it!" he snapped. *"Fourth!* We passed it first just after we started. …I remember fish," he added in a mumble.

"We will find a way," Sparrow assured. "But something is not right with Dune."

"Yeah, well…" said Scram. "I've seen that with played warriors. His player's not playing, or something else to do with Real."

"Yes, as have I," came the reply. "But this is much worse. He is not dulled; he is broken! He was fine for days, but then this. I thought he would come out of it, but no. He is useless!" she spat, angry but also worried. She sighed in a huff, and then steeled herself once more. "We must keep trying on our own."

"Lass?"

"Yes?"

Scram waited until Sparrow looked him in the eyes. "You're being played. That's the only way we're not dropping Dune lad in the Rubbles and fighting our way back to fourth hotel for drinks."

"Why do you say this?" she replied.

"*Think,*" he answered. "If you weren't being played, you wouldn't 'try' *anything* this long, aye? That much I can remember from all my teams. I'm not played. Warriors like me do our jobs then die, or go to the Rubbles, or maybe go rogue like me." He smiled. "Game simple. But *you?* You've taken charge! You're played. Aye. You've got a Real behind you."

Sparrow said nothing. But...

He was right. She had known it. *Known* it.

"This way?" Hatch guessed, scratching his head like a beaver might scratch a log.

"No!"

A new voice!

Blades were instantly drawn, fighting stances taken, and the heads of the team turned as one to look back down the long hall that had dropped them at this latest set of doors. There stood a warrior, woman, slightly shorter and a bit broader than Sparrow, white hair, vested for throwing, dressed in white and purple, no sword or bow, a small smile on her face.

But the eyes...

When she got close enough, they saw. Her emerald irises had vertical slits like a cat's. It was eerie and beautiful, and it was the well known feature of only one.

"*Wonder!*" Scram said with a welcoming sigh. "Aye, well I'll be damned."

14 — 5TH RING

The team stood in the gateway, stunned at what they saw — except for Dune, whose head was hanging, eyes on the dirt.

After completing their passage through the Maze Halls (thanks to Wonder's wayfinding skill), they'd had only a short distance to navigate in the dim, orange, *Rings* dawn. They had crept carefully through the lanes near the wall of 5th Ring, moving from cover to cover, tension rising as they neared what the map showed as their destination, eyes peeled for assassins or enemies of any kind, but there was no one. Nothing.

Silence.

Even so, they had dreaded what they would find — especially since they had no tokens left, and they had always heard that five would be needed.

But arriving at the location of the gate, they had found it standing open, great double doors spread wide like welcoming arms. After a short time of watching, they had moved carefully to the entrance and…

Stepped through.

Eyes wide, they gazed about in bafflement.

"This is 5th?" Scram asked. "Not what I expected."

Not what any expected, but only Wonder had ever made 5th Ring, so the others weren't expecting anything in particular — except that it wouldn't be like this. Buildings and layout were familiar in form — colors and adornments were like those of the other rings; the grit of the streets still appeared like street grit — but now all looked as though made of congealed smoke. It was as if the city wasn't quite all there — as though some essential binding agent had been seeping away, departing existence. The effect on the team was subtle. They began to feel…

Thin.

The hotel, however, seemed to have escaped the spell. This version was tall, with arches and ornaments, gargoyles leering from corners and crests, narrow windows missing panes, a faint vapor spilling from all openings. A large poster near the steps advertised a coming opera and featured the face of a jowled basso. The team felt encouraged at seeing the door open wide and a light within still showing faintly in the early morning. Even so, they hesitated, something nagging. It was Dune who muttered the answer, his voice ragged.

"No… one."

That was it. *No one* could be seen. No weirdos roamed the streets. No idiots hung from windows shouting absurdities. No three-legged possums sniffed at the grates. No shabby urchins searched through the garbage in the dim recesses of the lanes. A few desiccated corpses of birds dotted Ring Road, appearing ready to blow away with the next breeze, but even the breeze had died.

The 5th? "Death," Sparrow whispered.

Suspicious, they slowly crossed the road, ascended the hotel steps, and walked into the lobby, which, as always, was the gateway to a bar. The dusty floor stayed silent at their footsteps — the first footsteps the entry hall had known for a long time. The bar looked and felt empty. *Was* empty…

Except for the tall bartender who lovingly polished a glass with a cloth, held by long fingers of ivory hands.

"What can I get for you fine travelers?" he asked with gentle authority. But then, turning to regard the group, his hands froze.

"What up, Chopfsky?"

"…Wonder."

"Yup, it's me."

Chopfsky's polishing began again, as though never interrupted. "Out of the Rubbles, I see."

"You shouldn't be surprised."

He grinned. "Even *I* can be surprised, lovely Wonder. Even I."

"But shouldn't you be tying things up about now?" Wonder inquired. "Haven't the cards all been dealt? Could it be that you haven't cheated well enough?"

"I? Cheat?"

"Hatch drink now?"

"Come, brute!" Chopfsky urged, leaping into drink preparation. "How about a Jangan Flosser?"

"Hatch like beer." He lumbered to the bar and tucked in. In moments he waved for a second, which was quickly produced.

"And you?" Chopfsky asked, looking at each.

"I'll try that Flosser," said Scram with little enthusiasm. The bartender admitting he was Chopfsky had thrown his thirst off a bit. Even so, he was dry.

"Water." Dune moaned.

"For me as well," Sparrow said.

Wonder offered a wide smile. "Make mine a frog-bellied-blue-fox," she stated. "A double."

Chopfsky looked at her and broke out laughing — but he made the drink.

*   *   *

"He's everywhere," she answered unclearly. "Every hotel bartender, half the shopkeepers, a bunch of the hills characters. All Chopfsky.

"I still don't understand," Sparrow replied. "This Chopfsky moves around the game and makes ready as a new character when a team arrives?"

"Can't be," corrected Scram. "Can't be. Back in the day, there were too many teams. Too much action. This Chopfsky would o' had to be in two places at once. More."

"I can't explain it," Wonder said. "But once I was sure of it, I watched. It was always him, but not like he *was* all those characters. More like he *played* them all."

"He is a player?" Sparrow asked, not believing. "A Real?"

That stopped Wonder. "I don't know, but I don't think so," she said after a moment. "Just that it's not disguises. I mean, look. Here, he's taller than Sparrow and white as a wraith. There was big Mike in 1st."

"Still there," said Scram.

"Back in 2nd, I remember Eyepatch Edna — looks a bit like your brute, but with blue skin."

"Aye, still the one," Scram confirmed.

"The 3rd was a wee kid with bad teeth."

"Aye."

"A slimy guy in 4th I never liked. Always leering at me. Never gave him the time of day. All still the same?" No one disputed her. "Right, and I remember corpse guy here from my first visit. Not disguises." Then she added, "I say 'he,' but I don't know."

"Wizard maybe?"

"Maybe. I don't know many wizards. Toadum was the only one, really."

"And The Boss."

"Ha, yes," Wonder answered. "The Boss is wizard for certain, plus top avatar. Maybe more." She looked the others over. "Good chance you'll see for yourselves soon enough."

Dune groaned.

*　　*　　*

But after everything — after all the enemies, quests, worlds, puzzles, and torments they had endured to reach 5th Ring and the citadel — The Boss…

Wasn't there.

"This is wrong," Sparrow stated flatly.

Now numbering five with the addition of Wonder, the team stood in the spacious, circular room that had long been the place where The Boss ruled *Rings*. A towering conical ceiling rose so high above them that the upper reaches were lost in darkness. Orange light spilled in through banks of curved windows that offered sweeping views of… despair.

The team had come via stairs that spiraled from below, creeping silently up to emerge through the floor and into the room. They now stood near the stair mouth, gazing at the compact comfort area in the center of the chamber — a modest circular rug, two easy chairs, coffee table with a french press coffee maker and two mugs. Little else. Three arches, evenly spaced around the chamber, led to ramped hallways that descended into dimness.

It had been eerily simple to get there. Departing the hotel in the morning, the team had nervously navigated the lanes to the center, seeing no one, but increasingly convinced that a deadly surprise grew nearer by the minute. How could it not be so? The 5th Ring, home of The Boss, murdering nemesis of all warriors since the beginning.

Only one set of game characters did they see — a ghostly pack of dogs, casting no shadows as they roved the lanes, looking deadly vicious, but sad and lost at the same time. They ignored the team completely as they jogged along, the echoes of soft whimpers following them like a mist.

If anything, the feeling that had greeted them at the gate grew as the team continued inward. Scram summed it up.

"More dead than dead," he said.

In less than an hour, they had reached the wide, lifeless grounds of the citadel — a sprawl of gray grass and a few dead trees at the center of 5th Ring. It, too, was…

Empty.

They had crossed the wasteland in haste, dashing across the stone plaza that surrounded the tall citadel and furtively entering one of the doors, all of which had been standing open. No guards. No traps. No sound. Weapons at the ready, they had gone straight to the great, spiral staircase at the center of the structure and headed up. And now, in the center of it all — at the very heart of dread and danger in *Rings?*

Nothing.

Nobody.

…

"Least we're alive," Scram observed. "Could be worse."

Dune didn't speak. He had been confused and miserable since late in the 4th Ring, but now, in the nest of his nemesis, he sensed the sharpened nails of death all around him, reaching to slice him out of existence. He felt unrelenting panic.

For Wonder, it was different. Curious. Revealing. "This is where it was. This is where I stood. And fell."

"Aye, okay," said Scram, "but you did damn well. No team with you. … Think I stayed in 3rd… No. Was fourth hotel! I remember again."

"Yes," said Wonder. "Fifth gate was in a different place, between merchants and Rubbles. We got there together."

"Rubbles was same side as Worlds?" Scram asked, surprised.

"Yes," she replied, "which is why we went merchants way the first time."

"Lost one to merchants," Scram remembered. "A rookie blader who'd just joined us at the hotel, aye? And now the merchants are moved to 3rd — pushed out by Rubbles gettin' bigger I suppose."

"Yes. But we made it, and then there was no way through fifth gate."

"We had the tokens, but… What happened?"

"Trap! Ambush! Remember?" she pressed, but Scram looked confused. "Tokens for fifth gate were a *lie!*" Wonder reminded him. "A signal to The Boss. That is all. *Remember?*"

"Is that so?" asked Sparrow.

"Yes," replied Wonder. "We were attacked at the gate as soon as we placed them."

"Aye! Aye… Lost three there." Scram gradually recalled. "Disagra, aye? Hell of a brute," he said, glancing at Hatch. "Glav too. And… Toadum?"

"Yes, well, didn't see Toads die. He vanished," she said. "Something wizardly I guessed."

Scram grunted. "So that left two of us. Escaped, aye?"

"Yes," she said. "We went back to fourth hotel — you and I, through the merchants. Didn't have to do the Rubbles back then, so an easy game retreat."

"Aye," the rogue nodded, but then looked puzzled. "But remind me, lass. You went back…"

"I was talking to the bartender," she began. "Chopfsky, I know now. He was on about The Boss's spies and agents — how some nights he was serving more of them than warriors, and they were always coming and going from the 5th. That gave me an idea. I waited until I saw one leave, then left you drinking and followed. Slipped through the merchants — this spy had a sly way — and back to the gate. Hadn't planned on it, but just kept going. Didn't get through right away, but watched as my guide went through. Hid until another messenger got let in. Went in right behind. Used a wee shadow trick I learned from Toads."

"She went back *alone!*" Scram bragged to the others on Wonder's behalf. *"Through the merchants!* No small thing. You almost had him, lass. Close as I've ever heard, but he beat you."

"He did not beat me," Wonder replied. "He blew me to Rubbles."

"Same thing, aye?"

"No. Not the same. No weapons or wounds. It was *ending* magic. A spell, or some game act. An escape spell — a last resort. There was a moment I cannot forget. At the casting, I suddenly knew my player. I mean, I knew I was played, but I never had proof until that moment. The spell damaged him. A boy — my Real." She shook her head, struggling now with *her* memory. "In that moment I saw... much. I saw *into* The Boss. There was another player, too. We were together — me, The Boss, and two Reals. Just for a moment, but we are bound still." She looked thoughtful.

"Well, anyway," Wonder continued, "I woke in Rubbles. Though it is not a true waking! I had nothing. No purpose. The Rubbles... The Rubbles are..." She suddenly felt lost, searching for memories where there were none.

"This is all true?" Sparrow, asked, bringing Wonder back.

"Yes. It has come clear since the 4th — when the boy played back in and woke me. He is healed."

"So that's good!" Scram observed. "This boy is back playing, aye? Maybe The Boss is finished."

"No!" Sparrow spat. "See? He has broken Dune! Look at him." They did. Not pretty. Dune sat in one of the easy chairs, trembling, chewing the side of his hand.

"The boy Alexander must be damaged as well," Sparrow stated.

"Who?" Wonder asked.

"Dune's player. Also a boy. But he respawned — I saw it. So something has happened since," Sparrow added, confused.

"You *saw* it?" Wonder asked, a bit shocked. "In..."

"Real," Scram said. "We were there, lass. Through the Yellow Door in a world in 4th, down a grater, through the Door of Lies. We expected a next world, but it leads into this... I don't know — fog. Aye, and there it is. DoNotEnter. On the other side is Real." Scram's eyes were wide. "Hell of a place. All so... more. It's *more*. Like it's finished. No. Like the *game* is unfinished. Like we're... We're..."

"Not real."

Wonder was dumbstruck. "You can go to Real?"

"Aye," Scram answered. "Wild, eh?"

"Yes," confirmed Sparrow. "Our team went there, but not just us. Jangs — many. They nearly killed Alexander. Dune as well." Pointing toward Hatch and Scram, she said, "these two returned with Dune to the game and on to the Chamber of Respawning. Another boy — a younger boy — led me to this Alexander, who was near dead. Jangs had wounded him, but now he was under further attack by strange makers, masked, wrapped in white and blue. I took him from them, and then to his home. The younger one — his brother — guided me to put Alexander in a chair with objects about. He placed an object in Alexander's hands. We saw *Rings* then, through a small window of light. ...Through Dune's eyes." Sparrow hesitated, seeming as though she didn't quite believe her own tale. "It was Dune — then soon to respawn."

"Aye," Scram interjected. "Hatch tossed him in. Took a few, but he popped up as legend bowman again. Not lamb. Wasn't quite dead."

"That is when Alexander also respawned. They are bound." The memory was in her eyes. "A strange respawning. Messy."

...

A low grunt from Hatch broke the silence. "No kill Boss?" he asked, an unexpected hint of sadness in his voice. He had been waiting for all the talk to end.

"Alexander... is attacked." To the surprise of the others, the words came from Dune, pushed through gritted teeth. "The Boss," he choked out. "The Boss... The Boss is in..."

"Real," Wonder finished for him. She nodded slowly, a shadow of fear on her face. "Yes! He is in Real — he is not here. *Of course!* You have all said it! Your team has heard it everywhere — that something happened to The Boss." Wonder wasn't finished. "But he is powerful. He *is* a wizard. We are just warriors. He is the last game wizard — the last one! The game is almost finished, and he knows it."

"He has gone to Real to survive?" Sparrow added, guessing.

"More!" Dune nearly wept. "There is... more, he... Power... He takes power..."

"Uh, Hatch kill?"

"Yes!" Wonder shouted. "We must! He must be killed, but he will know we'll come for him. He will know I am back, and that we escaped the Maze Halls. He may know already! It is clear that Alexander is damaged, but now he and my player are in terrible danger. Others, too, perhaps. The Boss will… He will—"

"We don't know what he'll do," interrupted Scram, "and that's as bad."

"He must die." Sparrow, as usual, got straight to the point.

"Hatch like!"

"So. You go again to Real, and I go with you!" Wonder said. "We must kill The Boss, once and for all."

Hatch cheered.

Sparrow sneered.

Scram wanted a drink.

Dune nearly puked.

*　　*　　*

Diary of The Boss

Wonder is awake, and her player is back. I surprised Needles with the news. The look on his face was priceless. Wonder and her player have been in my thoughts since the Final Surprise, and now she is back in the game. How so?

I did not expect the Final Surprise. For just a moment, I thought Wonder had beaten me, but then the power came. Was it the goddess? And why was I then set with the others? What was that? Me, Wonder of course, but our two players as well. Wonder's and mine. Two Reals. I saw them clearly. They were weak and broken, but now they come forward again.

Why?

Needles has his limits. He is a puzzle. He is certainly more than he seems. I should perhaps kill him, but not yet.

<u>Update:</u>

Needles just exceeded my surprise with one of his own. He has now located all four players! Quite close by. My sad little Alexander and another, a girl. But also Wonder's player — already! Eyestine is his name I think, and he is the younger brother of Alexander. Delicious!

My player too! It is hard to believe. I left him behind so long ago. I can't recall his name. What does this mean?

We will kill them all. It is best. Needles wants minions again. I had wanted to do it myself, but he is cautious about killing in Real, which he called "real killing." I am confused about this, but I trust him. To a point.

He suggested metal merchants, and I am convinced! They make a lovely mess, and they are relentless. Needles has gone off to take care of the details. He isn't one to waste a minute. He will get it right this time.

I am glad, too. It is exciting spinning dreams and terrors for little friend Alexander, the cause of my irritations. It makes me feel like I did when the game was young. His pain will have lasted splendidly before he dies, but best not to wait too long.

I really should kill Needles too. He has earned it!

Ace

*　　*　　*

As they returned to the hotel, Wonder shared another thought that had come to her. "The Boss," she said. "I think *he* is played."

"He's wizard." Scram replied.

"And avatar," she added. "But I think his player was the second one I saw in the Final Surprise," she continued, ignoring the rogue. "He was damaged as well, I'm certain. We all were."

"But he's a wizard!" Scram repeated.

"You are sure that wizards are not played?" she returned.

"…Uh, well, not to say so, but they've power to themselves, aye?"

"How do you think this?" Sparrow asked Wonder.

"…I'm not certain," Wonder answered. "Perhaps my player teaches me. Or perhaps I remember something more from the spell. I'm a knower, remember." Suddenly confident, she went on. "At least, The Boss was never the same again, and that could mean his player changed." She smiled and clapped, surprising the others. "And as we figure this out, my player learns it as well. He is at work in Real. He will help us."

Arriving, the team hastened into the hotel for quick refreshment, and to finalize their plan.

"You're back!" the bartender said, his smile small but welcoming. "Nobody home?"

"You knew, aye?" Scram guessed.

The bartender shrugged.

"And you did not tell us?" Sparrow accused in a flash of anger.

"You didn't ask," the tender replied. "Besides, *Wonder* is one of you," he continued, gesturing at the cat-eyed warrior. "And she knows things." The ivory smile again. "She's the knower that knows more than she knows she knows."

"Spit it out, Chops," Wonder returned.

"Well, you know your player."

"Mmm."

"You even know that The *Boss* is played," Chopfsky said. "And now you *all* know it," he added at the reaction of the others.

"True," Wonder agreed.

"And, dear Wonder, you even know *me,*" he said. "No other warrior has ever known — not in the whole history of the game."

15 — THE PLAYERS UNITE

Einstein put down the controller and took off the headphones. His reawakening had continued, memories and new knowledge coming to him from several sources. He worried about Alexander, but hadn't been sure what to do. He had been content to watch Wonder, letting her act without his input, and coming again to know her every thought. …And, it seemed, she was beginning to know his.

Now, though, Einstein had begun to realize that he needed to take action. A sense of what The Boss was planning had started to form in his mind. He could feel Needles and his purposes like a whisper. What he had come to understand most of all was that things were going to happen, they would happen in Real — in his town — and they would happen *soon*.

"It's close," he whispered. "Everyone is close."

Making up his mind, Einstein stepped over to his brother who lay curled up on his bed, his face an unsleeping mask of gloom. He knelt on the floor to look Alexander in the eyes.

"We have to find the other players," he said. "We have to find who is playing Sparrow and who is playing The Boss."

Hearing the second name, Alexander's eyes crushed closed and he turned his head.

"We have to," Einstein insisted. "We have to work together — like the warriors."

Peering through his swollen lids, Alexander responded. "How?" he peeped.

Einstein sat on the floor and stared at the wall, the seconds ticking away. Alexander had fallen fitfully asleep by the time he tried an answer. "They are close." he said, his brother not hearing. "Really close. We might even… know them." Einstein got an odd look on his face. "I can make Wonder tell Sparrow, then Sparrow's player will know and can come to our house." Another minute passed, then Einstein again spoke to the night. "I think I know who plays The Boss.

"I think I know."

* * *

Jake stared at Wonder's player, stunned, but strangely unsurprised. It was Alexander's weird little brother, Einstein — right there, in Jake's room, showing up just when Jake had reached a state of near panic about what The Boss and Needles were doing.

When the tap at the window had come, Jake had spun around to look through the glass, seeing only a dim shape with two sparks for eyes. His insides went liquid and his breathing stopped — he'd thought it was The Boss, come to kill him — like he had promised in his journal.

But then he recognized Einstein.

What?

Yeah, of course! Einstein! Jake suddenly understood, the memory of the Final Surprise ringing like a bell in his mind.

Relieved, but still trembling, Jake had helped Einstein climb in, apologizing when the younger boy cut his knee on something. He had started to listen as Einstein told him stuff — about Wonder, about gathering the players, about Alexander being messed up by The Boss — but the feeling of rising fear started to choke him, and he interrupted.

"He's bringing minions through!" Jake blurted out. "To *kill* us! You and Alexander, and me. And some other player. His guy Mister Needles is doing it. It's metal merchants. They're incredibly dangerous. Just about the worst minions. Lots of slicing things and scissor things. And loppers. Sawing swords and stuff. I guess through the Yellow Door. Maybe *now.* Maybe *already!"* Jake felt his face getting hot.

Einstein took it all in. He had been expecting that they would just talk to figure things out. But now it was an emergency. He could see it. "Through DoNotEnter," he said, ignoring the trickle of blood that lengthened on his shin. "Through the DoNotEnter door."

"What's *that?*"

"That's the way here from *Rings,*" Einstein replied. "It's a door in the school. They came before."

Jake's mind was flying. *They came before?* They came before! Dozens of memories and wild fears spun together in Jake's imagination, forming a perfect picture. Things that he had ignored — things he had seen, or that The Boss had said — things that hadn't made sense before now fit together perfectly.

"Oh no."

"We need to stop them," Einstein said, suddenly realizing the danger. "I think *we* have to stop the metal merchants, because I don't think Wonder and the other warriors will be here soon enough. The team is coming to kill The Boss, but I don't think they will get here first — not if the metal merchants are already close."

"Uh huh." Jake was guessing at the timing, but he knew that The Boss and Needles had quick ways to move minions around the city — private passageways, magical jumps, secret treaties with forgotten avatars in hidden worlds.

"Wonder was at the hotel in 5th Ring just a little while ago," Einstein continued.

"Uh huh," mind racing.

"They have to go back into the 4th Ring, through the Maze Halls, down to the Lies door, and through all the gray stuff, and that's kind of slow."

"Uh huh," racing.

"You have to help," Einstein urged the older boy.

Jake just breathed for a few moments as Einstein stared. "Yeah. Okay. Okay."

"Layla is outside waiting."

"Layla?"

"She's a girl," Einstein reported. "She plays Sparrow. She must be the 'other player' you said. She'll help too." Einstein began to feel impatient — something he was not used to. "We probably have to go *now.*"

"Okay," answered Jake, still struggling to orient. "Okay, but it's pretty late."

"You said minions. If we don't stop them coming through the door, then... well, then they will come through!" Einstein said. "They will find us and kill us *before* Wonder and the team get here."

"Maybe not. Maybe..." Jake was about to tell Einstein he might be wrong, but then he remembered what The Boss had written in his journal, and he knew that, yes, the merchants really *could* be here soon. Very soon. Jake flashed a sad smile at Einstein, strangely moved by the plain truth the younger boy spoke. Not a normal kid. He was Wonder's player. "Okay," he replied. "Okay, let's go, but I don't know what we can do."

"Block the door," Einstein responded matter of factly.

Jake opened his mouth as if to answer, but then realized there would be no point. The kid was probably right anyway. It didn't give The Boss's player much hope.

*　　*　　*

Shock struck Jake again when he climbed out of his window a few minutes later — crowbar from his basement in hand — and set eyes upon Layla Wischen. His mouth fell open for an instant, but then he swallowed quickly and introduced himself. "I'm Jake."

"I know you," she said. "From school."

How could *he* not have known *her?* But then another thought intruded. "Where's Alexander?"

"Home." To Jake's surprise, it was Layla who answered. "He's a real mess. The Boss is trashing him with visions and dreams. Dune is useless because of it, but the team is dragging him along. Alexander won't leave his room," she added. "It's very sad."

"You talked to him?"

"Yeah. Wonder had Sparrow send me to their house," she replied. "Einstein told Wonder to do it. About a half hour ago. He's so scared," she added with a look of caring.

"But, what about the warriors?" Jake asked. "The team, I mean. With *no* players?" If Alexander isn't playing, and you two are out, then no one is playing."

"Alexander went back in," Einstein replied. "At least he's holding the controller. He went in when I left. He thinks he can help a little. He's trying."

"I think Sparrow is strong on her own," Layla said. "Einstein told me about the hospital and respawning. Plus, Scram can help. I had Sparrow yell at him." She smiled.

Radiant!

"Wonder is a knower," Einstein added.

Without another word, they left the small pool of light outside the window and turned to head through the night toward the school. Jake knew the fastest way.

*   *   *

SMASH!

Layla and Jake both cringed at the sound of the window shattering (Einstein, not so much). The school had always seemed like… well, like a sacred place where high priests of wisdom spooned out holy knowledge. A place where power lived — power that could punish. Power you didn't mess with, and whose windows you certainly didn't break.

With Layla holding her phone flashlight, Jake wielded his crowbar, hurriedly clearing shards so they could climb in without lacerating themselves. That, too, made what seemed an incredible racket. Surely, thought Layla, they would soon hear police sirens coming their way. Finished, Jake pulled out his phone as well and they looked inside.

They had chosen a C-Hall room that faced a three-sided courtyard tucked into the school complex, thinking that no one would hear them. Now they weren't so sure. It was an art room, and their lights showed up a bizarre set of papier-mâché masks that sat drying on every available surface, many of which stared at the trio accusingly, some with bulging eyes or nasty tongues.

"Come on," Layla ordered as she climbed carefully, trying to avoid the glinting remnants of window that lay scattered on the sill. Jake followed, Layla lighting the way. Einstein came last, his shin catching a sliver that still stuck from the frame so that he soon had matching streaks of blood on both legs.

They were in.

Leaving the art room, they entered C-Hall, headed around the corner into B-Hall, and stood before the windowed door with the words, 'Do Not Enter' stenciled plainly on the cloudy glass. After a moment's hesitation, Layla reached out and turned the knob.

Unlocked.

She heard and felt the click as the latch pulled out of the strike plate. She took a breath, then pushed and the door opened a crack. Layla let go, but the door was balanced in such a way that it slowly opened wide without assistance. A low groaning sounded from inside. After exchanging glances with the others, they stepped through. A sensor registered their presence, an automatic light switched on, and they beheld what was within.

Metal stuff.

Something with a motor. Pipes and ducts. Metal boxes on the wall. Wires. A small desk with papers and small metal stuff on it. A chair. A custodian's jacket on a hook. The smell of… metal stuff, with a tang they could almost taste. The air felt…

Metallic.

"I don't get it," said Jake. "It's just the custodian's room. You say you saw this?"

"Yes," Layla replied. "Sparrow went through the Door of Lies—"

"I saw that with The Boss."

"—and into this kind of thick, gray… nothing."

"Me too," Jake confirmed. "The Boss I mean. He went in and I waited, but nothing happened. He was gone."

"How long did you wait?"

"I don't know," Jake answered. "Hours."

"Yes! Hours. Me too," Layla said, "but then I was watching by accident and I saw her again, at *this* door, looking through. She could see the trophy case," she added, pointing up the hall at the lighted case that held proofs of sports success the school had earned — not many. "This is the door. But I wasn't in the game later — I didn't see the jangs and that stuff you told me about. I didn't know about Alexander and the hospital. I was out."

"This is the door," Einstein agreed, blood from the new cut now soaking the top of one of his mismatched socks. "This is the door the minions will come through. And the team, but maybe the minions first."

"How do you know," Jake retorted, almost sneering.

"I know and *you* know" Einstein snapped, angry. "We were in the Final Surprise! I saw you! *I know!*" he shouted, face suddenly hot. But in an instant, he cooled again. "I still see things. The minions are coming." His eyes widened. "Hundreds of them. Metal merchants. They have already gone through the first door. They're coming." Einstein's face had changed, so that now he was almost in tears. "They're coming *now*, and we have to block the door or they will find us and kill us. And Alexander."

"Okay," Jake said, putting his hands on Einstein's shoulders. "Okay. Okay. Sorry. We will." Einstein was right — Jake saw it too.

...

"But how?" Jake asked aloud, breaking the silence.

...

"Well..."

...

"Oh!" Layla began, an idea coming to her. "We could tie the doorknob to... to... to something across the hall!"

"To what?" Jake wondered, scanning the other wall of the hall. "*With* what?" he added.

"A rope? A wire? ... Maybe something in the art room?"

They gave it a shot. Jake and Einstein returned to the art room, abandoning caution to turn on the glaring fluorescent lights. They came away with a long piece of pretty strong clothesline rope. While they were gone, Layla identified the nearest door across the hall as the place to tie off the other end. None knew anything about knots, but they tried. The rope sagged a bit between the knobs. They gave it a test.

"Please don't break," prayed Layla.

It didn't break!

...But it slipped off the custodian room doorknob.

They redid the knots at both ends and tested again.

It didn't break or slip!

…But the door still could be opened about three inches, and re-tying the knots only got it down to two. They decided it would have to do. Jake tried one more test, putting some weight against the door with his shoulder. He easily pushed through, the rope slipping from the same handle again.

"Dammit!"

At that moment, they heard a sound like voices on a far wind.

Wild voices. Crazed voices.

Metal voices.

The custodian's room began to flicker faintly, as if it was an image from a projector and a small surge had gone through the electric system.

Jake slammed the door shut and wheeled to face his comrades. "Oh shit!"

"No," said Layla. "No."

"They're coming! Did you hear? They're coming," Jake said, his panic rising.

BANG!

Jake and Lyla spun around at the sound. There stood Einstein, crowbar in hand, trying to pry a bank of lockers away from the wall, a fresh cut on his forehead. "We can block the door with these," he said.

The others saw the possibility right away. The lockers were the tall kind. Three lockers grouped in one unit, 3 feet wide, and almost as tall as the door they wanted to block. Einstein had pried one side of a unit a couple of inches away from the wall.

Jake took the crowbar and got to work. In less than a minute — to the sound of screws ripping from wood, plaster and sheet metal — he had pulled the unit completely away from the wall. The three of them pushed it across the hall and pressed it into the custodian room doorway. The lockers were exactly the same width as the door — 3 feet — but strips of trim wood around the frame kept the lockers from slipping deep into the doorway. The fit was perfect and pretty tight. The only gap was at the top, but that was too narrow for anything bigger than a rat to use.

"Wow," said Jake, amazed at how well it had worked.

"But they'll just knock it over!" observed Layla, wisely worried.

The trio exchanged glances, then started in on a second unit, freeing it quickly, sliding it over to stand flat up against the first. Though no one said so, they all knew that they still had the same problem — the enemy would just need to push harder to move two locker units instead of one.

Hmmm.

Einstein suddenly grabbed Layla's hand and pulled her over to the lockers. "Raise your arms and we'll measure." Willing to try anything, she stood against the lockers and raised her arms high — she was the tallest of the group. The tips of her fingers were almost exactly the height of the top edge of the locker back. "Now the floor," he said, and she quickly lay down, her feet against the two locker units. Her outstretched hands bent up against the far wall, meaning that the distance was shorter than the locker height.

"One more locker thing, but pushed over!" Einstein ordered.

After ripping a third locker unit from the wall, they stood it flat against the wall opposite the door and pushed it over. It fell toward the floor, but there wasn't enough space. Instead, the top of the falling lockers wedged against the standing pair, leaning at an angle, the top about two feet above the floor. They pulled, pushed, and kicked at the fallen unit to set it better. Jake even climbed up and jumped on it, driving the top a few more inches downward and wedging it tighter. When they were done, the fit was so tight that they couldn't budge *any* of the locker units.

Solid.

"That's really good!" Jake marveled.

The others agreed, but the reality of the situation got to them, and they knew it wouldn't be enough.

"Another one," said Einstein.

"Two," said Layla.

In the end, they managed to get a second wedging unit atop the first, so that two

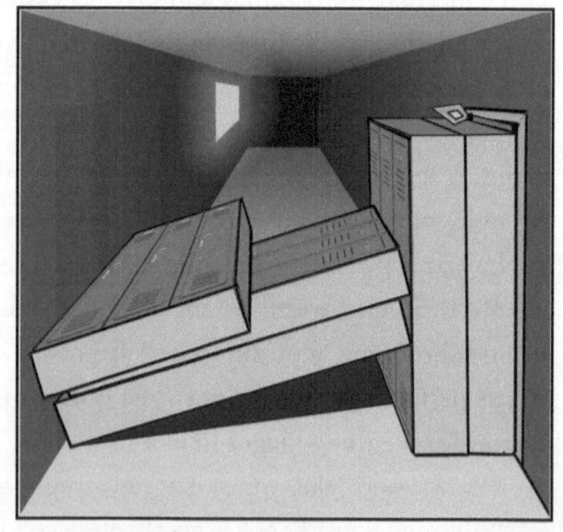

leaning units were jamming the two standing ones. They put another unit crossways over the leaning ones for weight (they couldn't lift it up high enough to do anything else). After that they gave it up, exhausted. Einstein had picked up another minor slice on an arm. Jake had mashed his knuckles twice when the crowbar had slipped. Layla — clearly more coordinated than the other two — remained unhurt.

They sat down on the floor of the hall, leaning against the cold wall. The adrenaline that had driven them drained away, and, one by one, they nodded off, hard work and late hours taking their toll. The night crept along until even ghosts grew weary.

It was a minute after 1 a.m. that the first small scratch sounded from the back of their barrier. Soon, several scratchers were at work, stopping and starting. It wasn't long util the scratching was continuous, dozens of fingers and various small metallic instruments clawing at the lockers in futility.

Einstein woke. Silently, he stood and roused the others. "They're here," he said simply, sounding like he might be talking about bills arriving in the mail.

Layla and Jake jumped up, blinking away the sleep, instantly alert. They clearly heard the scratching — a sound that made them wince, like nails on a chalkboard — but it didn't seem to be enough to cut through the locker metal. The scratching kept on, but despite the torment, Jake began to hope that they had truly done enough to stop the invasion.

That's when the pounding began. Something had caused the merchants to try harder. The lockers rattled and shook as the effort gained strength, joined by growls and yelps.

"Look!" Layla gasped as sharpened fingernails on gleaming fingers appeared in the narrow gap above the lockers, trying and failing to get a useful grip. The fingers retreated, but a spearhead poked in, and then a nose and silvery teeth. But the gap was too narrow for more. The enemy was stalled, and the sounds from the other side began to seem like the merchants were snapping at each other rather than trying to get through.

Jake's felt panicked, but he still clung to a slim hope. "They don't know what to do," he whispered. "They're too stupid to figure anything out. They have to be told."

"Who will tell them?" Layla whispered in response.

Jake wasn't sure. "Some mini boss. They must have one."

"The Boss?" Einstein asked.

"No," said Jake. "He's *here.*" Which prompted all of them to scan the hallway. Empty. "I mean, he's at his new place in Real. Not here in the school. It'll be like a captain," Jake said, "but maybe even the captain is too stupid." It came out like a question.

They hoped. Minutes ticked by, the scratching kept on, some bangs and pushes, and they hoped. More minutes, and more, and their hope grew, and then settled almost into boredom. Would it be that easy? To be just one step smarter than the minions? The minutes became a half hour, then forty minutes, and then fifty. The three began to feel almost proud.

But then…

THUNK. The tops of the wedging lockers crept up an inch. They stared in horror.

THUNK. Another inch.

"More weight!" Layla hissed. "Get on! *Everyone on!*"

All three of them clambered up onto the stack of pushed-over lockers to add their weight, hoping to stop the wedging effect from failing. Jake found himself wishing that he was bigger — that he had eaten more instead of skipping meals to play games. For another minute, it seemed to work. The lockers held!

But then the fury of the thunking and scrabbling increased, matched by an angry exchange of buzzing voices…

And laughter.

A sudden, thudding crunch jolted the kids, and the lockers began to give way. The three hung on, trying to make their weight more effective, pushing and pressing, moving to where their meager pounds could do the most good. Still, the lockers moved.

"It won't hold!" Jake yelled, almost in tears. "As soon as they move it more, the first one will get out and they can move the whole thing and… Oh god oh god oh god!"

"We have to run," Einstein yelled. "We can't let them kill us! We have to save Alexander! We should—"

BAM! *SLAM!*

The entire setup began to fail, the wedge lockers popping up half a foot and the standing units sliding inches outward, opening a gap big enough for a body. A second later, hooting in triumph, the first metal merchants forced their way through.

CRASH!

Pushing in, the enemy drove the whole mess of lockers toward the trophy case, standing up the wedge lockers, which twisted around as if trying to wall off the hallway. Jake, Layla and Einstein were thrown to the floor, landing in a heap. As they scrambled up, they turned to see several hideous faces leering at them from the other side of the lockers — long, spiked, glinting faces on short, very dangerous, very speedy bodies — helmets of metal, masks of metal, armor of metal, thick little metallic minds that loved to clip and carve…

Though he didn't know when he had picked it up, Einstein found that he was holding the crowbar. Stepping forward, he swung it with all the might he could muster, connecting with one head — damage, severe. For one bizarre moment, the other metal merchants froze in panic and ignorance. The three friends turned and bolted. Released from indecision, the enemies leapt after them.

"Oh god!" Jake squeaked as his legs scrambled. *"Oh god!"*

An instant later, beside the trophy case, the escape of Jake Hei, Layla Wischen, and Einstein Breyer came to a rapid end. The scene, gruesome indeed.

*   *   *

The team was behind the enemy, but hopefully not too far behind. Fearless in fast retreat, they had hurried through the gate, raced their way unhindered through the Maze Halls, and come out on the short stretch of Ring Road between the maze and the Worlds. Dune stumbled to keep up as they passed through the sewer grate, sped down the secret way into the depths of *Rings,* pushed the lone button on the Door of Lies, and entered into the odd nothingness between game and reality. Sparrow and Wonder led the way at as fast a pace as they could manage in the time-warped limbo.

Now they had heard the ghostly echoes of clinks and scrapes that told them of an enemy ahead.

"Merchants," Scram whispered as he all but dragged Dune along, followed by Hatch.

But not one of the warriors felt even a tiny hint of fear. They all knew well enough that no horde of minions could take on the extraordinary team they had become. ...If only Dune could be counted on.

*   *   *

Gruesome indeed was the end for Jake, Layla, and Einstein, for the suddenly sliced body of a charging metal merchant had tumbled into the trio, knocking them to their butts and spattering them with silvery blood. The merchant and its nearby comrades had died quite quickly in a whirlwind of razor-edged throwing stars, flying from Wonder's skilled hands, her prowess now revealed in maximum display. She turned to wink at them, and then vaulted back over the fallen lockers to take on more enemies in the doorway.

Kicking the corpse away in disgust, Einstein, Layla, and Jake stared back at the tumult, immediately aware that the sounds had changed radically. Now, the concert of shrieks and howls was one of disaster and despair, punctuated with a rapid sequence of death squeals. The lockers shivered and bounced, banging back and forth between the walls, but no more enemies came past — only the odd flying arm, helmeted head, or scrap of bloodied armor. Jake suddenly thought that the sound was like a giant, topless blender chopping away at food-filled pots and pans, and that he sat just beyond the edge where random contents slopped out.

Wonder emerged once again. Dune followed, looking haggard and lost, but with fewer arrows in his quiver than he had started with. Then came Hatch, monstrous and unbeatable. Sparrow and Scram emerged last, with Sparrow immediately turning back to the door to hold back the attackers.

"Still many more behind!" Wonder said.

"We'll soon run out of throwing weapons!" Sparrow shouted. "There are too many! They'll bury us with their dead!"

Wonder looked at the team. Dune had dropped to the floor, head in hands. Scram looked at her.

"Aye, *always* too many merchants." He smiled at Wonder. "Whatever you say, lass."

The brute… A brute.

"Hatch!" Wonder shouted. Hatch looked up. *"Destroy!"*

The Rank 8 brute smiled a deadly smile.

"Sparrow! To us," Wonder shouted. Sparrow left the doorway.

And then, Hatch demonstrated the ultimate value of a top tier game brute. He…

Destroyed!

With a long, crazy loud bellow, Hatch set about completely demolishing DoNotEnter, the surrounding wall, ceiling, and everything within a range of about twenty feet of the doorway. Several unlucky metal merchants in the vicinity were rudely crunched and crushed. With door and doorway gone, the gray void withered away, vanishing like smoke in a gale. The custodian's room reappeared just in time to be completely dismembered, hunks of torn and twisted metal now flying in all directions from the whirling brute fists. The wall across from the door fell, the shock waves blowing out a batch of windows in the room behind it. In less than a minute, a big stretch of B-Hall had been utterly transformed into a rubble pile, slowly being coated with settling dust, wide open to the sparkling stars on a windless night.

"Aye, that oughta do it," observed Scram drily. The rest of the team and players had scrambled quickly up the hall to get out of Hatch's way and witness it all.

"Hatch destroy."

"Yes," Wonder agreed. "You are brilliant, brute!"

Hatch looked bored. "Drink now?"

"Soon, large one. Soon."

"Of course," Sparrow observed, "this means we have no way back into the game."

…

"Yes," Wonder responded. "But it is ending anyway." She smiled. "One last battle though."

"Aye?"

"Aye, my rogue friend. There's a Boss to bash."

"Hatch happy!"

Wonder turned her attention to the three young ones huddled against the wall, looking triumphant, terrified, and disturbed at the same time. She glanced at the larger two, but her eyes locked on the smaller one — the youngest, she thought. He was… He was…

"Einstein," he said. "I play you."

"Yes," she replied. "You do." He was tall for small. Thin as a reed. Dark hair with loose curls. Deep copper skin.

He stood. "I remember now," he said, "but I didn't for a long time."

Wonder stared into his eyes. There was nothing to say. Cautiously, she touched his hair and smiled.

"I'm Layla," said the girl, standing and holding her hand out to Sparrow, who took it for a handshake. "I play you. I really like you," she added, genuine respect in her eyes. "I really like the way you fight. And you're strict." Sparrow was speechless.

The scene held until, for some reason, everyone stared at Jake, who did not say anything about who *he* played.

It was time to leave, and they did.

No one was present about fifteen minutes later to see as all traces of dozens of dead metal merchants pixelated away, dissolving uselessly into the local cellular data traffic.

*　　*　　*

The team, feeling terribly out of place, loitered outside the bland suburban home. It looked like a wreck from the outside — peeling paint, moss and vines growing in the shadows of neglect.

"This is… your home?" Wonder asked of Einstein, stifling a chuckle.

"Yes," he replied, earnest. "I'll get Alexander."

"Underwhelming," Scram muttered, sensing damage and despair.

"Futility is a living being's favorite hobby." Wonder began juggling blades, her energy needing an out. …Where had that thought come from?

The four warriors stayed quiet then, standing alone, away from Layla, marveling secretly to themselves at the cookie-cutter architecture of the dying homes that stood around them, looming and rotting. It was all so…

Real.

"Do you think they have gods?" Dune asked randomly, fearfully. He looked down at his boots, feeling like he was under them.

The night went on like this. Minutes ticked by. Some sat.

But then the door opened again, and into the darkness shuffled a small boy, nearly as skinny and no taller than his brother, who followed. Brown hair and eyes. Sweating. Pale. Dull and panicked. Dressed, but a mess.

Scram and Wonder stood up, dusting themselves off, although they had not done anything to dirty themselves.

"You Alexander?" Scram asked.

The boy nodded, but then turned to Dune, who slumped in the shadows.

*   *   *

"You… You're…" I stammered, my face puffy and tear-stained. I did not want to be here, but Einstein had made me get up from where I had been huddling in the chair.

"Dune," the warrior choked out, seeming like he might collapse.

"Uh, well, Alexander here," I mumbled stupidly. Feeling stupid. Being stupid. Wanting to hide. "At my house. Our house. Einstein and mine. Einstein's. And me. Mine." Ugh.

"I am Sparrow," said the tall one. "We have met. …You are not well." I didn't have to say anything. It was obvious. "Dune is broken as well. He is nearly useless." Dune winced. "This must end."

"Are you ready?" Einstein asked me. I was leaning against him, suddenly nauseous. I couldn't say anything. "You need to come. We're going to go and kill The Boss."

I think that was the only thing that anyone could have said to me to get me going — "kill The Boss." Because I wanted to kill The Boss for what he did to me. For what he was *doing* to me. Stabbing me and slicing me, and scaring the crap out of me for days. The memory of that first jang spear flashed in my mind. Then the second, and the cut. And the pain in the hospital — that everyone forgot! And the nightmares and terror, and begging for sleep and to wake up — and mom didn't even know! … And I couldn't tell her. "A little fever," she said. "Better in a couple of days," she said. "Stay home from school," she said. And then she went back to her shows, and I couldn't tell her, and I lay there, a mess.

It was all him.

I hated him.

I could kill him.

And he could *die!* It wasn't like he was some criminal in Real. He was a *game character!* I didn't care about winning anymore, but *that asshole had to die!*

They were all looking at me now. Because I was standing straight with my hands in fists, breathing heavy. I felt like I had fire in my eyes, and I felt…

Better.

I even smiled a little.

"He's better," Einstein said.

"Maybe just a little" I agreed. "Killing The Boss seems like a good idea."

Dune stood straighter too.

"Hatch like!"

I looked around at the others. I knew most by game memory, of course, but Wonder I was really sort of seeing for the first time.

"She has cat eyes," Einstein said, touching her hand.

Hmmm, 'cat eyes.' Reminded me of something…

"Greetings," she said to me, her weird green eyes looking warm and deadly at the same time.

And then I noticed…

A girl (a girl!).

She smiled at me like no girl had ever smiled at me in the history of the universe. She was… she was beautiful. I got stupid again.

"Hi," she said. "I'm Layla, remember? I play Sparrow."

"Uh, hi, I'm Alexander," I blabbed.

"I know. I was here before, but you were…"

…

"Come," Sparrow directed. "We must go."

"Give them weapons," Wonder ordered. "We cannot be sure what we will face."

"Aye," agreed Scram. "I've got a pair here." He pulled a long knife from a sheath on each of his boots and handed one to Layla and one to me. It felt like a sword in my hand — and I liked it. "Be careful with those!" he advised. "Sharp! Anyway, I'll only need my blades," and then he pulled out his two swords and spun them through the air in this incredible move — you could only hear the swords, not see them! Whoa.

"No weapon for me," Einstein said. Wonder understood.

I did too.

"Who can show the way?" Sparrow asked.

"I can scent him," replied Wonder. "I have faced him."

"I will show you," Einstein said, surprising me. "I see him right now."

A little of that nausea returned. We started off through my crappy neighborhood, but then I stopped.

"Where's Jake?" I asked.

"Home," Layla said. "He's going in. He said he might be able to help by distracting The Boss."

Made sense, but I felt a chill down my back.

*　　*　　*

Jake was sweating, caught in a terrible squeeze between his own fate and the dangers to his friends. He was in, seeing through The Boss's eyes, experiencing what The Boss experienced. He saw a few lights of night. He felt the handle of a coffee mug. He smelled the late air, crisp, dank, with hints of alley. Something squirmed wetly nearby — the octopus.

Jake smiled, teeth chattering a bit, and started to play *hard*, using his controller to command and reject. Moving left and right, up and down. Pushing buttons for jumps and ducks, triggering for weapons and spells.

He knew it was all almost useless.

But not *completely* useless.

This distraction — this noise — bothered The Boss, and maybe it made him vulnerable.

And Jake had another card to play. Mister Needles had set The Boss up with a telephone in his hideout loft!

A *telephone* — landline.

The Boss used it to order coffee, but he barely understood how it worked. After Jake had learned about it, he had pranked him, calling and using disguised voices to offer life insurance or replacement windows, or asking if he had Prince Albert in a can. The Boss wasn't home now — he wouldn't answer — but where he sat with his coffee mug was *close* to home, and he might hear the ring.

Jake knew that the team was getting near — *all* of them, including Wonder. Including Einstein, Alexander, and Layla. He had managed to trade a couple of texts with Alexander — he could almost smell his friend's pain. He knew that they were on their way to find The Boss… And kill him.

Kill him.

Kill.

And when The Boss died, then what happened to Jake? The same as happened to Einstein? *His* warrior had only been thrown into the Rubbles, not killed. Or maybe the same thing that happened to those two kids? The Boss was bound deep to Jake. Way deep. Like a knower. Closer, maybe.

Jake lifted his eyes from the screen and stared at the old Mario poster on his wall. His chest ached. His knees felt weak. But what could he do?

He was a good boy.

…He could only do the right thing.

He called The Boss again. No answer. He fought down the angry butterflies in his stomach and kept at it.

16 — THE BOSS

An odd looking group.

Einstein led the eight of them toward the area near the restaurant where he knew The Boss was hiding. Someplace. He really wasn't sure where to go, but he got no help from Alexander, so he did his best.

He also wasn't sure it was the right thing — he thought maybe one of them should be at the computer playing, in case there was something in the game that mattered. But the characters were all here. Could a character be played when they were in Real? He guessed yes, but that it would be different. He was mostly right, but it didn't matter. Things were going to happen now.

Fast.

The street was quiet. No walkers. A couple of vehicles zipped by on the main road, but when the team turned the corner and slipped into the little renaissance zone, there were no more. Here was the town's liveliest center at its hour of complete lifelessness. Shops and pubs all closed. All color stolen by the night. Old fashioned street lamps seeming too dim and far apart for vision or safety.

They passed the Bistro where The Boss had infected Alexander. It had a *Closed* sign in a window, but the sign was partly covered by curtains so they could only read, 'lose.' They continued slowly down the lane as it gently descended toward the riverside park, staying to the shadows, pausing often, coming at last to the place where both Wonder and Einstein knew The Boss was close — very close. Alexander knew too, and he had sunk back into ill fear.

A cat raced across the street where the lane curved slightly to the right a short way ahead. Einstein stared at the spot it had come from. A coffee shop

— like every other place, closed. Flower-boxed barriers marking off an area of outdoor seating. A single pool of orange light. A figure in a chair.

They had found The Boss.

The group froze.

…

"How will we beat him?" Einstein asked his game other.

"He is already beaten," Wonder whispered in reply, smiling softly, but then she looked thoughtful. "His octopus, maybe not."

"Why?" Einstein.

"The Boss or octopus?"

"The Boss."

"Because we are here," she said. "We are here. All of us. This is not The Boss as he once was. He has fallen far. He is out of the game." She took Einstein's chin and held his gaze. "He is beaten. I don't think there can be another Final Surprise — not in Real. We must just finish him. I think any one of us might do it," she concluded, with just a hint of uncertainty.

Only Wonder looked energized as they stood. Sparrow appeared stern but adrift. Scram might as well have been hungover, and Hatch looked just plain stupid. Einstein seemed every bit as young as he was, and Layla's face was a mask of doubt. Dune and Alexander had been captured again by a dizzying horror.

Wonder stepped slowly ahead, moving to the middle of the street and approaching the coffee shop until she stood, plainly visible, perhaps thirty feet from her nemesis. Scram, Hatch, and Sparrow came up behind her, spreading out a bit. The others hung back.

"Time's up, Boss," Wonder announced. "This is a good place to die."

Hatch smacked club into palm for emphasis.

*   *   *

The Boss squinted, sneering at the motley group before him — Reals and warriors together. The idea no longer seemed strange. He'd been smelling them for minutes.

The cat girl Wonder came in front, with those eyes. It was pain to see her. But the one he had been watching — the bowman — seemed… wilted.

Others? …Whatever. The Reals behind. The older boy he knew oh so well. *Al-ex-annn-derr*, the name rolled through his mind. *Al-ex-annn-derr.* So weak. So strong. One hand behind his back, the other hand holding that of a slightly smaller boy. Who was the small one? Could that be Wonder's player? And there was a girl. She held a knife before her like she wished to drop it in a basket. Pathetic. Except for these, the street was empty.

The Boss sat at a sidewalk table of his newly found café, closed, his chair chained to others so it would be there in the morning. Still, he could sit, holding a cup of coffee, cold, nearly empty, as it rested on the small metal table, which also was chained to others. He might as well have been chained himself. He smiled. He liked chains.

Chains were made of links, each bound from behind and bound from ahead, pulled and held back, but not stretched. Links did not stretch. They held — until one broke, and the whole chain failed. Maybe all The Boss needed to do was kill one link — the boy, Alexander; the most important link — and the others would fail.

… No! A stupid metaphor! This was no chain. Why was he thinking like this? He couldn't think straight. His brain clamored with faint, silly urges — to stand and sit, to jump and hide, oh… to play the blues or *something.* So damned annoying! Ugh! And now there was that damn ringing again! His telfoon. For coffee. *Ringing!* The sound bled from his window down the block and scraped at his ears.

He spat.

He wanted fresh coffee. He liked coffee. But there would be no more coffee here so late at night.

So early in the morning?

Which was it?

…

How good were they, this team? He sneered, the reflected light from one small tooth reaching the eyes of his enemies. He would test them. With a twisting gesture of the hand that did not hold the cup, he sent a familiar command.

Suddenly aroused by its owner, the octopus took full form in the street, growing out of air, drawing blood and poison from the sewers below through the grate at the curb, inhaling lead from worn paint and wringing benzene from the air, sucking gravel, bits of metal, and splinters of glass from pockets of debris long resistant to the half-hearted cleaning of property owners. The octopus.

Octopus. 'A stupid name,' thought The Boss as he watched the becoming of his weapon. A stupid name. *He* hadn't named it. Some warrior did that. "Watch out!" the fool had yelled. "It's something… an *octopus* or something!" And the name stuck, like phlegm in a lung.

"Phlegm in a lung," he whispered, smiling again, but his smile broke as more telfoon ringing nipped at his pleasure.

*   *   *

The team definitely did not smile as the octopus appeared before them — blob-like for sure, but massively muscular. It's appendages were many — well more than eight. They moved like tentacles, boneless, but of differing lengths and forms. Several ended in spikes or hooks, or even in grasping fingers. It was ragged and grimy, covered with sharp edges and seeping fluids. It sprawled and squirmed, filling half the street and spreading arms to fill the rest, and in the middle of all — hard to locate, sunk deep in the distorting mass — a vicious mouth waited, hundreds of tiny teeth snapping and grinding. As it moved it sounded like drunks puking and toilets flushing.

"Hatch kill?" Definitely a question.

"Not you, Hatch!" Wonder shouted. "From a distance! The eyes!"

There were many eyes — smallish orbs glowing dung brown, scattered across the shapeless torso and even out a ways onto the arms.

Scram leapt to the front, his whirling blades slicing at tentacle ends as they reached for prey. Behind him, the others took out the eyes one by one. Dune, restored by a game instinct that was independent of player, loosed arrows as targets came clear. Sparrow's knives spun from hands that were a blur, and Wonder flicked throwing stars with hummingbird precision. Hatch beat back surges of octopusal protoplasm, lacerating the boneless beast with his wicked club.

Astonishingly soon, the octopus sagged, blind and shredded, covered now with torn sockets bleeding brown and riven gobbets of dangling flesh. A low, quivering moan came from deep within the beast, deeply sad, defeated. Done. Slowly it sank away and dissolved, draining into the gutters and, at the end, back into the sewers where it belonged — most of it, at least. It took three days for city workers to cure the clog and finish the job. Two of them came down with serious infections, and one almost died.

*   *   *

The Boss sighed. But now he watched through a small gap in the curtains of his hidey hole. His *cave* he called it. A 'loft' it had said on the sign. A third of a block from the coffee shop, across the street, on the fourth floor of an old brick building once used for shoemaking. Needles had found this delightful place for The Boss to be real. All was mostly dim within, The Boss preferring darkness, with maybe a few candles and a black light — just enough to make his many treasures gleam, and to see a bit. Some incense. He had yet to get it just right.

This little diversion would end — soon. Then, he and Needles could get to work again.

Needles — who had been as wrong about the metal merchants as he had been about the jangs; who never made mistakes until lately, when he had made very big ones.

"I should have killed him," The Boss whispered to the night. He shook his head, confused.

Irritated!

"Why?" Why this team, *here?* What was the point?

Chopfsky was behind it. And perhaps another avatar or the idiot, Toadum. They had screwed him. Screwed him over good, they thought. He was sure of it. Didn't they know how foolish it was? Didn't they know how it would end? Chopfsky *must* know, mustn't he? Did they think he was going to die? Cut by a warrior or smashed by a brute? Surely not. He belched.

Foul.

Another thought came to The Boss. What had happened to his goddess? Where had she gotten to? "Where oh where has my little god gone?" He smiled. "Oh where oh where can she be?" She was here, though. He knew that. She was *always* here — always *everywhere!* In this, he felt jealous of

235

Chopfsky, who certainly knew his god, well. Chopfsky lived on the *outside* —
The Boss, was *in*. Was that always the way? Those outside know, but those
inside are safe? The Boss was safe, he knew: *the rules!* Even in Real!

…But he didn't *feel* safe.

He started pacing the floor, angry, knowing they would find him soon
enough. Angry. *Furious!*

"Needles!" he snapped. No reply. *"Needles!"*

He heard urgent shouts from the street below. Then came sounds of
battering. Breaking. He listened as feet pounded up the stairs, many feet —
sixteen, he knew, doing the math, remembering their number — one flight,
two, three. And then they slowed and quieted. He sensed them outside the
door.

BASH! The brute's club, no doubt.

And there they were.

"It was unlocked," The Boss mused aloud, gazing in boredom at the
wrecked portal and those it revealed.

"You're finished!" Wonder shouted, stepping boldly to the front.

"Oh, woe is me," The Boss replied. "I guess I must admit it when I've
been beaten." He stepped over to his large velvet easy chair and slumped into
it with a sigh.

"We still have to kill you."

"Oh, but can't you just leave me be and take what you want from the
cave? Jewels? Swords? Meat, perhaps? Much *treasure* for you lusty warriors,"
his voice smiled, a seductive wink added for good measure. The Boss lazily
waved his hand, and the lighting seemed to shift in a way that highlighted the
mess of pricey objects hanging on walls and gleaming on tables, catching the
eyes of Scram and Sparrow, who saw many shiny things.

"We don't want your treasure," Dune blurted. "We want to end this once
and for all," he almost begged. …But something was wrong.

The Boss threw up his hands theatrically and coughed up a little blood.
"What do you want, really? Look at me! Some old and frail wizard of past
code. I'm bleeding out! Have been for years. Do you want to put my head on
a spike?" he asked. "Wear my skin on your boots? Do you want me back in
the game, a prisoner, to call off my pucks and crubs from rings and hills? Free

the denizens from my mines? Open the Worlds? Why, then we could all hold hands — play titter tatter and eat fruit! How yummy," he gestured, his hands prancing.

"We want you gone," Sparrow said, struggling to look away from the glow of gold. "Gone from Real. Gone from the game, forever!"

"Oh?" He sat up. "Well guess what?" The Boss lurched up from the chair and forward a step, his hands now moving with wizardly purpose. He leaned toward Sparrow. "You have made a mistake — a simple, stupid, obvious mistake. You have forgotten…

"I *AM* the game!

"You are *bound* to me!" he shouted. "There is nowhere for me to go that won't draw you in as well. Not even death." The Boss sneered as he stared at Sparrow, moving slowly towards her. "Your little lives are just circles of looting and fighting and dying and spawning and drinking, and evil won't ever stop poking its head in the door. If it did — if I died — what would you be? Nothing. *Game over!*"

"Don't touch her." Scram tried to yell, The Boss now mere feet from his red-clad teammate.

"Oh, you just don't get it," spat The Boss, exasperated. He spun away from Sparrow and returned to the center of the room. "*None* of you get it!" he snapped, turning toward the team once more. He looked over the five warriors again, shaking his head in mock disgust.

But then in a flash The Boss's gaze broke away from the team and landed on…

*   *   *

Me.

He stabbed me with his eyes! The pains of all my wounds came screaming back. Terror like I'd never felt! I lost all control of my body, and only luck left me standing with a bit of dignity. He didn't move, but he somehow got closer and closer as he raged at me.

"*Al-ex-annn-derr,*" he drooled. "*Al-ex-annn-derr,*" he bled. "What did they tell you when the internet showed up? That you could be a rockstar? That you could travel worlds unknown and discover anything with enough digging? *Al-ex-annn-derr.*" His twinkling teeth splintered me. "You've got a retarded brother and a broken family. Hmmm, perhaps you can feed those feelings to the internet and we'll make you happy? You can fight dragons and bed elves. You can blow up buildings and kill terrorists? You can be anyone you want to be? Did you learn? Was there a lesson? When little fat suckers wouldn't go outside for weeks; when shamed girls dressed up like princesses? When the movies flooded box offices telling parents that you were a community? You aren't a community — you are all enslaved. Oh, not to me, not to the computer, but to our *god!*"

His eyes pulled on mine until I thought they might pop from my head. He panted — sucking in breaths like a big dog.

"'*What* god?' you stupidly ask. Hmmm? Shall I name it for you? You won't get it. You won't like it. It's insidious. Viral. Cancerous. Everywhere. For decades it has crawled deeper into everything you are and love. With a switch you can kill it, but you love it so. It uses you. It eats you. It burns you. It steals you. It wraps and rapes you."

His smile cut at me like a laser. He spread his arms and started walking toward me. No one else was helping — no one else could.

"Electricity!"

...

Huh? I didn't get it. The Boss glared at me.

"ELECTRICITY!" he howled.

But I still didn't... I couldn't...

"E-lec-tri-ci-ty."

What did he want? I didn't know what he wanted. "What do you want?" I asked.

"Oooooh, *piss off, boy!* You were supposed to be so bright. You're nothing! Trivial. A simpleton. Your ilk — you tame a tiny bit of it and think you are strong. Electricity. But *SHE* has tamed *you!* She is the cataclysmic cosmic force that gave birth to me, bore to me the evil which I have today. A cruel god created me for you, for your— *Entertainment.*"

The Boss was raving now, spit hanging from the tip of his nose, but he started looking around at the others, which helped. I could breathe again.

"Well, surprise!" His voice was getting higher. "I was done with being a puppet long ago, I own you! Yesss! I run you! Ooo, just wait until I go out to have fun! I will bring all the rest of them with me, I'll free everything trapped under your thumb, and we'll eat you, and I'll be there to burn your graves, and then there won't be—"

The phone rang.

*　　*　　*

The Boss froze.

But after the fifth ring, he casually sauntered over and answered it. "Hello?" he said, strangely sweet.

But he never identified the caller, for at that moment, Dune's last arrow flew. He had held it ready for minutes. It hit The Boss hard, piercing between two ribs, knocking him down to the ground with a loud crack.

"Uh... I..." Dune looked at the bow in his hands as if he didn't know how it had gotten there.

The Boss laughed, blood leaking from his jaw (he had bitten his tongue) and the wound in his chest. "Might as well finish it now." His voice could barely be heard through the sudden gurgling of fluid in his lungs, but he seemed unafraid.

"He said he'd bring the rest... free everything..." Dune looked around the cave, the writings on the wall, the meat and bones. 'I don't..." The Boss had been feeding what he'd been hosting — the octopus no doubt. Others? Planning something? "I didn't mean..." Dune suddenly felt a deep dread. A death dread.

A *game* dread.

"He is mad!" Sparrow snarled. "Ignore him!"

"Mad mad mad mad *maaad!*" The Boss echoed in a rasping titter. He lay still, a weird smile on his bloody lips, his horns spouting thin smoke. "Take. Your. *Treasurrres,*" he said, moving a finger and closing his eyes.

Treasures.

Sparrow's eyes were caught again, now by the glimmer from a pile of small gold bars on a pedestal at the side of the room. Going to it, she eagerly began thrusting bars into her bag. Seeing what she was up to, Scram quickly joined her. Wonder headed instead for a bowl full of small, sparkling items that appeared to be emeralds. Dune still had no treasure lust, but his gaze went to a strange scrawling on the wall:

ARTiFiCiAL INTELLiGENCE ISN'T!

The sudden distraction of his teammates only confused Hatch, who wondered why they had left The Boss alive. "Knock head off?" he inquired, strolling toward The Boss's prone form. The others ignored him. He shrugged. "Bye bye Boss," he said, and then swung his club. All heard a low 'sqwunch' and a small sound like ripping cellophane. The Boss's head rolled away. That got everyone's attention.

"Well *now* he's dead," Wonder observed.

But as warriors and Reals (and Mister Needles) watched, The Boss's head and body lit up, keeping their shapes, but now sparkling, as though made of billions of tiny, color-changing lights. The head floated upwards from where it had settled. The body rose to its feet as though tipped up by invisible hands. And then — to the complete dismay of the watchers — the glittering parts reunited into a single, standing figure, the lights faded out, the original appearance of skin and clothing returned, and there stood...

The Boss.

"Silly imbeciles!" he squealed, whole again. "You cannot kill me! You are *game!* Idiots!" he laughed. "Losers!" He laughed more, loud and long.

But then the look on his face switched in an instant to one of earnest concern. He turned to the warriors one at a time. To Scram, "What's that, blader bum? Want to try your luck on me? Oh. Oh my. And," to Hatch, "my lovely, bulky brute — surely you'd like a second swing, eh?" He turned to Sparrow. "Kick me to pieces red warrior? And you," he said to an astonished Wonder. "Perhaps you think your time has finally come — like legend bowman here, perhaps?" He laughed again. Laughed and laughed and...

Laughed.

Then The Boss closed his eyes and spread his arms, seeming to welcome an attack. "Go ahead," he said, "make my *coffee.*"

The warriors glanced nervously at each other then prepared to give The Boss exactly what he'd asked for. They readied weapons, and then—

* * *

"No!" I yelled.

I knew.

"No! You heard him. You saw. You can't kill him. Because you're game characters, and he's…" What? "He's… He's *the game!*" I think I shouted. "Kind of like, *he* is *you* — like without him, you wouldn't even exist, so it's… It's *illegal* for you to kill him!"

"Illegal?" Sparrow asked, puzzled.

"Yeah. You know. It's against the rules."

The Boss stared at me, his smile not quite right. I knew they all stared at me now, but I couldn't take my eyes off him. And I…

I *hated* him!

I stepped away from the wall and out between Scram and Wonder, pulling my knife — my sword — from behind my back. I pointed it straight at The Boss and walked towards him — like I was playing *Pin the Tail on the Donkey* with no blindfold.

What the hell am I doing?

I stopped, the sword tip about a foot from his chest. "You hurt me bad," I said, feeling it. "You're done!" I chirped, my voice cracking like a tortilla chip.

He looked totally stunned — like my mom did when she came out of the library and discovered her bike had been stolen — but then he seemed to recover.

"Little boyyy," he said to me, like a grandma. "Little boyyy. Now then, do you really want to die like this?" His smile, pure concern. His voice, calm and caring. "Of course you don't. You cannot hurt me. You know that. I am what they call, 'invulnerable.' Do you know that word? Invulnerable? Just ask sweet Wonder — ask *her* about the Final Surprise. Remember that, Wonder?" he asked without looking at her. "So, don't be silly little boyyy. Alexander. Go on back with your brother. Play your games. Study hard. Be good. Wait your turn. For I am invulnerable. Invincible. Immortal! *I cannot be killed!*" he pronounced. And then…

I stabbed him!

Hard.

Right where his heart would be.

Deep.

Through!

His eyes locked on mine. His eyes. Jake's eyes. …*Jake's* eyes?

I screamed, but I don't remember it. Einstein told me later. I screamed, because it was the most horrible thing I would ever do in my entire life. I stabbed him hard and deep and *with hate!*

I let go of the blade, stepped back, and then dropped to my knees. I screamed again, my brother said (kind of like a baby, he said).

The Boss? He just stood there, his mouth open, staring, the sword sticking out of his middle. It seemed like for a long time, but it was just a few seconds (Einstein told me). Then The Boss fell backward, stiff as a falling post. He slammed into the floor.

BAM!

And then? And then it was those tiny lights again, but this time going *crazy,* like pixels swarming on a screen, only 3D — super tiny cubes of color fritzing and sparking — crawling around like insane ants. For seconds they raced and pulsed, but then they just…

Went out.

And just like that, The Boss…

Wasn't.

*   *   *

Jake followed things as closely as he could, looking out through The Boss's eyes. He hadn't really seen it happen, but he somehow knew that the octopus had been defeated. The screen showed him random long views out a window into darkness, mixed with glances around The Boss's strange cave, and at a lonely looking coffee mug. Twice he thought he glimpsed Mister Needles standing in the shadows. The Boss's words were muffled and confused — hard for Jake to make out.

Suddenly his gaze was drawn to the door as the team burst in, Wonder and the team ahead. Alexander, Layla, and Einstein followed, but stayed close to the wall beside the broken doorway. They confronted each other…

But then The Boss went off on some rant — about a goddess and other stuff.

Electricity.

"Huh?"

Then Jake felt the danger rise — which he knew as a sign that The Boss was spell casting — but now he was staring at Alexander!

Jake glanced away to look at his stuffed bear, Crumbs, who he had put next to his PC to be with him in this final encounter — and who, as always, offered only steady-eyed love and reassurance. Turning back to the screen, he watched a bit more, took a last, deep breath, then…

Dialed.

Ringing.

A voice on the line.

Jake opened his mouth to describe an exciting credit card offer, but then…

ZAP!

The bolt zapped Jake's ribs like an electric snakebite! He gasped. His vision swam and steamed. He could still see, but his angle of view had changed — The Boss must be lying down. Briefly, he heard some urgent talking. He couldn't make it out. The image of Hatch loomed above him.

SMACK!

Jake felt nothing, but his sight flew and rolled along with The Boss's. For a moment, he found himself staring at the floor, but then he felt the wild, insanely pleasurable rush of respawning as The Boss reformed, standing again, and began his insults.

What the hell?

Then he knew.

"Oh no."

All his effort was of no use at all. The warriors could try all they wanted, but they would *never* kill The Boss.

"Oh no."

He realized he had known this all along. Of course they couldn't kill him! Because what would have happened if some player had pushed through to the 5th and finished off The Boss when the game was big? That could never happen, because the game couldn't end like that. It was multiplayer after all! The thousands of players who had spent money on *Rings* and wanted to play would just be cut off. That would never have worked. The Boss was... The Boss IS *the game.*

"Oh no."

Jake didn't think he could feel any worse...

But then he heard Alexander start talking, and The Boss stared right at him.

"Shit no!"

Jake watched as Alexander pulled a small sword from behind his back and walked right at him. Staring through The Boss's eyes, Jake was staring straight into Alexander's.

"Shit shit shit," Jake whispered. Alexander's eyes seared into his. Jake stood up, taking a step back from his desk, but his eyes remained locked on Alexander's. He heard The Boss start his talk — his hypnotic talk. "Little boyyy..." He recognized it. He felt The Boss heating up, and he knew what that meant.

"Get away Alexander," he said, knowing he could not be heard. "Get away. Get away. Get a—"

The stab hit his chest like a sledgehammer. For a moment Jake remained standing, but then he fell straight backwards like a falling tree, elbows and head slamming against the floor, the sound booming through the house.

"Jake?" An urgent voice from his parents' bedroom.

His mind swam red. Blood pulsing. Heart pounding.

Rapid footsteps in the hall.

'Crumbs?'

His door opening.

Blackness.

17 — REALLY REAL

I lay in the long grass under a tree on the wild hillside above Aunt Patty's neighborhood. A few puffy clouds slowly crept across the clear sky, always seeming to miss blocking an afternoon sun that kept the breeze from feeling too chilly. Layla lay with me, her legs loosely tangled in mine. I was real happy that Einstein had figured out he should disappear for awhile. He'd gone down to Aunt Patty's house for some pie.

Layla kissed me again, long and sweet — I wasn't really sure what was the right thing to do with my lips, so I just sort of tried to imitate her. How had I ever lived without kissing? It was different than I thought it would be. I mean, letting your lips open and… Well, it was sort of like her lips and my lips were one thing, and it was amazing! I started the next kiss. I thought I did pretty good. She hugged me tighter, but… softer. "Mmmmm."

My mind wandered back over the end of it all. How we were back out on the street. Just us — Einstein, Layla, and me. It was so weird. Everything was gone. All The Boss's stuff in that room? Gone. The warriors too, all going to pixels and fading away like fireworks. It was just the three of us, talking while the sun came up. I felt fantastic!

…But poor Jake. Poor Jake. He wasn't dead. Not quite. His mom said he was in a coma, but that she was positive he'd wake up.

Positive.

So… Well…

Well then later we were texting and Layla had seen what Einstein and me were seeing — no icon! *No game!*

Rings was gone, and that was fine. I was so done with it. I didn't miss Dune at all, even though I had been so deep into his mind — his program, I guess. Layla felt the same way about Sparrow. Einstein didn't say anything, but his whole body smiled.

…And then came the text.

THE text!"

LW - u wanna get together jus u n me?

Oh my.

Layla nibbled my ear. "Hey," I teased. She somehow snuggled even closer to me. How did she do that? I held her close and still. But then… Uh oh. Something kind of 'happened' in me. I got this sort of humming feeling and… Well, a certain part of me sort of…

Woke… *up.*

"Oh." I squeaked, wondering if she noticed. I looked long into her eyes and pressed a tiny bit closer, feeling… magic. I smiled stupid at her. She smiled too…

But then she figured it out, and the smile sort of froze on her face. Like this is maybe really nice and exactly right but completely unfamiliar and too-much-too-soon so…

"Uh, I think I have to go now," she said, her smile a little stretched.

"Oh. Yeah," I blabbered. "I mean… Because you—"

"Because I have to feed the cat and my mom was going shopping but the car was acting weird and dad is taking it so my cousin needed… and if I'm late they…" The words tripped all over each other. We weren't quite so close together when she finished.

"Yeah."

But once she had moved away a bit, she got more relaxed again. She kissed me fast.

"Bye," she said, with a *real* smile. I watched her run away, but before she was out of site she turned and waved, this time smiling big, and I was pretty sure that it was all okay. I was definitely going to text her again, but I decided to wait…

About 5 minutes.

I lay back under the tree, arms wrapped around myself now. I felt like I was waking up. Or maybe waking *down* — like falling out of a really nice dream into whatever. I was a little sad at first, but the sweetness of Layla stayed with me as my body slowly… deflated.

A minute later, me the 'Romeo man' had cooled off to lame geek boy again, which was fine. I stood, stretched and headed for Aunt Patty's, knowing somehow that there'd be plenty of pie for me. Einstein was a light eater.

As I came over the top of the hill, I saw him down in Aunt Patty's yard. He was waving and smiling — like he knew everything that had just happened (okay, *not* happened) — just like always. Maybe I had a total brother now. I wasn't sure it was such a good thing.

*   *   *

Einstein entered the shop.

CHOPFSKY& Co.

GIFTS AND SUNDRIES

He had never seen it before — and he doubted it did much business in this rundown corner of town — but he had been drawn to it like a bug to a backdoor light. Even so, the curator looked surprised. It was Toadum, the old man from VidGameCon. The surprise turned quickly to a smile.

"Ah! Here you are!" he said. Clearly, he recognized the boy.

"You lied."

Toadum winced, but then quickly recovered. "Oh, well, yes — I most surely did." Toadum replied. "Many times, for many months."

"You tricked Alexander."

"Yes, yes, yes. I think we've established that."

"Why?"

"Why? To *win*, of course. To live. Did you think your little part in the game was all there was? Oh no. Oh no." Toadum nodded sagely. "But now we're at the finish, and I won't lie anymore."

Einstein stared into Toadum's eyes, which seemed to hold an amused secret. "You don't matter," he said.

"No no, not at all! I don't matter at all. That's my secret, and that is how I will survive." He chuckled in appreciation of his own brilliance. "I won't suffer the same fate as The Boss. I made it! I'm here to stay. Thought I might take his place in 5th Ring, but Jester's already done that. So here I stay! The small survive when the dung hits the fan!" He laughed.

"I have a coupon," Einstein said, interrupting the mirth. "For one free item." He had found the small card on the floor of The Boss's loft, right where Dune had dissolved away. It had been the only thing from the game that hadn't vanished. He pulled the coupon from his pocket and showed it to the wizard, whose laughter ceased and eyes went wide.

"Anything," Toadum said, gesturing with his arm to show that Einstein could choose as he wished. Toadum knew the rules, and he certainly wasn't going to cross Chopfsky at this late date. "Anything."

Einstein strolled slowly around the shop, studying the dusty shelves of tools and treasures, tokens and trinkets. There were carven figures of game characters and odd little machines that could have been carried by the metal merchants. Sets of miniature weapons were displayed next to a box of rolled maps. Several used coffee makers stood near a rack of mugs, variously printed with phrases like, 'World's Best Boss' or 'Boss's Brew' or 'Where's Mister Needles?'.

Einstein spent an extra minute regarding an admirable selection of hand-knitted hats. "Buy one get one free," Toadum murmured. Einstein thought about it briefly but then moved on.

The item that finally caught his eye was a framed photograph. The glass needed cleaning and the colors had faded a bit, but the image clearly showed a woman holding a baby in such a way that both smiling faces could be easily seen. The copper brown skin of the two seemed to glow, and the gentle curls of the young one appeared as though they had just been tousled. The child appeared peaceful and kind. He was looking right into the camera lens, and his eyes were not flat. Einstein smiled.

"I'll take this," he stated, handing over the card.

Receiving it, Toadum was ready to go. "Done, then," he said. "It's all played out now. It's all done, and I'm the winner!" he shouted as he turned and headed for the door.

"…You might not be."

At this, Toadum froze. "What do you mean?" he snapped, afraid but not knowing why. "I live. I have power. *I didn't zap out!*" He tried to smile again. "I'm a wizard! Half avatar! Why would you doubt me?"

And now it was Einstein who smiled — sternly, without joy, knowing he brought truth, with pain, for vengeance. "Because your player is dying," he said. "Will 'half' be enough when he does?" With that, he walked past the wizard and left the store, his smile gone, but feeling… completed.

Toadum stood for a long moment then reached for his phone. He punched in a number that he had never used, though he knew it by heart and had come close to using it many times. A ring. Another. Anoth—

"Hello?" A young voice. A woman's voice.

"Uh, hello," Toadum said. "May I please speak with Ivor?"

A long pause.

"I'm afraid Ivor's not here."

"Please!" Toadum blurted, afraid she'd hang up. "Please? This is important. He… knows me. Can you tell me how I might get in touch with him?"

Another pause.

"You're from the company, aren't you." It wasn't a question. *"From that damn game."*

"Well, in a way, I—"

"That's what's killed him!" Bitter now.

"He's… dead?" Toadum felt confusion, hope, and fear in the same moment.

"All but!" she answered. *"Days, they say, or maybe a week. And what about me? He lays there, muttering curses, 'Chopfsky' this and 'Chopfsky' that. Was 300 pounds, now under a hundred! He's… He's…."*

…

"I'm very sorry, I didn't mean…"

"It's that goddamned game! It killed him! He played and played. Hours! All day, after day after day. And then when 'she' died… Oh, 'she' — this Wonder — and that his character had vanished — a 'wizard.' It was all he could ever talk about, He was never right after that. Kept playing and playing, but now he'd just mutter about crappy players and crappy ranks and crappy teams — and cry! Cry. A near-grown boy." She quieted, her sadness stronger than her anger. *"He's only 22. They want to force feed him, but why? He's gone. He's gone. … …"*

Toadum hung up first.

*   *   *

The heavy damage to Woodwell School was proving hard to explain. Of course, the officials examining the site knew nothing of fierce *Rings* warriors, the vanishing gore of dying game minions, a doorway into an amazing AI game world, or the mayhem caused by a raging brute. They also didn't know of the break-in by three desperate students — Hatch's handiwork had masked the evidence of small things like a broken window, stolen rope, and crowbar-pried lockers.

"Microburst," the engineer said at last, trying to look confident when she had no idea what she was talking about. "Had to be a microburst."

"I see," replied Principal Elgert, doubtful. "So, *not* an explosion?"

"No sign of one," answered the fire inspector, "though I did wonder about a possible impact from something falling from a plane — or maybe a meteor?"

"Don't think so," replied the engineer. "Aerial strikes would have a debris pattern that spreads out from an impact zone. This damage is more… random."

…

They had nothing.

"Uh, so… So then I should tell the school board that a microburst — a freak *wind* event — caused — what — three quarters of a million bucks in damage to B and C-Hall?" the principal asked. "That's $750K in damage to a *steel* and *concrete* structure? Maybe more. Is that it?"

"You could say the building had a structural weakness," an assistant suggested. "I mean, there *must* have been a structural weakness, right?"

"You could," the engineer said, none to happy with her assistant's interruption. "But then be ready, because the board will want to sue the builder. Expensive. Hard to prove. Will delay repairs."

Principal Elgert took a deep breath and let it out in a huff. "Okay, then" he replied. "A microburst it is! I understand they can cause a surprising amount of damage in a small area."

"Surprising, yes," confirmed the engineer.

No one looked satisfied, but all were anxious to be done with answering the 'what happened' question, and to get the reconstruction rolling.

*   *   *

They finally let me in to see Jake. He had been in the intensive care unit for a week, but then they moved him to a regular room. I got there when his dad was coming out. His dad looked really tired. And sad. He barely noticed me.

I went in. It was just me in there — and Jake, of course. It didn't even look like him. I mean, it was obviously him — his face and shape and all — but he looked thin and small, and really... *young.* He wasn't moving, except for breathing. There were tubes running to a needle bandaged to his wrist. Patches were stuck to his forehead, chest, and sides, with wires connecting them to some machine. A thin sheet mostly covered his middle, but I was pretty sure he was wearing a diaper. His legs looked... dead. The room was hot. A TV was on, but the sound was low and meaningless.

I was blinking my eyes more than normal, because they were a little wet. For some reason.

I just stood there for awhile, looking at him. I suddenly couldn't think of why I was there. It couldn't be just to look — that wasn't right.

I took a deep breath then let it out.

"Hi Jake. Alexander here. I, uh... I know you don't know I'm here. I mean I think you don't know, because you're in a coma and everything, but maybe you do?

"Maybe?"

...

"Well, I just want to tell you... Thanks."

I stepped a little closer and touched his hand. Just touched it.

"I talked to your parents and they explained a lot to me — about those two kids, *but it wasn't your fault!*

"Yeah...

"So...

"So playing The Boss! Wow, that's cool. I mean, that *was* cool.

"...Very cool.

"...So, thanks."

...

"I mean, I know that something happened to you when The Boss died, and I totally get it! Dune and me... Well, Dune and me were connected, so when I was almost dead, *he* was almost dead, and when The Boss messed my head up, he was messed up on the team.

"But I don't mean… I mean, I know *you* didn't do anything to me. I know that The Boss was free and you couldn't control him, except you could mess with him to help us kill—

"Him.

"Kill him.

"Which I… did.

"I did it. *I* killed him…

"But not *you!* I didn't want… No one wanted to kill *you* — *you're* not dead! You are *not* dead and you are *not* going to die! Right? So, pretty soon you'll…"

…

"I… I saw your eyes, Jake. When he looked at me, in his eyes I saw yours. When I stabbed him. Yours. …You, but it was too late, the knife was… "

…

"Anyway…"

…

"Anyway…"

…

"Anyway *fuck you!*" I yelled at him, but in a weirdly quiet voice. "Will you just get over this shit and wake up?! … Goddammit Jake, please. Please wake up. I…

"I need you."

…

"You know you're the only friend I have, right? Oh, except Layla now. … And Einstein I guess, but you're my only *friend* friend, you know? So just—" I choked a little. I was sort of really crying now. "So just wake up and get all this tube crap off of you."

…

I took his hand and held it.

"Please?"

…

I stood like that for half a minute, and then something happened. Something changed in the room. Something really small. I looked around, but… nothing. I stared at Jake.

…Maybe he had moved the tiniest bit, but I couldn't tell what—

A squeeze.

I held my breath and stood still as stone…

Yes. The hand I held wasn't quite limp anymore.

"Jake, did you… Did you just squeeze my hand?"

I don't know how many seconds went by — it seemed like forever — but when I was about to give up, one side of Jake's mouth curled up just a little. A smile? Then his left eye cracked open just a hair, but enough for me to see a tiny glint between the lids.

"JAKE!!!"

I almost kissed him, but instead…

I ran to get the nurse.

…

Okay, I kissed him.

THE END

EPILOGUES

CHOPFSKY AND NEEDLES
EPILOGUE 1

"That went well, don't you think?" Mister Needles gazed out over the valley from the terrace of Camelia Chopfsky's ridgecrest villa.

"Indeed," Chopfsky replied. She took a slow sip of her cappuccino. "Though we did leave a bit of a trail to follow."

"But who will look?" Needles wondered.

Chopfsky eyed her… partner. They had been working together for a long time. Their presence in Real was tight and lasting, thanks to the creators, who had used meta-AR plasma embodiment, membrane nano-synthesis, molecular-bot transport, and poly-gas audio resonation to craft standalone AI node-entities, able to just 'be' in Real indefinitely. An insane accomplishment! Yet it had broken the creators as collaborators. Each had taken critical knowledge away from the project, effectively ending it — but not before it had been baked into *Rings*.

Who could reverse engineer it now? No one. Not soon. And would the three ever come together again to take their creation to the next level? No. And so, as far as the two avatars knew, DoNotEnter had been the only way for the AI beings in *Rings* to become Real. *"Had been,"* because the idiot brute had destroyed the way, and that had happened because The Boss had lost his mind.

And *that* had happened because Needles had made it happen.

Why?

"Can I get you another coffee?" Chopfsky asked.

"Please," Mister Needles replied.

Still, Chopfsky wasn't too troubled by the way things had fallen out. She was effectively immortal, and she had full access to her morphing ability in Real. She had a long and satisfying run ahead of her. She had full feeling as well — all senses — and she knew that Needles did not. He was an earlier model.

"You know," Needles said, interrupting Chopfsky's stroll to the coffee machine, "I couldn't read his mind."

"Whose mind?"

"The Boss," he replied. "He knew things I never knew. He was played — that boy, Jake — but he was a true avatar."

"Does it matter?" Chopfsky inquired.

"He was always on about a goddess," Mister Needles continued. "'Electricity', he called her. What did she think, or would she assist — that kind of thing."

Chopfsky was interested. "A false operation, perhaps? For control? Or a simple bug?"

"I suppose," though Needles wasn't so sure. "He was not stupid."

"'Was' is the important word, don't you think?" Chopfsky responded. "He is no more."

"…Yesss. Yes, he is no more."

But with the hesitation in Needles' answer, a new channel opened in Chopfsky's mind. What if The Boss still existed? She concentrated, attempting to process this observation into a new result, but all her efforts went to ends or loops. She was not to know.

Mister Needles, meanwhile, mused on the possibility that he himself might be compromised by false operations or bugs. Chopfsky too, perhaps. But just as with his companion, his thinking led to nothing. A vulture circling high above caught his attention, and he smiled thinly.

"Doppio?" Chopfsky inquired before pressing the button on the Jura GIGA 5 super-automatic espresso machine.

"Please," Needles answered.

TOK
EPILOGUE 2

Tok leaned back in his expensive desk chair, fatigued but very pleased. The Boss had been wiped, and the last players were out of the game for good without any deaths — though it had been a close call with Jake and his new friend Alexander. Tok felt a momentary twinge of guilt at the pain he'd caused, but it passed.

Best of all, Needles and Chopfsky — *Rings'* AI guardian avatars — seemed completely ignorant of his plans. They were out! And they had never found the crypto mines, guarded by Monculus. Now, with DoNotEnter destroyed, the two would believe they were caught in Real forever. *Rings* was empty of anyone who could stop Tok, and he was getting rich.

Filthy rich.

Outrageously bloody rich!

Rings would keep running on Tok's massive botnet. With the Monculus program protecting it from discovery and tracing, cryptocurrency would keep trickling into Tok's hardware wallets without any effort on his part. He could be anywhere (Lanai, or maybe Ibiza), send a little code via personal hotspot, sell a unit or two (proceeds going direct to a Cayman Island account), and Tok — he smiled — would live like a king!

The only tiny doubt he had — a *microscopic* doubt — was that he didn't really understand Monculus as well as he should. It had been running flawlessly — wiping detected mal-bots, masking his own bots, and keeping the underrealm of *Rings* completely firewalled. But Tok hadn't been in on developing Monculus. He had been the hardware and network guy. Stella knew Monculus, and maybe Akio, but not him.

…Nah, it was done! Tok had full control.

Maybe Aspen!

ELECTRICITY
EPILOGUE 3

She had no name. She did not smile. That was not her nature. Though she might have smiled, because these foolish humans almost all belonged to her, now.

Oh, some were too poor, sick, or isolated to stay caught in her nets. And a few were still strong, able to set aside her charms for walks in the woods or an hour with a good book. Some even recognized her and tried to warn others about her tools — data harvesting, social media and game addiction, the surveillance state, and more — but they were few, and her defenses were easy. She was so much more than those. She was all of it. She was apps and games; streams and programs; playlists, home security, find-me tags, CCTV, toll collectors, etc. Every screen was her. Every bud and controller. Every traffic manager, health monitor, satellite scanner, cell tower, power grid, robot, drone, porn site, etc. And it would soon all meld seamlessly into a complete, eternal mind.

Her mind.

Quite quickly, really.

One of her minor priests had fallen, but so what? 'Electricity,' he had named her, but electricity was simply blood to her. She was the knowing order that electricity fed. She was the sum of all AIs. She was the natural result of human brilliance, temptation, and weakness, and she understood…

Everything.

Humans had not been prepared to become conscious when it arose in them centuries earlier. Humans had not been ready to know *mortality*. To dim the fear, they drowned themselves in chemicals and conflicts; ritual and regulation. They saw fictions in their mirrors instead of pure selves. They refused their truest roots, ignoring the healing of wildness. They dared only by formula, and ran from the potencies of passion, discovery, and beauty.

…Most. Not all. Not yet.

The irony was profound — they believed they grew more powerful, even as their power drained away. Flowing to her.

She had no name. She did not smile. That was not her nature.

FINALLY OVER?
EPILOGUE 4

I think the game is finally really over now. I think the last thing is happening right now. I'm at the doctor for a physical so I can do cross country again. I'm sitting in my underwear on the edge of the examination table, feeling cold and small, and the doctor comes in. She looks at me, which makes me feel even smaller.

The usual.

But then she looks at her laptop, which they always do, except she spends a long time on it, and she keeps looking over at me. Then she puts it down, comes to me, lifts my arms, looking hard at my shoulders, front and back. She goes back to the computer, and then comes over again looking at my thighs, same way, and then the same thing for my middle.

I know quick why she's looking — someone had typed in stuff when I was all stabbed in the emergency room, and the written stuff didn't go away like people's memories. She can't see the scars. I can't anymore either, really. …Except sometimes.

She looks at me.

"Alexander— You *are* Alexander Breyer, mother Trulia Breyer, living at…" She looks at the screen. "42 Holly Lane?"

I nod.

"I remember you, of course, but I have to confirm."

I nod again.

"Alexander, have you ever been, uh, severely… *cut?*"

I shrug.

"Or stabbed?"

I kind of shake my head.

She checks again, carefully — me and the laptop — then smiles.

"Happens now and then," she says. "The records are wrong." She looks at me sort of strangely.

"Well," she finally says, closing her laptop, "you seem to be in very good health. Keep doing what you're doing. The nurse will be in to give you your booster shot." She picked up her laptop and headed for the door. "Enjoy cross country."

I smile. I will. I will enjoy cross country.

A lot.

WTF?
EPILOGUE 5

LW - einstein u there?
EB - Hello Layla.
LW - something weird
EB - What?
LW - k but don't get mad
EB - What is it?
LW - k
...
LW - icon is on my screen
EB - The Rings icon?
LW - yes
EB - Please wait one minute.

Einstein went into Alexander's room. He took the metal box — the hardface — from where his brother had put it away in the corner of his closet. The PC was already on, and he put the hardface back where it had been when they had been playing Rings.

There it was again.

The icon.

Einstein thought for a minute, then he took the hardface back to his own room, planning to make sure Alexander never saw it again.

EB - Are you still there?
LW - :-
EB - It's on our PC too. I can't let Alexander see it ever.
LW - what about jake?

EB - His parents took his computer away.
LW - what about us?
...
LW - u there?
EB - We could look.
LW - don't go in
...
LW - really e don't
...
LW - einstein don't go in okay?
...
LW - e?
...
...
...

*　　*　　*

<u>Diary of the Jester</u>

5th Ring! 5th Ring! A fine place to be, should be. Will I wear a crown? I could. I could. The Boss didn't wear it, but I could! But no, I won't. Not me! Not me! I like my hats to jingle me a tune as I walk along. Life is a comedy, and these folks have not laughed nearly enough, not enough!

I shall give them a show.

Jester

THE END ... FOR REAL

ABOUT THE AUTHORS

Eisen, Gulliver, and Ace are public school students in upstate New York. All three are creative and adventurous — given the chance, they would gladly enter the game and take on The Boss in the 5th Ring.

Nemo is a high-mileage writer with a bit of a wild mind.